Never Kiss a Hotshot

Annie Mick

Cover design: Josh- Pro-X Design

Contents

Never Kiss A Hot Shot

Prologue

"Straight flush. Beat that muddahfuddahs." I grin cockily and lay my cards down, face up, on the cot – a temporary sacrifice by one of the tent mates while we kill time. We don't play for money; we keep a tally on who buys the beers next time.

"Muddafuddahs?" Silas belly laughs as he tosses his cards in the losers' heap. "Have we called a limit to swearing? What's next? Oh shoot, darn, and double hockey sticks?"

"Nah." I tip a teasing chin and grin at our youngest comrade. "It's Conroy's first time out. He's still adjusting. I was afraid if I mentioned mommies, he'd be pulling out pictures and calling home for a phone hug."

Conroy's face pulls into a sly grin. "If I pulled out a picture, Bellamy, it would be the nudie your sister sent me."

As if by reflex, I'm on my feet and diving across the makeshift table, cards flying everywhere; Conroy's T-shirt fisted in my hands as I knock him to the floor. "Touch my sister and you're a dead man."

"It was a joke! I don't even know your sister," he sputters while three sets of hands yank me off of him. With six strong arms holding me back, he apparently feels safe as he lies on the floor and smiles cockily. "And if you really do have one, I sure hope she's better looking than you. Besides, I'm more of a MILF guy. Can't beat experience. What shape is your mother in?"

"You're lucky we don't let him loose, smartass," Silas growls in warning. "There's a limit to pushing your luck, Conroy. Ex-girlfriends and cousins, maybe. Little sisters are a death sentence."

"Now I know." Conroy nods stiffly, then follows with another cocky grin. "You still haven't told me what shape your mother's in."

Rendering a couple snorts and laughs from the guys behind

me, he's found his place. This guy is going to fit in easier than any I've worked with, besides Silas. He's ballsy, a smartass from the word 'go'. Gives as good as he gets.

I roll my eyes as I relent and extend my hand to help him off the floor. "You couldn't handle my mother. She'd beat your ass black and blue."

His eyes dance with mischief as he pushes his luck once more and bobs his eyebrows a couple times. "Would she tie me up with her apron strings and use a wooden spoon?"

Conroy was a perfect fit, for a long time. Until . . .

Chapter 1

Roger

"You're going to kill us, you know that, don't you?"

Silas breathes hard as he drops to the ground, his limbs tired from trekking three miles through rough terrain with a fifty-pound backpack over his shoulders in ninety degree heat and a time limit of an hour to finish. I've been at this for two years. He has no idea. This is child's play. Another week and that time limit is going to be cut by ten minutes.

Why increase his anxiety? He'll find out soon enough.

Six more weeks and fire season starts. The adrenaline will kick in and the anxiety will be long forgotten.

He lids lower as he eyes me skeptically. "You sure this is really part of Hotshot training or are you doin' some kind of hazin' shit?"

I don't even attempt to hide my laugh. I'm a year older than Silas; his Captain and Hotshot trainer. When we're out in the field, I don't demand my men call me *sir*. We're soldiers, there is protocol, but this is a whole different world. The battlefield they're training for is hotter than hell. Our enemy is a torturous bitch that wipes out whatever gets in her way, and leaves nothing behind but remnants in the form of embers and ashes. This would include anyone who gets caught in her blanket of fury. We work together, a team, a chain that cannot afford a missing link.

The men do follow orders – that goes without saying – but this is physical and mental training that often leads to a lifetime of work in a specialty field. Some become Hotshots for life, some firefighters, some smoke jumpers, some a combination of both. The Army will train you, prime you, and give you the tools for success. It's up to the individual as to whether or not they use them. In the world of fighting wildfires, you stay fit – on and off season – because if those flames ever get close enough to lick the underside of your ass, you'd best be ready to kiss it goodbye.

One goal is to make these men as strong, fast, and able-bodied as they can be. The ultimate goal is to make them aware of their surroundings under any and all conditions in order to survive the challenges that will await them on the unpredictable battlefield of hell.

"No hazing, Silas," I reassure him with a chuckle and toss him a canteen. "But you'd better be ready to nut-up for tomorrow."

He pops the screw top on the canteen but before he takes a drink, his curiosity wins out. "Why? What's tomorrow?"

I wave a finger toward the wall adorned with the square-patterned, knotted climbing rope. "You're gonna shoulder that same bag up and down that wall."

He laughs confidently. "That's no big deal. I can handle that."

Shooting him a side-eye, I lift a brow. "Ten times."

"What!?!" He looks as if he's ready to cry, as are the others who have overheard.

Tossing him a Gatorade this time, I grin. "Drink up. You need the electrolytes."

Silas Mitchell and I have become good friends over the past two years. We're currently stationed at Fort Hood in Texas. His rank is 1st lieutenant and he's so close to promotion, I struggle to remember his lower rank because of that friendship. He trains hard, is goal oriented to finish his service commitment, and move on to seasonal auxiliary Hotshot with a city-based firefighter job somewhere close to his family in Scottsdale, Arizona – another thing we have in common. His dad is a four-star General, so the Army life was nothing new to him. However, somewhere around the sixth year, he decided the Army was not the retirement plan he wanted and considered training with the Woodlands Crew.

"We still got the weekend off, don't we?" he asks, hopeful the schedule hasn't changed.

"We do." I gather my own backpack and hoist it over my shoulder. "Three days, actually. Best enjoy it while you can, Mitchell. We've got some rookies starting next week. I plan on using you to help break 'em in."

His entire demeanor changes as his eyes widen in surprise and he hops to his feet. "You're gonna let me lead?"

"I think you're ready, don't you?"

"Hell yeah!" he says without missing a beat. "This calls for a celebration. You wanna hit that titty bar in Waco with me?

Jarvis says the one in Austin ain't bad either so we can try that one if you want. Choose now though. I ain't wasting driving time doin' both. I'm lookin' to get laid."

"I'm not looking to catch the clap, Mitchell," I deadpan, then shake my head and turn toward the Jeep. "I can drive five miles off base to a quaint little bar, find one set of titties, a firm ass, and get her off more times than the amount of miles you'll be driving to get lucky on sloppy seconds."

"Waco is sixty miles away!" he yells indignantly. "You can't get a woman off sixty times in one night!"

I turn back, smirking. "I've taught you everything you know, Silas. Never said I taught you everything I know."

His gaping jaw remains open so long, I'm afraid it's going to lock before he finally inquires, "You got an instruction book on how to do that?"

Pinching the bridge of my nose, I groan. "Oh for God's sake. Get in the Jeep before I leave you out here with the sand fleas."

Chapter 2

Roger

The *Twilight Club* is as it is every time I can sneak away from the base without the usual entourage. This is my place of peace and quiet; my secret. A little hole-in-the-wall gem hidden on the outskirts of Harker Heights. No cowboy hats or oversized belt buckles worn by deep southern-accented Billy Rays looking to get laid after too much beer and boot scootin'. Just dim lights, a soft classy piano bar with an actual talented musician at the keys, and an atmosphere that speaks of bourbon a whole lot more than Budweiser.

I don't dress in military garb when visiting my favorite haunt. A simple button down, blue jeans, and street boots do the job. My hair is short, but not buzzed. There's enough on top to run slender fingers through it, tug on as their thighs squeeze. My facial hair grows so fast I have a five o'clock shadow by two, and since I haven't shaved since yesterday morning, there's enough stubble to leave a nice whisker burn behind. Is it intentional? Absolutely. Some women love a military man. Some women hate us. I'm not looking to be loved . . . or hated. I'm just looking to relieve a little tension.

Having reserved a room at the Hampton Inn down the road for three nights gives me a place to stay. Yes, I could have gone to Waco with Silas; could have gone to Austin, too. But why waste the time and miles? It's clean here, comfy. Definitely classier. And the women usually supply the place to go, leaving me an easy out, after putting them in a post-sex coma.

Scouting the room once in the door, I note a few open tables; some occupied by couples, some by small groups of hungry women, and an empty seat at the semi-circle tabletop around the grand piano that's been custom built to accommodate ten. There are a total of three open stools at the lengthy bar—also custom designed with a layer of pennies buried under an inch of resin—the most inviting of which is next to the one at the end. It's occupied by a head of gorgeous auburn curls that fall over slim shoulders, leading to a tiny waist atop a perfect ass, noted as she reaches forward, using the rung on the stool to lift herself up to snatch a napkin from the bar.

Yup, I've found my place to sit.

"You saving this lucky seat?" The stool is pulled out and my ass halfway planted on it before my question is finished, and examining what I hope to be lovely icing on a damn nice looking cake. My first big mistake.

I've seen my share of pretty eyes. Blue, green, brown, hazel, little flecks of gold spread throughout some of them. But hers? The single most, indescribable shade of . . . is that emerald? Jade? Peridot? It's some kind of jewel, but it escapes me as I try to catch my breath. They're icy, but not in a cold way. They're fucking gorgeous. The kind you find on a painting that follow you around a room wherever you go. Porcelain skin, pert nose, full lips, a mouth made for . . .

"Why would you think it's lucky?"

. . . and a voice I'm going to hear in my dreams for the next decade. Sultry, a tiny rasp that mimics a slow song.

"Because it's next to the most beautiful woman in the place."

She chuckles softly. It's sexy as hell. She's not trying; it's just . . . her. "Nice pickup line. Does it usually work for you?" She lifts the glass of amber liquid to her lips and takes a slow sip. Not a beer, no fancy martini, nothing fruity. Whiskey. Classy.

"I wouldn't know," I confess. "I've never used it." It's the truth, sort of. Asking if she was saving the seat was nothing new. A lucky seat? Nope. Much like the bar, this seat felt custom made for my ass. Hell, women were usually willing to give me their seat so they could sit in my lap. I don't take credit for my good looks – I inherited them. Doesn't mean I can't use them to my advantage.

She shoots me a knowing glance. "You mean you've never had to use it."

Damn those eyes. Hypnotizing. She's seeing right through me. Lying to her would be painful, and just plain wrong. There are sixteen cardinal points of direction on a compass, and a wise man would run for any of the fifteen that point away from her. Me? I'm zoomed in on the one that doesn't. I feel a pull to this woman, an instant attraction; as if this isn't a coincidence.

I smile sincerely. "How about a refill?"

She sips the last of her current drink and sets the glass on the bar. "So long as you realize," she turns toward me and lifts a brow, " – it's not going to get you laid."

"Oof," I react dramatically and slap a hand over my chest. "Whatever will I do?"

She grins wryly. "I recommend a cold shower."

My shoulders rock with uncontained laughter before I extend my hand. "Roger. And whom do I have the immense pleasure of keeping me company?"

She studies my hand for a moment before lifting her gaze to mine, hesitating, then extends her delicate one to shake it. "Savannah."

Savannah. It's beautiful. And while, for some odd reason it sounds familiar, I want to whisper it in her ear as I . . . Ah, the city. That must be it.

"Savannah," I repeat on a whisper, savoring the way it rolls off my tongue, studying those eyes once more. "It's beautiful. Like the city. Is there a last name to go with it?"

She smiles coyly. "*Just* Savannah."

"Well, *just* Savannah," I flag down the bartender to order our drinks. "– how about I buy you dinner and we can fill in the blanks later?"

"You're still not getting laid, Roger."

"I have access to a cold shower." I grin and wink. "The best things in life are worth waiting for. I'm a patient man."

Watching her visibly shiver is worth it. I'm not only patient, I'm persistent, goal oriented. I knew what my goal was when I sat down, but my curiosity has been piqued, and exploring her mind seems almost as interesting as exploring her body.

Almost.

Chapter 3

Savannah

My goal this weekend was to spend a few nights alone. There is no privacy in the barracks. There was no privacy in the hospital. I was determined to self-train sleep without dreams, slumber without background noise. Prove to myself I'm capable of nocturnal solitude without night terrors.

My goal in coming to the *Twilight Club* was to find a place with a small number of people, relaxed ambiance, and maybe some soft music. Sitting in the corner of the dimly lit bar was my strategy: stay well-hidden and you don't get hit on every two minutes. It took me two months to find this cozy little hideaway. No loud noises, no fellow soldiers, no concussion bombs, no unruly crowds. Best of all? No country music. I don't hate it – I'm simply not a fan.

The last thing I'd anticipated was seeing him. *Captain Roger Bellamy.* Why did I tell him he wasn't getting laid? I have all night. Three full lazy ones, if I didn't have to be back in uniform before entering the base early Monday morning. I have a room at the Hampton. I certainly had no intentions of sharing it with anyone. I suppose if we used his, I could sneak out early and still make it in time. Or, settle for one night only and disappear in the wee small hours.

When's the last time I took an entire weekend off base? When's the last time I put on civvies and makeup, wore my hair down? Put on a dress and heels and felt like a lady instead of a soldier? Good God, I even shaved my legs . . . not to mention a few other parts! Granted, it was all for me, but still.

Hesitant enough to give him my first name, I wasn't about to give him my last. Had Silas ever mentioned me? What I wouldn't give to spend one single night with the Captain. He is what dreams are made of. From the sweet and passionate to '*am I going to be able to run in the morning for drills?*' kind of dreams. I can only imagine all the things he could teach me. I have fantasized about the man since the first time I saw him interact with my brother . . . from a distance. We've never met.

Oh, yeah. That is why I told him he's not getting laid.

My brother. Silas Mitchell. My goofy and loving but overprotective, obnoxious, *'Just because I do it doesn't mean you can',* brother. He and Roger are best friends. Which would make me off limits. Hence, the very reason we've never met. I've never met any of Silas' cronies, nor has he met mine. Those are the rules. I don't need him banging my crew mates – who can't shut up about him or Roger – and he would just as soon not be teased about his little sister. We also don't need to be hit up for fix-ups.

The women love them, though they seem to be only a

fantasy, as both he and Roger are very disciplined officers, and neither of them touch the goods on base. I internally roll my eyes when the women comment, then reluctantly agree they fill out fatigues quite well. There's only one backside of the duo I've ever checked out, but if your gaze is in the general direction, no one notices. Pretense can be your best friend when need be. Truthfully, I stay hidden as best I can. Red hair has a strong tendency to stand out. Therefore, mine is skillfully tucked under my cap at all times.

No, on base, my brother and I are virtual strangers with the same rather common last name.

That's not to say if we ever needed each other we wouldn't be there. We would. In a heartbeat. Just like we were as kids. Six years apart, but thick as thieves. When your dad is gone ninety percent of the time, and you move from place to place as an Army brat, you find strength and solace in your loved ones. We were each other's stronghold, Mom was our base, Dad was our iron grip. We always knew he was out there, somewhere, and that love could cross oceans if it had to. That man could make us feel a hug through a computer screen better than anyone. And when he got home? Every minute of his time was spent in fervent effort of being a dad in lieu of an officer.

How Silas and I ended up on the same Army base was sheer happenstance. It definitely wasn't in my plans. I was stationed at Fort Sam initially for combat medic training, then overseas for two years, before I ended up here. I had planned to reenlist for another four years, but you know what they say: the best laid plans . . . .

Since being back I've learned Silas is in training for Hotshots, headed by the infamous Roger Bellamy. The Woodlands Team. I can't imagine my mom being very happy about it – if he's even told her. Dad's another subject. He won't hold judgment nor will he interfere. I kinda wish he would in this case. That's a combat zone larger than life and a horrible way to die if you get caught in it. Helluva long way to healing if you don't die when you get caught in it.

Dad certainly had his say when I went into combat medic training. He's thrilled I won't be reenlisting when my stint is up in four months, and heading back to Arizona to continue school in the medical field. He and Mom both have had all sorts of *recommendations* and/or suggestions on the matter. I should have plucked something out of the air, i.e. orthopedic surgeon, cardiologist, etc. so they would give it a rest. As it is, I stupidly told them I hadn't decided.

I have decided though. I love the medical field, but there are limits for me now to being hands on again. Maybe an x-ray tech. Possibly . . . .

Rule #1: go in with a plan. Even if it's a lie. When the time comes, you can then tell them you've changed your mind.

"I see those wheels spinning. How many thoughts can a redhead hold?" Roger sets his glass down and turns on his stool, elbow on the bar, giving me his full attention.

"Endless." My finger traces the rim of my glass. "The trick is to sort them into stacks and figure out which one to tackle at a time."

He nods slowly. "I don't detect the typical southern accent. Are you from around here or visiting? Maybe here for work, *just* Savannah?"

His subtle effort at gaining a last name makes me chuckle. I'm not a liar, so I choose omission instead. Harker Heights is far enough off the base to not connect the two. If I say I'm a former combat medic, currently stationed in the base clinic, the enchanting banter would be over. A captain with a sergeant? Not in his lifetime.

"I'm in town for a couple days. I work in the medical field, *Roger*." I emphasize the lone first name he gave with a lifted brow. "What is it you do?"

"Army," he says without hesitation, a touch of pride in his tone. *Damn, points for honesty. Here in civvies, he could have said accountant and no one would be the wiser.*

"Lifer?"

The inquisitive look he gives me nearly makes me cringe. That wasn't exactly a civilian reaction, or question. He studies my face for an extra beat before answering, "That's the current plan."

Covering my tracks the best I can, I react nonchalantly. "My dad was Army. You stationed at Hood?"

His shoulders relax. "I am. Non-duty weekend. Three days of bliss. Been a long time."

I smirk and tilt my head. "And you were hoping to get lucky."

His laugh only adds to the perfection of the smile. Blonde, straight white teeth, sincerity reaching all the way to the corners of bright blue eyes, and dimples that I'm sure he was teased about all his life.

"I already have." He slides the menu the bartender dropped off minutes ago in front of me. "I met you. Eat here at the bar or do you want a proper table?"

I lift one shoulder in a slight shrug. "It's cozy here."

His gaze drops from my eyes to my mouth and his tongue slides slowly along his bottom lip. "And proper is so overrated."

Lifting my menu to study the few selections the club offers, I cling to my resolve. I am so out of his league. I'd be the brunt of every joke on base.

"She didn't even know how to grip it."

"Starfish."

"I had to show her how to do everything."

"I wasn't looking to be a teacher!"

"I'd swear I was banging a virgin."

Newsflash: Because you were!

"Still not getting laid, Roger."

He leans in so close his breath whispers across my skin. "I don't need to get laid to feel lucky, *just* Savannah. Tell me you're free for the weekend."

The bartender appears before I can answer, giving me a welcome reprieve. "Have you decided what you'd like?"

Roger grins as he looks to me. "Burgers and fries? I'll take you for prime rib tomorrow night. There's a fabulous place down on the edge of town."

"Burgers sound good to me."

He holds up two fingers and tells the bartender, "Two burgers and fries. The lady and I are having the same thing."

The bartender collects the menus. "You got it. Refills on the drinks?"

"I'll just have water," I tell him. I haven't finished the one in front of me and it's my third. Loose lips sink ships and I still need to get back to my hotel, to my own room via Lyft. It's only eight blocks away, but it's long after dark and walking alone, in heels, might not be the smartest thing to do.

"One more for me with a water, thanks," Roger says, then turns to me. "So, it's settled. Prime rib tomorrow night. How would you like to spend our day tomorrow?"

Wow! There was a question in there somewhere. Just not the kind that gave me a choice . . . or an out. More forcing one of my own that sounds a lot like *what the hell?*

Chapter 4

Roger

Coming on strong with women isn't exactly my MO. I don't need to. I'm simply a guy who knows what he wants, when he wants it, and precisely how to go about getting it. In the field I'm calculated, disciplined, focused. There is nothing casual about my job. My goal is to always finish what I start. The more challenging it seems, the more I like it.

Which brings me to this evening and the woman next to me. She is a challenge. The women I meet are thrilled to spend the few hours we roll in the sheets together. Rarely happy with the cold goodbye that follows, but I'm a creature of habit. I like my bed one way and one way only. Cold in the morning, a party of one, and only distant memories of the night before. Memories that are washed away with the first cup of coffee.

"*Our* day tomorrow?"

Instead of furrowing her brow, she lifts it. Rather than narrowing her eyes, she widens them in curiosity. Instead of pressing those full lips together, she opens them slightly. And if she doesn't change that facial expression, I'm going to lose all control and answer her question and kill that curiosity with a kiss not fit for public viewing. Deep breath in, slow release.

I reach for a lock of soft auburn hair and twirl it around my finger. "Do you have other plans, *just* Savannah?"

Those green eyes narrow the slightest bit, but she doesn't lose focus and stares straight into mine. "What if I do?"

"I'll ask you to change them."

"Here ya go," the bartender announces, setting two plates loaded with burgers and fries in front of us, followed by bottles of ketchup and barbecue sauce. "Drinks will be right up."

"Why me?" Savannah breaks the silence halfway through the meal. I've given her time to decide. Not that I would have given up easily. I will take whatever time she's willing to give me tomorrow. I just wish I knew why.

I swipe the napkin across my mouth. "Eighth wonder of the world." I lift my water glass and tip it in a cheers. "I plan to figure out what it is."

She thinks on it for a moment before holding up her glass as well. "Ten o'clock at the Hampton. I'll be waiting outside."

"You won't have to, *just* Savannah," I say with a wink. "I'll meet you in the lobby. I'm in room 312."

"You're at the Hampton?" She eyes me warily, as if the odds are unbelievable or at the very least . . . suspicious. There are only two hotels in town. Literally, the odds are 50/50.

"I am." My lazy smile grows as I tilt my head. "What room

are you in?"

"Not 312," she deadpans.

Redheads are a bit of a fascination for me. I know a dye job when I see one. Blondes and brunettes are easy to come by; they blend into a crowd like camouflage. But a true redhead? A green-eyed redhead to boot? Two percent of the population on both fronts. Rare as a blue diamond. I read a study once that said redheads have more orgasms than the average woman as well. I wouldn't know; I've never had one. My convo with Silas rings in my head as fresh as my last sip of whiskey as I drain my glass. *"You can't get a woman off sixty times in one night!"* Maybe not tonight, but I do love a challenge.

"I can always switch rooms," I proffer with an unmistakable invitation that has never failed me.

"Lobby at ten o'clock." She arches a no-nonsense brow. "In the morning, Roger."

"Can't blame a guy for trying. Come on." I chuckle and extend my hand to help her off the barstool after throwing a handful of cash on the bar for our meal, drinks, and a good tip for the bartender. I can't even say I'm disappointed. She's gorgeous, a forty on a scale of one to ten, but she's not easy. She's classy. I've never been made to work for it, but I kinda like it. There is a first time for everything. "You driving back to the hotel?"

She shakes her head and snatches her clutch off the bar, retrieving her phone from inside. "No, I was going to call a Lyft. It's long after dark and the safer option."

"It's not that far and the weather's nice. I'll walk you back," I offer. "We're both headed that way. If you'd like, we can have the bartender snap a pic of my ID to guarantee you won't end up on the evening news tomorrow."

Corbin Reeves, former Army and the bartender who has overheard my offer, chuckles as he gathers our plates. "I can vouch for Roger. He'd kill a man for hurtin' a woman. He'd never be the man to hurt a woman."

Savannah's eyes flit between him and me before she crinkles her nose and bites her bottom lip. *My freaking kryptonite.* "I'm in a dress and heels."

My gaze travels an unbelievably fit body from her head to her toes, as if to confirm what she's just said. Legs so long they could wrap all the way around my back and lock at the ankles. "I see that. I can always carry you piggyback if your feet get sore."

"My dress will ride up my thighs!"

I shrug as if it's nothing. "I won't be able to see it." I place my hand on her lower back and lead her toward the front door. She's only got half of her thighs covered as it is. "Besides, my hands will be too busy covering the bottom of your ass cheeks to keep them hidden from public viewing. It'll give me a chance to practice my Braille. Let's go, Savvy."

God, I hope her feet are killing her by the first block. Added bonus would be that she's wearing a thong under that dress.

Chapter 25

Savannah

"Have you gone through the applications I gave you last week?" Dad asks before forking another bite of mom's pot roast. I leave tomorrow morning to go back to base, and both he and mom are counting the days until I return. Little do they know, I've been researching schools for months and my plans are not to live under their roof, no matter where I attend. My VA education bill as well as my experience have worked to my advantage for the OR tech career I've finally decided on. Even online classes wouldn't convince me to live at home. I have never lived alone – not even sure I'll like it – but one never knows until they try.

I have enough money saved to cover living expenses for a year in comfortable accommodations, and I'd been eyeballing teaching hospitals in Phoenix. Banner Medical has already accepted me for their program that starts in two months. Just far enough away to breathe and close enough to prevent a heart attack for them.

"Don't need to, Dad. I have plans of my own."

He drops the fork and it clatters against the China. "Tell me you didn't reenlist."

I nearly laugh at the notion. "Not hardly. I've been accepted at a teaching hospital in the Phoenix area. They have an excellent OR tech program."

"OR tech?" My mom's voice is an octave higher than usual. "Savannah, I thought you wanted to be a doctor."

Shooting her a wry look, I remind her, "When I was ten. Since then I've also wanted to be an astronaut, a deep sea diver, an acrobat, and a plumber."

My mom's burst of laughter spurts wine faster than she can catch it with her napkin when she notes the sour look on my dad's face. "A plumber?"

"Only their foreman, Dad." I roll my eyes. "So I could tell them to pull up their pants to cover the cracks of their asses. You should have seen the guy that came to fix the sink one time. Silas told me it's where they stash their pens." I catch a sob with the memory of my brother. "Handy for the customers to sign the work orders."

Mom is out of her seat as fast as Dad is and they both lay arms over my shoulders. "I'm going to miss him so much. We never told anybody on the base that we were siblings, but I always knew he was there for me if I needed him. No one knew until the day he left and he came to say goodbye instead of texting. I think he somehow knew he wasn't coming back."

"Savannah," Dad's shocked whisper comes from my left.

“Why would you and your brother hide being siblings?”

I let out a pitiful laugh. “Silas and Roger were pretty hot commodities, Dad. The women drooled over them. I didn’t need my bunkmates badgering me to set them up, and he didn’t want to be teased about his little sister.”

He tips my chin up, his forehead crinkled in curiosity while his eyes are narrowed in suspicion. “And the day they left is the first time you met Captain Bellamy?”

Squaring him straight in the eyes, I reiterate, “I told you that was the first time Silas introduced us.”

He plops back down in his chair, disappointment radiating off of him.

“Neither one of them knew, Dad. Roger had no idea that I was Silas’ sister . . . or a soldier.”

“How in the hell did you hide that? You were on the same base!”

Twirling the stem of my wine glass, I eye the bottle on the table and contemplate draining it before spilling the sins of his daughter. “Roger and I met in Harker Heights one night on a weekend leave. It was only supposed to be that weekend, but it turned into more. He hid nothing about who he was. I lied about everything. We worked on opposite sides of the base. I was in the clinic all day.” I shrug. “I kept my hair tucked under my cap, head hung low. A lot of looking over my shoulder.”

His eyes are wide, skin flushing with every breath. “How long did that go on?”

“A few months.” I hear the shame in my reply, but feel not one ounce of remorse. I loved the man – still do – and wouldn’t trade one moment we shared.

“Oh, Savannah.” My mom’s whisper of disappointment is enough to put another tear in my heart.

“Young lady!” Dad’s fist comes down so hard on the table it

makes me startle. "Do you have any idea how many rules of conduct you've broken?!"

The legs of my chair scrape the ceramic floor as I scoot it back in a hurry. Throwing my napkin on the table, I glare at him. "Feel free to report me, Dad. It's over. And the only thing broken is my heart. Thanks for caring. I'm going to finish packing. I'll be out of here in the morning."

On the way to my room, I hear my mom scolding my father. "You put that temper in check, Dirk. She's not one of your soldiers, she's your daughter."

Half an hour later, three light taps on my door are followed by my dad's soft voice. "Savannah, can I come in?"

Swiping the back of my hand across my cheeks, I call out, "It's open."

He takes a seat on the bed next to me and places a gentle arm across my shoulder, pulling me in for a side hug. "Sometimes we dads have a tendency to speak before we think. I have a tendency to forget I'm the luckiest man in the whole world." His voice cracks and he sniffles as he squeezes a little tighter, resting his chin on my head. "The best kids, best wife. My daughter was out in the line of fire saving lives while others were home deciding what dress to wear to some club." I feel his chin on my head when he shakes his. "You fell in love with him, didn't you?"

I nod against his chin. "Yeah. He said he loved me, too."

"I don't doubt that, sweetheart. I saw the way he looked at you." He draws his head back to hold my gaze. "Roger's got a lot on the line here. You need to consider what he has to lose, and men can get really stupid when it comes to love. We can still arrange it so you finish out the last few weeks right here on . . ."

"No, Dad. It's over." I stand from the bed and toss the last few things into my duffel. "I'm doing the rest of my time at Fort Hood. I have people there I'd like to say goodbye to and I want no hitches in my service record."

A soft sigh leaves his nose that he tries to hide. "Your mother and I would be happy to pay for school."

"I earned these benefits, Dad," I remind him. "Let me use them."

His mouth twists. "Can we upgrade your apartment?"

"You don't even know where I'm going to live yet! I'll be fine."

"Buy you a car?"

"Dad," I huff and point to the door. He rises and slowly makes his way to the door, but before he can leave I toss in a little food for thought. He's Army, he's tough, stubborn, and a little on the hard side. "Hey, dad?"

"Huh?"

"Sometimes a good old fashioned I'm sorry would be a whole lot simpler and a lot less expensive."

He stares at me for only a moment before his face splits in a grin. "Come 'ere, *Trouble*." I laugh at his nickname for me. He pulls me into a hug and rocks me back and forth. "I'm sorry for being so harsh. All you ever have to do is call. I love you."

"Love you too, Dad."

"Wanna go for ice cream?"

Warm, wet tears find their way to the surface. Dad hates ice cream, but he'll eat an ice cream cookie sandwich once he's scraped out the middle. It's always been about the simple pleasure of watching his kids enjoy a treat.

"Shall I bring the spoon so you can scoop it out?" I giggle.

"Nah. I found this brownie delight shit they're serving now." He slips his arm over my shoulder to lead me out the door. "There's almost no ice cream in it. It's not bad."

Chapter 5

Savannah

Savvy. Well, it's better than *Peaches.* Savvy gives me credit for having the ability to use good judgment. Peaches only reminds me I was the *oops* baby after Mom and Dad had a quickie one drunken, horny night outside the base near Savannah, Georgia, and the condom broke. At least that's what Silas used to tell me. Truth is, I was named Savannah due to the location of conception. I never said my brother couldn't be a real ass when he chose to.

I'll walk barefoot or develop blisters before I let Roger carry me piggyback. I wore a thong under this dress in order to avoid panty lines, and he would be palming literal ass cheeks in order to keep them covered – because they're naked otherwise.

I simply wanted a weekend to feel feminine! To let my hair down, wear lingerie that wasn't cotton or a sports bra, to shave above my knees, wear perfume, apply makeup, polish my nails.

Three blocks later I'm feeling the burn. The balls of my feet are on fire, my arches are being stretched to the point of no return, and I feel every pebble under the soles as I take another step. The top of my fourth toe on the right foot is also starting to rub. Never have I yearned for my broken-in Army boots more than I do at this moment. Soaking my feet in an ice bath on a Friday night was not my idea of a good time. Wearing Band-Aids for the next week doesn't sound too enticing either.

"This was not a good idea." I stop suddenly, pondering whether I should strip my shoes off, call for a Lyft where I stand, or let Roger practice Braille with my ass cheeks while he lets me ride piggyback to the hotel.

Roger doesn't release the hand he's been holding since we left the *Twilight Club*. "Two choices, Savannah." He turns to face me fully, then uses his free hand to palm my cheek – the upper one. "Over my shoulder or piggyback."

My glare should speak for itself, but I add to it just to be clear. "So you either get to see my fanny or feel it."

The buttons of his shirt are being undone one by one as I fight to keep eye contact and not stare at a chiseled chest leading to sculpted abs. His eyebrows lift in a dare as he detects my struggle before he strips his shirt off his shoulders and wraps it around my waist, tying the sleeves together in front. His breath is warm on my skin as he leans close and speaks softly in my ear, "If you wore a skirt long enough to cover your ass when you bend over, we wouldn't be having this dilemma, sweetheart. No one will be seeing that fine ass tonight. I won't be seeing or feeling your *fanny* until you give me permission. Now, over my shoulder or piggyback?"

Feeling as if I've been scolded, had my virtue kept intact, and a bit claimed at the same time, I sheepishly whisper, "Piggyback."

He grins wolfishly. "Safe choice. I never said I wouldn't bite it." He turns his back to me and squats. "Hop on. Your chariot awaits."

I swear he is bouncing with each step on purpose. His forearms are under my thighs in order to hold me up while my shoes dangle from two of his fingers after he stripped them off my feet. His shirt covers my ass, but my skirt is bunched up around my hips with the stretch of my legs in order to wrap them around his waist. With every rhythmic step, the tiny scrap of silk between his bare back and my aching core may as well be nonexistent. Every time I try to adjust my hips to ease the agonizing ache, he simply hikes my thighs higher, making for more friction. The more I try to separate us at the waist, the more stimulation my nipples receive. The more I try to hold my nipples away from his bare back, the more my crotch rubs. It's a lose/lose situation. I am ten seconds away from a dry hump orgasm, in a vertical position no less, and he knows it!

The orgasm hits like a runaway train – fast and unstoppable.

My forehead drops to his shoulder as an unbidden moan rises all the way from my chest into my throat and releases somewhere out into the universe. My body trembles as I try to suck air into my lungs. My thighs quiver with the effort to squeeze them together as the pulses between them pound a beat I'm sure he can feel, and my toes curl on now outstretched legs before every muscle in my body eventually begins to relax.

"Well, that was embarrassing," I utter into the crook of his neck, the masculine scent one I will never forget.

"That was sexy as hell," he returns, boosting my thighs up a notch and continuing the journey toward the hotel. "You ride horses bareback too?"

I slap his shoulder on the opposite side while burying my face deeper into the bend of his neck, my humiliation crushing any self-confidence I've worked so hard to rebuild. "I think I hate you."

He laughs heartily. "Baby, you can hate me like that all you want. Can't say I've ever had a woman get off riding my back before, but I guarantee you, my saddle on the front rides a whole lot better."

Be still my thighs.

The entrance to The Hampton appears like magic, but Roger doesn't carry me inside. Instead, he sets me down approximately twenty feet outside the doors with a clear view to the inside of the lobby, then turns to shield me from its view.

"I'm going to do the gentlemanly thing here, *just* Savannah." He reaches under the tail of his shirt and adjusts the hem of my dress so it rests where it's supposed to once again, but leaves the shirt in place. "Our agreement was to meet in the lobby at ten tomorrow morning. How are your feet?"

My feet? Are you kidding me? The man just got done setting my every last nerve ending on fire and he's worried about my feet?

Shooting a quick glance down at my bare feet, as it would seem I'd forgotten all about them, I stammer, "Um, fine?"

He holds my heels out for me to take. "Good. Wear sensible shoes tomorrow. There are some waterfalls not far from here that I'd like to show you. It's peaceful, a nice place to walk. You interested?"

If I don't look away, I'm going to cry. An actual date. The gentlemanly thing. The fantasy of the Army base is asking me for a date.

"Yeah," I accept with a nod. "I'm interested."

I fumble with the knot on the sleeves of his shirt that

he tied around my waist, but he halts my efforts with gentle hands. "Keep it for now. Feel free to wear it for PJs tonight and return it to me in the morning. It's almost like being in bed with me."

My lips tip as my cheeks flush. "I just may do that. See you at ten, Roger."

"One more thing." He tips my chin with two fingertips. "It's gonna be a cold shower no matter what, so I may as well make it worth it."

Yeah, that gentlemanly thing? It lasts for all of five seconds before that hand firmly grasps the back of my neck and maneuvers full control of a kiss I'd pay good money for; leaving me breathless.

He leans his forehead on mine and squeezes his eyes closed. His voice matches his military rank of captain, demanding and gruff, as he commands, "Now, go get on that elevator, to a room I don't know the number of, before I beg and plead for it." He drops a soft kiss to my forehead. "Goodnight, my little green-eyed eighth wonder."

Chapter 6

Roger

I could be getting laid. Hell, I could be done getting laid . . . five times over! But instead, I'm lying here with the TV on trying to cover the sounds of guests returning to their rooms with no consideration for those of us trying to sleep. Doors slamming, kids tromping down the hall as if on a sugar high from hell. Good! I hope they're up early in the morning making life a living hell for the parents who can't control them. I should make note of the rooms they enter, so I can make their lives a living hell come six o'clock in the morning when I plan on leaving for my daily run. Walk the halls and randomly pound on the doors. If nothing else, wake the kids up as I loudly announce ice cream being served at the continental breakfast bar. What the hell. It's practice for the nieces and nephews when my little sister, Ruthie, has a few of her own.

Who am I kidding? The kids in the hall are not the reason I'm awake. I can sleep through a football game at a stadium next door paired with a hurricane and a tornado. Conditioning. Gunfire might be a different story. The snap, crackle, and pop of flames as they close in is another.

The cold shower I took was futile. The hot one following with a little self-help was of minimal relief. Would she have come to my room if I'd asked? Would she have invited me to hers? *Just* Savannah. What I would have given to be able to see her when she let go. Look into her eyes.

Damnit, why did I kiss her? I want to do it again. I want to do it now. I don't do romance. I do sex, and I do it well. A little too well tonight. Hence, getting her off with a piggyback ride. My goal was to warm her up, edge her a little, but I never expected the explosion of pure pleasure as she rode out her orgasm against my skin. That was a first for me, probably for her too judging by her embarrassment. But I'd do it again in a heartbeat just to hear her moan. Feel her thighs squeeze around my middle. See those toes curl as she stretched her legs. And passersby had no idea what was happening. So composed. So disciplined. So fucking perfect. There's no show with her. You get what you get, and I really liked what I got. Damn! I liked what I got.

So, why am I not getting laid? Good question.

She had told me I wasn't going to, and I wasn't going to push my luck . . . tonight anyway. I'll see her tomorrow morning at ten o'clock in the lobby. Never say never.

And with that thought, my eyes close and sleep starts to take me under.

If that knock on the door is kids replacing ding dong ditch with knock-knock ditch, there will be hell to pay. A quick glance at my watch on the nightstand reveals two o'clock. Whoever it is at the door had better be ready for my jerseys because I'll be damned if I'm grabbing pants. If they can't handle the wood, that will be a *them* problem. If Silas somehow figured out my treasured place of solitude, that will be cause for murder. Running a slow hand down my face and over my scruff, I throw back the sheet and work my way across the room to the door.

Utilizing the peephole reveals a damn better sight than kids. She's in my shirt, clutch in hand, as her eyes give away the fight or flight instinct that wars within.

"Savannah?"

"Um," she starts slowly as she tries to peer past me through the open door. "Is it possible for me to . . ." Female laughter rings behind me from inside the room. "Oh God," she lets loose a shocked whisper, then glances at the natural phenomenon known as morning wood bulging in my jerseys. "I-I didn't know you had company. I'm sorry." She shakes her head, holding her hand in the air as she turns away to make a fast dash back down the hall. But I'm faster, though not as gentle as I should be. It's two o'clock in the morning and while my reflexes might be quick, my brain hasn't caught up yet. That, and if I let the door close, we're both locked out. Jerseys and wood might not be a welcome sight in the lobby – unless the front desk clerk is horny.

"It's the TV, Savannah. I was using it for white noise," I explain once we're both in the room. The entry light is on, and my arms are wrapped around her shoulders in an apology for grasping her elbow too hard. "Did I hurt you?"

"No." She shakes her head against my chest, though her answer is rushed.

I tip her chin up, but she won't look at me. "Hey, eyes up here. Talk to me." My voice may not be harsh, but I really need to work on my delivery. She's not one of my soldiers. She is all woman, and apparently in need as she lifts her gaze and I note the redness, the worry, and what I swear is fear in her eyes.

"Can I . . ." she hesitates, "can I stay here with you?" She sucks in a small gasp and her eyes go wide. "Not for sex. I meant, can I sleep on the sofa?"

Taking her shoulders in my hands and bending at the knees so as not to seem overpowering, I virtually demand, "Did someone make you feel unsafe?"

"No! No!" she denies vehemently. "The noises, I-I mean the noise, I can't sleep. I was hoping it was quieter up here."

Up here. Aha, she's on a lower floor. I could ask if she put in a complaint with the front desk, but the fact that she's here supersedes the reason why. So, instead I take her clutch and set it on the coffee table, lead her over to the king size bed, and adjust the blanket, folding it back so she can climb under. "Hop in."

She crinkles her nose. "I'll take the sofa."

Stepping back to the entry, I snap the light off, return to the bedside, pick her up by the waist and toss her onto the mattress. "Neither of us will be sleeping on the sofa." As she starts to weakly protest, I crawl over her body to the other side, and pull the blankets over both of us. "Grab the remote and shut off the TV."

The mattress shifts with her weight as she reaches for the remote and the room is suddenly blanketed in darkness as the episode of whatever was playing comes to an end. When I hear the remote touch the nightstand as she sets it down, I snatch her around the waist and tuck her back tightly against my chest, breathing in her feminine scent of coconut and vanilla. "I should probably mention I'm a cuddler. Goodnight,

Savannah."

I've never cuddled in my life. Never had the desire . . . until now. Something tells me I won't want a cold bed in the morning, nor a party of one, and I definitely won't want coffee to wash away this memory.

Chapter 7

Savannah

After that kiss in front of the hotel and something to look forward to tomorrow, not to mention that earth shattering orgasm—that which I'm still trying to figure out the logistics—I was sure I could find uninterrupted sleep tonight.

Falling asleep was no problem; staying asleep was. If the door across the hall hadn't slammed when it did, I'm pretty sure the inevitable scream would have awakened the whole floor. The timing was perfect. I was seconds away from the point of no return: when laughter was replaced with screams of pain, the color green was replaced with crimson, and limbs were torn like paper. The same dream that haunts me on a regular basis.

I'd been offered an honorable discharge after, but I fought it like a bad case of dysentery. I didn't feel a few broken ribs, a shoulder dislocation, and a concussion were reason for medical discharge. The physical injuries weren't their main concern though. It was PTSD due to how they happened . . .

Britt had told me to call her if I needed her this weekend. Brittany Sunn is my best friend on base; my confidant. She knows my struggles to get past my past, and she's made it her personal mission to help me do so. But I didn't want to call Britt tonight. For some reason, room 312 was whispering my name. And if I didn't answer the call, I would be pacing the floor until I wore a hole in the carpet.

He doesn't ask why I'm here, other than to inquire if I felt threatened by someone in the hotel. *How do you explain only the ghosts of your past?* I can see he has more questions, but he spares me. Small wonder he's a leader – a captain. I told him I'd take the sofa, then he literally tossed me on the bed, and told me where I'd be sleeping. He now has me wrapped in a cocoon of safety and comfort – as if he knew I needed it.

"One more thing," he whispers against my neck, then kisses the tip of my shoulder. "Skip the makeup tomorrow. I like those freckles."

Well, that should prove what a mess I was when I showed up at his door. I had removed all my makeup, brushed my teeth, and went to bed in his shirt and a pair of panties. And apparently, he approves.

The room is dimly lit by the sun streaming through the crack in the curtains when I slowly open my eyes. The urge to fight the stronghold around my midsection is strong, until I remember whose it is. Slow breath in, slower breath out. What the hell time is it?

Reaching for the arm around my waist, I gently pry it loose, slowly lift it away from my body, and attempt to slide out from under it.

"Where do you think you're going?" The low rumble of his chest vibrates against my back and makes me shiver as he tightens his hold and tosses a leg over mine. *Oh, oohh. Sweet baby Jesus. Mary and Joseph too.* I thought his arms and pecs were firm. They've got nothing on the tree trunk rubbing up against my backside.

"I was going back to my room," I lamely explain. "To get ready for our day together. You said we were going to see some waterfalls."

"I haven't forgotten, Savvy." He buries his nose in my hair and breathes deeply. "Damn, you smell good. So much better than my quarters on the base. Just give me a minute to savor this."

"Your quarters on the base?" I chuckle softly. "Doesn't sound like I have much to compete with."

"I don't know about that, baby. Army issue linens and a half flat pillow are pretty hard to beat." He splays a hand on my belly, presses his erection against my backside, and moans into my neck. "Total lie. I've never woken up so hard in my life." He heaves a painful sigh and sits up quickly. "However, I promised you waterfalls and if you don't get out of this bed, the only waterfall you're going to see is what's coming from the showerhead while I take you underneath it." He smacks my butt cheek. "Go! I'll meet you in the lobby."

I skitter out from under the sheets and snatch my clutch from the coffee table. Turning before I'm out the door, I see him watching me go. He is the perfect specimen: propped on one elbow, sheets to his waist, a chest built by years of hard work and training. If my crew at the base knew I was here, they'd be absolutely giddy for me . . . and extremely jealous. We didn't even have sex, and it was the best night of my life.

"Thank you for letting me stay."

"You got a swimsuit?"

"Yeah."

"Wear it under your clothes." He winks. "You're gonna love the waterfalls."

The door closes softly behind me and I make my way toward the elevator back to room 210. Swimsuit? I brought a bikini because I thought I might utilize the pool once or twice while I was here. Why would I need it if he were only going to show me waterfalls?

Oh God, if he's anything like Silas, he sees *No Trespassing* and *Do Not Enter* signs as invitations. The yellow tape they use at crime scenes always meant 'enter with caution' to Silas. He told me if it were truly off limits, they would use red. Orange street cones were targets. Again – not red. He thought the 'Do Not Feed the Animals' signs at the zoo were stupid. *"It's no wonder they eat people if they get too close. They starve the poor things."* We lost him one day when he lagged behind at the zoo. Eventually we found him – sitting at the window of the gorilla exhibit next to an orangutan on the other side, performing what he said was sign language. Later that evening he told me the gorilla signed he preferred little redheads for dinner. Then informed me he had given the ape the code to get out of the zoo, and left the key to the house in a special place so he could find me after we had gone to sleep.

It was the only mean prank I remember my brother ever pulling. My mom found me hiding in my closet that night, terrified, sobbing, waiting to be eaten. I was five, Silas was eleven. He gave me his dessert every night for years thereafter, taught me how to ride a bike, always let me choose the weekend activity, punched a kid for calling me 'carrot top', and watched every classic Disney movie ever made with me – even after he was a teenager. We became best friends – at least he became mine – all due to a guilty conscience. Maybe a sense of obligation. Possibly a chat with Dad. But in the end, I cried when he left home. He cried when he left home. But he never failed to stay in touch, send gifts when he found something unique, call on birthdays, and made sure he was there for my graduation.

At ten o'clock sharp, I step out of the elevator to find a smiling Roger in a T-shirt and quick-dry nylon shorts, a backpack over his shoulder, and two carryout cups in his hands.

"Ready?" He holds out both cups. "Thought you might want coffee. Cream and sugar or black. Your choice."

He doesn't strike me as a cream and sugar kind of guy. I picture him as a black, hot, the stronger – the better type. "Cream and sugar if you don't mind."

"Thank God," he breathes in relief, and sips on one as he hands the other to me. "Not one much for dessert in a cup. Tell me there's a swimsuit under there."

"There is," I confirm, glancing down at the romper I wore over the bikini, and my comfy Chucks for walking. No Band-Aids needed this morning, but I did put on cushioned invisible socks to protect the reddened areas caused by the heels from hell. My hair is tied up in a messy bun and the only thing close to makeup on my face is tinted Chapstick and a coat of SPF-30.

"Good girl." He taps my nose with his index finger and winks. "Glad to see you didn't forget the freckles. I may have to do a little exploring and see where else you're hiding them."

Chapter 8

Roger

The Jeep sits at the curb outside the lobby where the rental service dropped it off minutes ago. I could have rented the typical mid-size car, but there are some back roads I travel when visiting the waterfalls here. That, and it gives me access others aren't aware of on the backside. Hence the reason for her swimsuit. Is it legal? Not for the general public. I, however, have an ex-Army park ranger buddy who allows me access to a few places the GP isn't allowed. I've never brought a companion, but I don't anticipate any problems. He's expecting me and knows I'd never violate a privilege.

Parking the Jeep in front of a diner down the street from the hotel, I tell her, "I'll be right back."

"Where are you . . ."

The half door is closed before she can finish the inquiry and I'm back out in less than three minutes, handing the bag to her as I start the Jeep. *Yeah, I called ahead.* "Hope you like breakfast burritos. Hash browns, cheese, scrambled eggs, and bacon all wrapped up in a tortilla." I turn to her and wink before pulling out into traffic. "All the delight in one bite."

Savannah opens the bag and breathes in a nose full of deliciousness. "I love them. You only got two, though. Where's yours?"

If I could record the sound of her laugh when I shoot her a feigned look of indignance, I would. Music. It's a first – an original, genuine. I want to be the reason for a thousand more. *It's one weekend, Bellamy,* I remind myself. You do one-times, not lifetimes. You're already pushing the limit; making an exception for her. You've never shared your sacred place with anybody. Give yourself a pleasant memory of a woman you may want, but can't keep. Consider it penance for those you've walked out on. You're Army, a Hotshot, a career man. Fuck her behind the waterfall; the one place you've never shared, and never will again. You can still take her to dinner, enjoy her unrivaled sense of humor, her body, get lost in those eyes for one or two nights. But the waterfall . . .

"Take a bite. I'll hold it for you." Savannah holds a half wrapped burrito in front of me; only the top portion open so it doesn't fall apart.

"Ladies first."

"This one's yours," she prods, nudging it closer to my mouth. "I'll eat mine when you're done."

"Take a bite, Savannah," I order slowly. "Be sure to leave a taste of your lips on it. It's that or I pull over now and taste them myself."

"Well, we wouldn't want to be late for the waterfall, would we?" She chomps down on a bite and moans in delight, the sound reminiscent of last night as she squeezed her thighs, curled her toes . . . "Oh my God, this is good."

"Put it in my mouth, Savvy." My jaw tics as my restraint is losing the war.

"Huh," she says as if puzzled. "I always thought the man says put it in *your* . . ." She stops suddenly and clears her throat, as if embarrassed. "Never mind."

Little tease. I snatch her wrist and hold the burrito in front of my mouth. "You're right, but you're not on your knees. I'll be sure to remedy that." I help myself to a generous bite of breakfast and speak around it. "But only after I've been on mine."

Half an hour later, we pull into the scenic park that leads to the falls. Once there is no other traffic around, I turn onto an access road blocked with a heavy iron gate adorned with a *Do Not Enter* sign, and veer the Jeep through the small opening at the side.

"What are you doing?" Savannah spins in her seat, searching for onlookers that may be ready to report a lawbreaker. "The sign said do not enter."

"Yeah, I saw that," I say with a shrug, navigating the pits in the rough terrain before bouncing onto the access road. "Looks like smooth sailing from here."

"Roger!" she shrieks. "I can't afford to get arrested for breaking state laws!"

Squeezing a delectable thigh, I reassure her, "I'm allowed back here. You really think I can afford to get arrested? The Army would bust my chops. I got a buddy who's a park ranger here. Gives me access."

"Oh." She calms quickly, but points her finger in warning. "But if you're lying, you're the one in the driver's seat so it's you who's going to jail. I'm an innocent party to your antics."

I snatch her hand out of the air and suck that finger into my mouth before I nip it gently, making her gasp. "Total truth. I'd never put you in jeopardy, and I hate liars." I drop a kiss to her knuckles and let her hand go.

She sits back in her seat and stares out the passenger side at the heavy foliage. "It's pretty back here."

"You ain't seen nothin' yet, Savvy."

The water is so clear you can see the bottom of the pool that sits off to the side at the top of the falls. There's no current per se – just a slight flow for filtration. Man-made, supplied by the falls' water, and used by only the chosen. Graduation of depth from one end to the other. A small inlet and matching outlet; designed by genius engineers. Totally surrounded by greenery, and most importantly – private. I drop the duffel on the ground, yank my T-shirt over my head and toss it on the duffel, then carefully place my shades on top. Looking to a stunned Savannah, I toe my sneakers off and smugly order, "Strip."

"What?!"

Gently, I slide her shades off and set them with mine. The little one-piece outfit she wears is nothing more than T-shirt material. If I weren't a gentleman, I'd tear it off of her, so instead I squat down and tap an ankle for her to lift her foot and allow me to remove one shoe – and sock – at a time. I stand and slide a thumb under a strap of the outfit covering a swimsuit I'm dying to see. "Strip. We're swimming. Did you forget?"

"You didn't say we were swimming!" she sputters. "You said we were seeing waterfalls."

"Why else would you need a swimsuit, Savvy?" I reach for the other strap and begin to slide them off her shoulders simultaneously.

Her mouths twists as she apparently considers what she

hadn't this morning. "In case we got wet?"

"You are adorable." I laugh as I slide the straps down her arms. My breath catches in my chest as I take in the hot pink bikini revealed to me when the outfit falls around her ankles. I've seen fit, but Savannah is *fit – with a perfect side order of soft.* I don't know what medical field she works in, but it sure isn't plastic surgery. There is not a mark on her flawless, natural body. Toned abs, curved hips, and tits that don't bubble up and over the top with silicone implants. Creamy, porcelain, untouched skin with a few freckles I want to count as I trail my tongue over every one of them. My slow and sly smile spreads from ear to ear. "And you are definitely getting *wet.*"

Chapter 9

Savannah

He hates liars. Seems I'm the champion this weekend, and it would seem he's an innocent party to my antics rather than me to his. Is it really a lie though? I didn't approach him at the Twilight Club. I have not *technically* told him any lies – I've simply not disclosed the whole truth.

One weekend, Savannah. You want an experience – not a ring on your finger. You have four months of service left. He'll never know. Keep your head low, your cap on, and your tail tucked between your legs. Self-preservation. He'll...Never...Know. And neither will your brother.

Roger picks up my romper and tosses it next to the duffel,

then extends his hand for me to take. "Ready?"

"As I'll ever be."

The water feels like heaven. It's cool, but not cold. Crisp. The base and walls of the pool are cemented smooth river rock; easy on the feet. The depth increases the farther we wade in and we're soon treading water. I study the mechanics and design of the small body of water. There's an inflow from the spring and it flows back out at a slightly lower pitch about thirty feet away; a virtual filter.

"This is man-made, isn't it?" Roger nods. "So who uses it?"

He swims closer, his intentions clear as he places his hands on my waist and moves us toward the shallower water until our feet touch bottom. "Right now, us. Nobody else is around." He reaches for a damp, fallen tendril and smooths it away from my face. One light peck to the corner of my mouth, another to my jaw, before his mouth crashes to mine in a fervent kiss; leaving the memory of last night's far behind. He wraps an arm tightly around my waist, bringing us skin-to-skin. "Legs around me, Savvy," he orders gruffly, using his free hand to slide under my thigh and coax it higher around his hips. Like a good soldier, I follow directions and fight the gasp that begs to leave my mouth when I feel what greets me when I do. He's hard! So, so hard!

My back hits the wall, the cool air breezing over my skin is little respite from the heat I feel from my head to my toes. We are a tangle of tongues and teeth, nips and tugs. My body arches and my thighs squeeze tighter around his waist as he drops the cup of my bikini top and takes a nipple in his mouth.

"Roger," I whimper shamelessly. "Please."

"Told you I'd get you wet," he whispers, dropping kisses across my chest on his way to deliver equal time to the other nipple. "Damn, you're beautiful. You sure you want this?"

"Y-yes," I nearly plead.

Reaching for the ties on my bikini bottom, he undoes each one slowly as if unwrapping a gift and squeezes each butt cheek as the back half slips off, while the front remains trapped between the two of us. "Gonna have to loosen your grip with these thighs, baby." He seizes the opportunity the moment my thighs allow, slides it out from between us, and throws it over his shoulder behind him. He's in thigh-deep water, and reaches under my right one to unzip a pocket on his shorts, removing a condom from within. Dropping his shorts enough to release the beast, he wraps it quickly.

"You make it so tempting to want more." He kisses me gently, slowly, then lingers as he gazes into my eyes. "I'm not gonna lie. If I had more to give you, I would, but I'm not that guy, *just* Savannah. I will promise you, though, I am never going to forget you." He lines himself up with precise aim, and thrusts.

I really didn't mean to yelp. I didn't mean to tear up, either. I definitely didn't mean to leave fingernail divots in his shoulders – well, not enough to draw blood anyway. But then, he could have been a little gentler in his delivery. You know, ease in, an inch at a time.

"Tell me that did not just happen." Trying to read his expression is difficult. Anger? Shock? Judging from his wide eyes, furrowed brow, and bristled tone, my best guess is both. Apparently condoms really don't dull the sensation. Pretty obvious he knows he broke the barrier. At least he hasn't pulled out, taking half my insides with him.

My nose crinkles as I choose the easy way out, and simply state what he's told me to, "That did not just happen?"

"You're a virgin?!" he snaps, incredulous.

"Not anymore."

He stares, jaw set hard, not moving a muscle save for the twitch I feel from the appendage my vagina is really starting to enjoy, leading me to believe it either turns him on or he can't help himself. "Why me, Savannah?"

"You're *my* eighth wonder, Roger," I answer honestly. "And if you stop now, I will hate you every second of every day for the rest of my life."

His eyes soften, and he palms my cheek with his rough, callused hand and swipes at a tear. "Bellamy," he whispers then follows with a kiss that matches its tenderness. "Roger Bellamy, and stopping would be the hardest thing I've ever had to do, but I would if you wanted me to."

"Good thing that's not what I want." I press my lips to his in an effort to reignite the passion. His need to give me his last name only reinforces his integrity. My first time shouldn't be with a first-name-only hookup. He also made it clear he can't give me more than this. *Honesty.* Little does he know, I'm well aware of who he is, what he does, his rank. I wouldn't be here otherwise. On the other hand, I shouldn't be here. *He hates liars.*

He pivots his hips with purpose, grinding against my most sensitive parts as if he knows my body better than I do myself. A slow, passionate build before he sets my world on fire with movements I didn't know were possible. I'm desperate for release yet reluctant to have this end.

"Roger . . ."

He bands a tight arm around my waist, one hand in my hair as he gently tugs my head back, full control of every determined thrust and movement. "Eyes on mine, Savvy. You should never forget your first time."

As if I ever could.

If there was wildlife in the trees, I think I scared them off. My hope is if there were any people that overheard, they mistook my howl of ecstasy for an exotic bird.

Chapter 10

Roger

Who was I kidding? She should never forget? It was me who didn't want to forget. Her whimpers and moans, the shuddered breaths were driving me crazy. I needed to see her eyes, watch her come undone for me. I've never been invested in a partner before, other than mutual satisfaction. I've never looked a woman in the eyes during sex. Hell, most of the time I was behind her; one of my favorite positions. *Disconnect*. Intimacy was for saps. Eyes are the window to the soul, and I've never wanted to bare mine.

Right now, I wish I hadn't looked into Savannah's. Her eyes tell stories I want to hear. They inspire poetry, music; break hearts. And I know mine is going to be one of them, because for the first time in my life I don't want to walk away. But she will. '*Only here for the weekend*'. Definitely penance.

She breathes heavily, resting her forehead on my shoulder. I'm still inside her, still hard; no desire to leave for fear if I do, she won't invite me back in. My fingers are wound in her now extremely messy hair knot, and I kiss her temple. "You okay?"

Her shoulders tremble against my chest and I fear I've made her cry, until a muffled giggle escapes. "I didn't mean to be so loud."

"Aw, you weren't trying to inflate my ego?" I hold her tighter to me, stealing the opportunity to feel her bare skin on mine.

"I just hope none of your buddies heard it."

"It's okay, baby." I rub my hand over the smooth skin of her back, and chuckle. "They'll wait 'til I'm here next time to give me high-fives."

She lightly slaps my shoulder. "They probably do it on a regular basis."

Those fingers I have wound in that messy bun maneuver her head so she's looking up at me. "I've been coming here for years and I have never brought anyone up here with me – especially a woman. You broke my waterfall cherry."

She looks skeptical as she questions, "Never?"

I shake my head. "You're the first, Savannah. And if you ever come back around after this weekend, look me up and I'll be more than happy to bring you back." I drop a soft kiss on her mouth and utilize the perfect segue now that it's presented itself. "Of course, you would need my number, and I get long enough leaves sometimes that I could always come visit you, which would mean I need yours."

She looks pensive as she bites her lip and nods slowly. "That is how that works, isn't it?"

"We're still on for dinner tonight, aren't we? I made reservations for two. I'd hate to eat that prime rib by myself." I shrug. "The burgers last night weren't bad, but I eat Army food all the time. A nice restaurant and you on my arm sounds really good right now."

Her forehead creases. "I only brought one nice outfit with me. Unless the restaurant likes shorts and T-shirts, I think I'd better pass."

"My room loves shorts and T-shirts, and I love pizza." I wink and drop another kiss to already swollen lips. "What do you say?" I refrain from telling her my room is open to naked and pizza as well, but we can save that for later.

"I like pizza."

"Then you can stay the night again." I don't pose it as a question nor as an offer. I want her with me. I want every last minute I can get with her, *before the end*. Because there is always an end. Fire season starts in two months. I will take any and all time she's willing to give me in the interim.

"I think I'd like that," she whispers.

Not sure when my dick made its way out of her, because she feels so damn good in my arms, but we do have to get her dressed once again. The thought of skinny-dipping does cross my mind. However, I should probably find the rest of her bikini before we take one more dip. That, and I haven't given her the tour of the actual waterfall yet.

"Let's get you back into your bikini." I set her on her feet and hide my whimper as I slowly raise the cups over those delicious breasts. *Goodbye for now, ladies.* I remove the condom, tie it off, and toss it on the ledge behind her to collect before we leave.

Moving away from the wall and out into the middle again, we both start the search for what should be the easy-to-spot bright pink scrap of swimwear, but find the pool void of anything other than crystal clear water. My eyes track the only path it could have taken just in time to see the last of the strings spill over the wall of the pool to join the water flow toward the falls. I really should have paid attention to my aim. Maybe slid the crotch to the side and worked around it, untied only one string. But I'm greedy, and she felt so damn good.

"Oh shit," I mutter, watching it go. It would be futile to dive for it. It's hardly worth battling the current. That little sucker is long gone. Yeah, this is going to be a day to remember. Unfortunately, it may also be one she wants to forget.

"Where are my bottoms!" Not really a question; more a panic-laced demand.

My military instincts are to deescalate a seemingly impossible situation – I've handled my share – but right now, Savannah looks like a one woman war zone and I'm not sure I could win the battle. Maybe I should have given her two orgasms – the calm before the storm. Damnit! What was I thinking? My dad told me once to never tell a woman to calm down unless I wanted the reverse results.

I approach from another angle and aim for humor. "You ever gone commando?"

"Roger *Bellamy*," she enunciates my newfound last name through a clenched jaw. "Where are my bottoms?"

"Best guesstimate?" I grimace and tilt my head toward the opening. "Probably at the bottom of the falls by now."

Chapter 11

Savannah

That was a three hundred dollar bikini! Worse yet? Not *my* three hundred dollar bikini! Britt insisted I take it and enjoy the sunshine by the pool – and attract a hot one-night stand at the hotel as long as I was there. The only swimsuit I own is black, one piece, and covers more than my sports bra and running shorts. Personal shopping hasn't exactly been a high priority.

"What do you mean at the bottom of the falls?" My voice is shrill, my bottom half naked – unfortunately still throbbing as well as a bit . . . stimulated – and in need of coverage to get out of this pool.

He does look remorseful, though that twinkle in those sparkling blue eyes makes it questionable. He treads water in one place and curls his finger. “Come here.”

“Why?”

He grins. “Because if I come to you, you may kick me in the balls. And I really need to kiss you right now.”

“That’s not going to fix my dilemma,” I snap back, though being kissed by him may make me forget it . . . temporarily.

“I’ll fix it, Savannah. Whatever it takes.”

Tipping my chin in challenge, I ask, “Are you going to give me your swim shorts?”

He lunges without warning and wraps me in his arms, burying his face in my neck. “I’ll give you what’s inside of them.”

I giggle at the sensation of facial whiskers tickling my neck and wrap my arms around his shoulders and my legs around his waist. “I’ve already had it.”

“So you don’t want anymore?” He tempts me with a thrust of his underwater erection and a deep moan.

“I didn’t say that.”

“I’ll buy you a new swimsuit.” He thrusts again. “Tell me you’re on birth control and I’ll buy you twenty. I only brought one condom.”

At 22 years old I am nowhere near ready to start birthing babies. Given my nightmares, I’m already waking up at two, four, and six. Yes, I’m on birth control, but I’m not stupid. Double or nothing; protection that is. My career path options do not include sore nipples, stretch marks, and daycare choices. I haven’t been around kids enough to know if I even like them.

“Oh, you’re buying me a new suit,” I draw back from his hold and narrow my eyes, “but it’s a condom or a cold shower.”

"You drive a hard bargain, boss."

"And you drive a hard babymaker. I think you bumped my uterus."

He laughs so hard he not only causes small wakes in the water, but wakes up body parts that don't need the stimulation as much as they need coverage at the moment.

"Come on, sexy," he says, carrying me toward the water's edge. "Let's get you dried off and into your clothes."

"I still don't have any bottoms."

He squeezes my butt cheek and moans. "Baby, you've got the sexiest bottom I've ever seen."

We spend a couple hours venturing through the park, admiring the waterfalls, and taking a few pictures. When he asks to take a picture of me to remember the weekend by, I panic. What happens if he uses it as bragging rights and Silas sees it?

"No! I don't do pictures!" My hands fly in front of my face before he can snap the shot on his phone. I've already been stupid enough to give him my real first name. It's not the rarest moniker, but it's not exactly common either. What the hell was I thinking?

Roger pulls my hands away from my face, and as I look up to see his, I'm met with what I recognize from the base anytime I catch a glimpse: a soldier, a leader, a commander. Steely blue eyes, mouth set in a straight line over a firm jaw that's currently ticking the slightest bit on the left side.

"Come with me," he demands in a voice so low I feel it more than hear it, as he leads me toward the parking lot. Once at the Jeep, he spins me so my back is against it. His skin is flushed with anger, eyes blazing with a heated glare. "No pictures, huh? I won't ask if you're married since I took your *virtue* only hours ago. That leaves me little to play with. Running from the law? Runaway? How old are you, *just* Savannah?"

That's what he was thinking?

I tip my chin, indignance glowing. "Hardly a criminal. And I am twenty-two; perfectly legal," I enunciate each syllable harshly. I've earned every damn one of those years. Sometimes feel like I've lived twice as long, through twice as much as those years would quantify. I love harder, feel stronger, and cry softer for it, but it doesn't hurt any less.

"Twenty *fucking* two," he grinds out slowly, like it's poison on his tongue, staring as if in disbelief. He laughs sarcastically. "Well, you played the grownup like a pro, sweetheart. Dress up like a real lady, sit in the bar and drink whiskey instead of some fruity shit. Find a real man to pop your cherry instead of a college boy. Good job."

My hand has never moved so fast or so hard. Definitely carries an impact as the slap stings my palm and causes Roger's head to snap to the side. "Fuck you, Roger *Bellamy*." I shove my way past him and head for the entrance to the park – I think. We came in from the west; east would seem the sensible way out. There are shuttles, buses, Lyft rides. Now, if I can only get some bars on my phone, I could make arrangements. Hell, I'll hitchhike if I have to.

What an asshole! Age does not define experience, character, maturity – *time of death*. Some of them could have been college boys, but instead they chose the military.

Chapter 12

Roger

Twenty-two?! Even after hearing it, I still can't believe it. Damn, that slap stung! She has more class, sass, and spirit than any woman I've ever met. She's tenacious. An adult sense of humor. There is life lived in those eyes; wisdom. She came to my room because of the ("*noises*") noise. Tell-tale sign and I missed it. There's a big difference and she was quick to correct it. She didn't ask for more; I did! She's not a clinger; I am! She's only two years older than my little sister! The sister I nearly pummeled Conroy for making a joke about. Good God, has she even finished college? *In* the medical field, or working her way toward it?

I hop in the Jeep and fire it up, determined to find that mass of red curls and set her ass back in the passenger seat. I'm the one who drove her thirty miles away from her hotel and I'll be the one delivering her back to it. I'm not an asshole. What I am is seven years older than she is and should know better. I'm Army, a career man. I'm also a Hotshot. You can play with us, but don't stay with us, unless you want to get burned – figuratively. We're not a risk worth taking.

Her footsteps are paced, solid, resolute; much like a soldier's. So unlike the feminine walk in her heels last night before I put her on my back. It has to be the difference in the shoes, though I sure didn't notice it ten minutes ago. I felt bad when I stripped those chucks off at the pool and saw she had socks underneath to protect a bit of redness on a couple toes. I should have put her on my back straightaway out of the club. So stubborn. But so damn beautiful.

"Get in, Savannah." I coast the Jeep slowly next to her on the road out of the park when she doesn't stop.

"Fuck you!"

"You can do that when we get back to the hotel." I mentally kick myself as soon as the words leave my big fat mouth. I'm a natural born smartass, and it serves me well . . . on most occasions. Today is not one of them. I'm not supposed to want her.

"In your dreams," she sasses back. "You weren't that good the first time."

Whoa, ho, ho. She is pissed. And damn quick with a retort. "Is that why you screamed my name, Savvy?"

"That was only to feed your ego. Figured you needed something to brag about to your Army buddies." She studies her phone as she walks, probably checking reception. "Might want to leave out the part that you were with a youngster. Go find yourself a *real lady* and leave me alone so I can arrange a ride."

Damnit! She is hardly a *youngster*; simply *younger.* And so damn beautiful.

I speed ahead, shut off the Jeep, hop out and backtrack to where she stands. "Get in the Jeep. I brought you here, I'm taking you back."

"No thanks. I'd rather walk with a grizzly. Maybe I can find a college boy on my way." She smirks. "Who knows? Now that you broke me in, if the frat house is having a party tonight we could . . ."

She yelps as I snatch her off her feet and carry her bridal style toward the Jeep. "You make a scene and the park rangers will come running, *just* Savannah," I warn. "Keep in mind, I have a clean record and a spotless reputation. Half of them know me. You can ride back with me or in a police car. Take your pick."

"I don't think I hate you anymore," she grumbles against my shoulder, but doesn't fight my hold. I relish how well she fits, until she lifts her chin and scowls. "I know I do."

The ride back to the hotel is uncomfortably silent . . . for me. I miss our banter. I miss touching her without reason. I miss her smile. Apologies have never been my strong suit. My only soft spots have been for my mother and little sister, and even they think I'm rough around the edges. I do owe her an apology, though. She didn't do anything wrong, and I don't want her to hate me.

"Savannah, wait!" The little shit was out of the Jeep and hit the ground running once I was barely parked, and is now halfway across the parking lot. She is quick – I'll give her that – but again, I'm faster. "I'm sorry," I whisper into the crook of her neck, holding her a foot off the ground by the waist. The scent of her hair mixed with the lingering scent of the pool makes me wish we were still there; that I'd spent more time easing her into ultimate pleasure. The way her body fits with mine at any angle, the race of her pulse in perfect beats with mine convinces me we meld better than any two people on the planet. "You are the realest lady I've ever met. I shouldn't have said what I did. You scare the shit outta me, Savvy, because you're the first woman I've ever met that I don't want to forget."

"You will though." Her breath catches as she fights a sob. "As soon as you go back to Ft. Hood. It's the Army way of life, right?"

Setting her back on her feet, I turn her gently in my arms and see the fallen tears. "The Army can only own so much of me, Savannah. They can't have my heart. You already stole it."

A pitiful laugh escapes and she swipes at her nose. "It's only been a day, Roger."

She's right; it has. Nevertheless, exploring the possibilities has fast become a high priority.

Fisting what's left of her messy bun, I murmur against her plush lips, "You work fast, my little thief." I capture her mouth as if it might be my last meal. I need her to stay. I haven't gotten her number yet. If there's a way to see her again – even if only on a sporadic basis – I'll take it. Something to look forward to.

I've always had a purpose in life, but I've never had a reason.

Chapter 13

Savannah

This wasn't supposed to happen. It wasn't that he was irresistible, he was untouchable – by so many standards, so many rules. We won't even touch the golden one – my brother. Silas might be able to forgive me – someday. The Army, however, will string me up by my heels. An officer with enlisted? Fraternization is not frowned upon – it's prohibited. I'm as illegal as a dimestore hooker in Louis Vuitton on a Sunday afternoon.

Untouchable is a bit like a dare to me. You know how it is. You always want what you can't have. Just a little nibble, maybe a finger swipe of frosting from the birthday cake before it's cut. But I never expected him to be the whole damn dessert.

So, here I am in room 312. Sheets over our naked bodies, backs against the headboard, sharing pizza and beers after working up a hefty appetite. Three guesses how we did that.

"When do I get Savannah's last name?" Roger asks, setting his napkin on the nightstand next to his empty bottle.

Knowing it was only a matter of time before this bit me in the ass, my heart still races. "It's *just* Savannah." I shrug. "Like just Cher or just Sting."

He takes my hand in his and snickers. "You know who Cher and Sting are. Interesting." He studies our hands, then lifts a brow. "Your pulse is 92, sweetheart. Which would mean you're either anxious for my dick again, or a lousy liar."

How does he do that? Nailed it, on both accounts.

"Roger," I whisper, guilt washing over me from head-to-toe as I stare at our joined hands. "It was supposed to be just the weekend. You already told me you can't give me more."

He takes my cheeks in his palms. All the hardness I've become accustomed to through observation is washed away as he promises, "I would try. Damn, Savannah, I would try. I'll meet you more than halfway at every turn. I'm not always available, the job takes a lot, but I'll do my best. I'm not asking for all of you, but a part of you is better than none."

I should confess, right now, right here. But I fear it would change the dynamic of every relationship that mean the most to me. Silas will hate me. Dad would be so ashamed. Roger would probably report me. The Army would end my career – what's left of it. Proving myself and furthering my education depends on finishing what I fought so hard for. Could I keep up this charade for four months?

"Can that part of me be *just* Savannah?"

He thinks on it for a moment. "Compromise. You keep your last name to yourself for now in exchange for your number."

"Two compromises," I counter, holding up my index and middle fingers. "You get my number, but no last name. And I get a promise that what happens here stays here. No swapping stories with your Army buddies, no pictures, no first name either. It's not that common."

He eyes me warily, forehead creased and eyes narrowed. "That's a helluva compromise, Savannah. Now give me the reason."

I look him straight in the eyes and blur the truth with the biggest bucket of whitewash – or bullshit – the best I can. If I word it precisely, it's not a total lie. *Semantics.* "My job. We provide medical supplies and services for military. There are rules against fraternizing with military personnel, for which I signed a contract."

Okay, I said 'we' instead of 'I'. I provide the bandages when needed. I do provide services in the clinic on the base. Finally, my job is a clinic medic until my stint is up. Neglecting to mention I am Army is debatable. Unless I get caught.

He is out of the bed as fast as he can throw off the sheet. "Then what the hell are you doing here with me!? I told you I was Army when we met!"

"I won't be doing this job forever!" I match his yell then throw the sheets back and reach for my shorts on the floor, yanking them over my legs. "And we were supposed to be a one-time thing until you turned it into an eighth wonder thing." My tank top is apparently in no man's land as it's nowhere in sight. I truly doubt the fellow hotel residents would appreciate a show, so I start my search – topless.

Roger stands on the other side of the bed, arms folded over his chest, buck naked, watching me. I pick up a pizza crust from the nightstand and throw it at him. "Do you have any modesty at all?"

He catches it easily and takes a bite, chewing slowly then speaks around it. "Nope. But if you want me to cover it up, I need the whole pizza, sweetheart. Extra-large, please."

I glare at his obnoxiousness; the casual pomposity. "You are so full of yourself."

"I'd rather you be full of me." He curls his finger slowly. "Come here."

"No!"

He smiles cockily and whisper-sings my name, "Savannah, come here."

"Why?" I feel my resolve weakening and know he can hear it, see it.

"Because I really need to kiss you, my little eighth wonder."

"Then you need to come to me," I demand, standing my ground, though I feel my toes grip the carpet for extra support to stay strong.

Step by slow steady step he makes his way to me until we're toe-to-toe. "I will come to you as often as I can. Have you ever been tempted to break the contract rules before?"

"No."

"So, I'm the first one?"

"Yes."

"Will I be the last one?"

"Yes."

"Then it doesn't matter, *just* Savannah." He delivers a kiss I won't soon forget, and a promise I know I can trust. "No one needs to know. This is us. Our secret." He gathers a handful of hair and tugs my head back gently. "Now, let's get something straight. We are not a one-time thing, we are a once in a lifetime thing. I can't promise you forever, but I promise you me for now. Give me your damn phone."

Thank God I switched to a Texas area code when I came back from Afghanistan.

Chapter 14

Roger

"Tony in his office?" I interrupt the front desk clerk as she checks out another hotel guest. I've got approximately half an hour to be out of here and on my way back to base. Savannah left at the ass crack of six o'clock this morning, but only after I caught her trying to sneak out at the even darker ass crack of five. We didn't need a proper farewell; we needed a proper 'see ya later', and I needed an estimated timeframe. *Two weeks.*

"If you'll let me finish what I'm doing, I'll be happy to take you, Mr. Bellamy." The desk clerk shoots me the same salacious smile she does every time we cross each other's paths. Had the customer not been within earshot, pretty sure she would have offered to *take me* in the broom closet on the way. It wouldn't be the first time. Not that I've ever indulged, but today it sounds repulsive. I want my real lady.

"I know the way, thanks."

Rounding the counter to the door labeled 'manager', I help myself to the doorknob, sans knocking first. Tony sits at his desk full of strewn papers, the glow of his computer screen reflected off his glasses.

"Bellamy," he greets me with a wry tip of his mouth. "I see you've yet to learn the art of knocking."

I rap my knuckles on the open door three times. "Better?"

"No," he deadpans, pulling his glasses off. "Would it make any difference?"

"Never has before." I shrug. "I need a name."

"I find asshole usually comes to mind when I think of you." He chuckles at his jab at me. "Will that do?"

Tony and I served together for two years before his stint was up. He's a Texas boy through and through. Older than I am by ten years, retired military, and happy as hell in civilian life. Has a wife and a couple of kids, but has struggled to kick an old habit. He has a tendency to stray.

Closing the door behind me, I state my case. "She was on the first or second floor. We spent the weekend together. First name Savannah. Didn't catch the last one."

"Didn't catch it, or she didn't throw it to you?" He leans back in his chair and snickers. "No fuckin' way, Bellamy. We don't disclose the names of our guests, you know that. Did she steal something?" He picks up his coffee cup and on its way to his mouth, he hesitates and sappily sniffs. "Oh wait, was it your heart?"

Eyeing the ceiling, I twist my mouth and feign confusion. "Was that two or three in the morning I caught you skinny-dipping with your secretary in the hotel pool?"

I meet his red-faced glare with a raised hand in pledge. "The only time I'll ask a favor for a favor."

He starts tapping keys on the board to his desktop. "And you wonder why asshole comes to mind," he grumbles. "No addresses. No phone numbers."

"Already got her number, Tony."

"You got her number but no last name?" He eyes me with raised brows. "You sure she's not a hooker? I don't need any trouble in my hotel."

A virgin hooker? No way. I gave her the ultimate experience this weekend. I showed her how it could be, and she was so receptive and eager to learn. I promised her discretion, and then I asked for exclusivity. Me. The guy who likes his bed cold, his women once, and his coffee hot . . . alone. I did not promise I wouldn't search for her last name. And I knew exactly how to get it. Fine! I'm an asshole.

"She's not a hooker, dumbass." I glance at my watch. "Would you hurry it up? I'm due back at base soon."

He stares at the screen then squints. "Ho-ho-holy Toledo. You spent the weekend with this? Damn, son, did you break anything?"

"Last name, Tony," I spit, my teeth grinding hard. Apparently she takes a good driver's license pic.

"Michelle," he answers brusquely. "And you'd better not let anybody know where you got it."

"What? You must have the wrong woman. I said last name."

"M-i-c-h-e-l," he enunciates, as if I'm daft then shrugs. "Maybe it's pronounced with a hard C. I don't know. Mickel, Michael. Maybe she's French." He squints as he looks at the screen once more, and nods slowly. "Yeah, she could be French. Soft C. Definitely a soft C. I've only got a headshot from her ID, though." He turns to me and bobs his eyebrows. "Maybe a D?"

"So far outta your league, old man." *And young enough to be your daughter, I think to myself. They're a firm C and fucking perfect.*

"Roger Bellamy's been bitten by the bug." He eyes me knowingly and laughs, then starts singing, '*Michelle, ma belle*', as I slam the door behind me.

Savannah Michel. I like it.

"You look like shit." I set my tray of food on the table and take a seat. His skin is a little pale and his lips are dry.

Silas stuffs a bite of food in his mouth and speaks around it, "It was worth every minute of lost sleep. Two in Waco on Friday night and I lost count in Austin between Saturday and Sunday." He tips a crooked grin of satisfaction and gives a mock salute. "Reporting for duty, sir."

"Did you wrap it?" I swear sometimes it feels like I'm teaching a locker room full of horny jocks. Do not drink and drive – this applies to cars *and* women. Unless of course you want to be raising little soldiers while you're still one yourself.

He grins cockily. "Twice for good measure, a couple of times."

"You sure you weren't just seeing double?"

He winks. "I was definitely seeing double. I just can't seem to remember their names. Tawny? Tallulah? Somethin' like that."

"No more alcohol until fire season is over."

"I know the rules. Had to get it outta of my system."

"Hydrate," I order. "You're gonna need it. We got the rookies to deal with, and that means show 'n' tell."

He grimaces. "I know. If we can't do it, we shouldn't expect them to. Do you know how sore my legs are? One of those women showed me some Kama Sutra moves that I'd nev . . ."

"Do I look like I want to hear about your weekend?" I quickly cut him off, shooting him a glare that can only be interpreted as *do not continue.*

"So, how was your weekend?" he asks innocently enough – until he smirks. "Did you give her sixty?"

Taking a moment to recall what he's asking about, I smugly answer, "I lost count after sixty nine." It's true – sort of. "Eat up. We've got training to do."

He stops chewing and studies my face. "Are we talking about numbers or . . ."

"Shut up and eat, Mitchell." I shove a bite of food in my mouth. I love the guy, but sometimes he is slow as mud.

"Just one more question," he insists.

"One," I indulge him with a roll of my eyes.

"How come you're still hungry?" He laughs so hard he nearly falls off the back of the bench.

Slow? Maybe. Smartass? Definitely.

Chapter 15

Savannah

Ten weeks later

The *Woodlands Crew* has been training hard, day in and day out. Fire season started a month ago and this year has been dry as the Sahara desert. Silas texts me on a regular basis, always lets me know when they're leaving; anxious to get out there and do battle with Mother Nature. They've done two runs already – a fire started in the eastern portion of the state due to an idiot throwing his butt out the window – and another started by lightning strikes that was nearing a community.

Neither of those calls have interfered with Roger's and my weekend meetups in Harker Heights. I feel it's only a matter of time – it's inevitable – but every two weeks, like clockwork, we find comfort in each other's arms. My room rented on another floor hides a duffel with Army fatigues, boots, and a cap in it, as well as who and what I really am. It's reserved ahead for another three weekends, every two weeks. It should have never started, much less continued, and will end soon with my discharge and departure.

He hates liars. I do too. But now I see how easy it is to become one. I'm in love with him. The real Savannah. The one that isn't lying about who she is. What I am doesn't define what my heart wants. My lie will only hurt me. In a little more than six weeks, I will be history in the state of Texas. He has no idea I'm leaving. My number will change. I can take my battered heart home, Silas will never need to know, and Roger can move on.

The door to room 312 stands open as he waits for me to step off the elevator.

"Damn, I missed you." He pulls me into his arms like a long lost lover. The smell of roses lights up my olfactory sense the moment we step into the room. On the bed there are red rose petals strewn from one end to the other. On the coffee table sits a charcuterie board and a champagne bucket with a bottle of chilled sparkling cider next to two champagne glasses. Roger explained weeks ago that alcohol is prohibited during fire season, and I explained if he was abstaining that I would as well.

"What's all this?" I ask, taking in the perfect setting for romance sans the typical liquor. Roger is many things: a gentleman, a generous lover, but romance is doled out cautiously. *Not forever, for now.* Admittedly, there have been times I questioned if he was trying to convince me or himself. But dreams are for little girls. I learned not to put too much stock in them when I watched others lose theirs without notice.

"This," Roger starts as he slides my purse off my shoulder, tosses it on the sofa and slides his arms around my waist from behind, "is the perfect backdrop for a man to tell his woman he loves her."

Grateful he's behind me, because as many times as I have dreamed of hearing it, my heart shatters. It can never be real. *My lie will no longer hurt only me. And if he discovers the truth before I'm discharged, his career is on the line. Don't tell him, Savannah. You brought this on yourself.*

"Y-you love me?" I stammer.

He turns me in his arms and in his eyes I see everything I haven't given him. *Honesty.* "Yeah, Savannah, I do. I don't know what I can promise you, but know that I love you."

I know what I can't promise him, but for the first time since the night we met, my armor drops and I don't have to consider my response before giving one; *an honest one.* "I love you, too."

I receive the best kiss of my life at 7:42 p.m. Friday evening at the Hampton Inn in Harker Heights, Texas.

Little did I know, it would be the beginning of my end.

At four o'clock in the morning, Roger's phone rings on the nightstand. He shoots up quickly and nearly drops it before answering.

"Bellamy." He scrubs his hand down his face and shakes his head as if to clear it, then scratches at his scruff. "Where? Give Silas Mitchell the green flag for prep. I'll be there within the hour. Tell him I'm on my way."

He disconnects and rolls back toward me. "I gotta go. They got a helluva canyon fire in Arizona they're calling us in for." He leans in for a kiss. "Go back to sleep, baby. The room is paid for through Sunday. Keep it. I'll see you when I get back."

He's in Captain mode. The sheet is thrown off and he's in the bathroom, relieving his bladder before I can blink. He's back out seconds later, buttoning his jeans as he's slipping his feet into his shoes. My back is ramrod straight as I sit up in the bed, watching his methodical movements. Shirt buttoned, watch buckled, wallet placed.

The soldier in me is nowhere to be found. He said my brother's name. Helluva fire in Arizona. No, right now I am simply a woman in love, and a little sister, who is scared shitless.

Roger leans over the bed, cups my chin, and leaves a kiss I won't forget. I can't forget, because . . .

"I love you, Savannah. Keep the sheets warm for me."

I wait five minutes before I open the hotel door to dash down the hall to the stairs that lead to my room on the second floor. I'm not staying in his room without him. I'm not staying in the hotel while a good portion of the base will be prepping to send soldiers out to do battle with Mother Nature. I may not be part of the prep team, but I can watch from afar, chew my nails, say a prayer, ask silent forgiveness from both my brother and Roger. Once in my room, I change into fatigues, tuck my hair under my cap, gather my things and toss them into my duffel. Waiting ten more minutes to ensure Roger has left, I call for a Lyft and head for the lobby.

There is no sign of Roger and no cars in the drop off out front, so I wait for my ride at the curb; duffel bag on my shoulder. *Helluva canyon fire in Arizona.* He must have meant Antelope Canyon. I saw the news on the TV in my room earlier. It's massive. Multiple homes and thousands of acres already gone.

It's nearly six o'clock by the time I get checked in at the gate, another half hour before I'm passing the crowd near the mess hall. The camp is in high gear for a Saturday morning, more boots on the ground than normal, air traffic is busy.

"Peaches!" My heart nearly leaps into my throat when I hear my brother's holler from yards away. "I've been looking all over for you. Where the hell have you been?" It would seem I'm not the only one who's heard him, as a few other soldiers making their way toward the mess hall stop dead in their tracks and stare.

He knows better. And Peaches? Are you kidding me? Turning slowly, I mentally prepare to throw something at him – maybe my fist. That is, until I see his expression. *Excitement, anxiety, and . . . fear.* Even worse for me, a red-faced, tight jawed, fuming Captain Roger Bellamy standing next to him.

Chapter 16

Roger

"Not bad, Silas." I clap him on the shoulder. "You even got Conroy outta bed and dressed."

"He was the easiest of the bunch," Silas jokes. "Was in the middle of a wet dream. He had more trouble pullin' his pants over his dick than he did wakin' up."

Conroy rolls tired eyes at Silas and flips him the bird. "I told you before to tell your sister . . ." he stops and holds up a finger. "Pardon me, your cousin to stay outta my dreams and I wouldn't have this problem."

Silas pinches the bridge of his nose. "It's too early for this shit, Conroy."

"Agreed." I scowl at Conroy then scout the rest of the room. "Go get some breakfast, guys. Plane is two hours out. They're running late. Hydrate like your life depends on it, because it does."

Once they've filed out, Silas stops at the door. "I gotta go do something first. A text isn't enough this time. She's gonna kill me, because nobody's supposed to know. Her stint is up in a few weeks, but I don't know how long I'm gonna be gone, and if I don't come back at all . . ."

I land a quick slap across the back of his head. "We don't ever go out with that attitude. We never say *if* we come back; it's *when* we come back! Is there something you're not . . ." My brow scrunches. "Whoa, wait a minute. You're seeing a woman on base? You'd better tell me she's an officer, buddy. You know the rules."

He scoffs and grins wryly. "Actually, she's a Sergeant. And if by seeing her you mean family dinners when mom and dad come to town, or in passing in the mess hall then yes, I am seeing a woman on base."

"Your sister is on base?" I point to the ground as if verifying the logistics. I knew he had a sister, just like he knows I have one, but they've always remained faceless little creatures. "Here? Why didn't you tell me?"

"She didn't want any of her unit hounding her about her sexy brother," he says with a wicked grin. "And I didn't want any of you bloodhounds drooling around my little sister. She's not exactly ugly. She was a combat medic, but got assigned to the clinic here until her stint is up. She's been through hell and back. Got more balls than a bouncy house." He backhands my bicep. "Come on, I'll introduce you. That way, if anything should happen . . ."

"Knock it off," I grind through a clenched jaw. "Nothing is

gonna happen. Now, what's her name again?"

"Peaches." His teasing lilt makes me think he's done it for years.

"Oh yeah," I grumble as we head out the door. "And that's why you're her favorite brother, too."

"I'm her only brother," he announces proudly. "She has to love me."

Ten minutes later, Silas has apparently spotted who he's searching for amongst a crowded movement toward the mess hall. He yells across the compound, "Peaches! I've been looking all over for you. Where the hell have you been?"

A lone body moving against the flow of traffic, wearing fatigues, hair tucked tightly under her cap, slinging a duffle bag on her shoulder, stops cold in her tracks. As I watch her turn toward her brother's voice, I stop cold in mine.

I left the woman in bed not two hours ago. I told her I loved her. I've spent the last two and a half months falling deeper and deeper. I know every inch of her body. I know I'm the only one who's ever enjoyed it. I took her fucking virginity.

Savannah M-i-c-h-e-l, my ass. Tony had taken his glasses off, fixated on her picture more than the letters I was interested in. Dumbass. It's Savannah Mitchell; just like her brother. Small wonder she didn't want to give it to me. Medical services, supplies, contracted . . . to the fucking Army! She's not my little eighth wonder. No, she's a pretty little liar and a thief.

The scowl she apparently had prepped for her brother vanishes immediately when she notes my presence. The duffel falls off her shoulder. Her eyes fly open wide with the lift of her brows, and her cheeks flush hotter than with any sex we've ever had. I've seen her mouth take on that shape, but it was a whole lot more inviting at those times – before I knew the lies it could spew.

Silas glances between the two of us, and thankfully

misinterprets the situation. "For God's sake, Peaches, he's not the second coming. He's a Captain, too old for you, and he does dirty things in the bedroom." He backhands me across the stomach. "Quit tryin' to scare the shit outta my little sister. Savannah, Captain Roger Bellamy. Roger, my little sister, Sergeant Savannah Mitchell."

My face is frozen in the same glare it was once she turned around. The chevron on her sleeve brings all her lies to light. "Sergeant," I grit through a clamped jaw.

Silas' description of 'more balls than a bouncy house' rings true as she stiffens – chin squared – and salutes. "Sir."

"Uh, I thought this might be a little less formal." Silas removes his cap and scratches the back of his head then turns to me. "She ain't like the others, Roger. I truly doubt she's gonna try to bounce on the Bellamy boner."

My glare shifts to the idiot next to me. "Do what you came to do." While I yearn to walk away, I can't make myself, so I wait and observe.

"Sav, we got a big one we're headed out to battle," Silas explains as he takes her shoulders in his hands and bends at the knees to accommodate the height difference. "I know you're pissed at me. We had a deal and I broke it. But you're only a couple weeks away from discharge. I wanted to see you before I took off. You might be gone before I get back. Don't be mad, please?"

Her eyes pool with tears as she studies her brother's face, slightly shaking her head. Not sure if they're all for him, but it wouldn't matter. We're done. "I'm not mad, Si. What the hell? You probably just gained me fifty new friends." She sniffles. "It may only last until you fuck and duck, but . . ."

"Hey, hey," he scolds then pulls her into a hug. "Ladies don't talk that way."

"I notice you're not denying it," she grumbles against his

chest through a sob. "Why did you take this stupid job?"

He props his chin on the top of her head and rocks her back and forth. "So I can go straight into the fire department when I get back home." He snickers. "And capture gorillas before they go after little redheads."

She releases a sob and slaps his arm. "You ass." She pulls her head back and looks up, pleading through teary eyes, "Please be careful."

He taps the tip of her nose. "Always. Who would drive you crazy if I weren't around? I love you, Peaches."

"I love you, too. See you when you get back." She dares a quick glance at me. "You be careful too, Captain Bellamy."

"Your concern should *lie* with your brother," I nod once, "*Sergeant* Savannah *Mitchell*." She flinches as another tear rolls down her cheek before I can turn away fast enough.

On our way to the mess hall to grab a quick bite, Silas grunts, "You coulda been less of a dick. Peaches is one of the best people I know. Those balls I was talkin' about are made of steel."

As he's chewing my ass for being harsh with his sister, I text a certain number I used to love sending messages to. *"I hate liars, JUST Savannah."* The moment I hit send, I wish I hadn't. What a pussy's way out. I'd rather shake her, demand an answer, and then have angry sex one more time to get her out of my system. I want to hate her – my little green-eyed eighth wonder – but I can't. Right now I'll utilize this anger to fight the bitch known as Mother Nature that's burning forests and homes, and concentrate on bringing my men back safe.

This is why I always used to . . . how did she put it? Ah yes, *fuck and duck.* And when we get back, Waco and Austin will be my starting ground. Harker Heights has lost all of its appeal.

Chapter 17

Savannah

Britt slaps her arm over my shoulder when she sees me standing frozen to the same spot I've been long after Silas and Roger have entered the mess hall, staring at my cell phone. *"I hate liars."*

"Got something you want to share?" she whispers. "Apparently it hasn't been the two hottest men on the base, so I'll settle for the secret. Spill."

She eyes a few of the gawkers who remain close by and waves her hand in a shooing motion. "Nothing to see here. Go eat. They're in there anyway. Better hurry. They're about to go play Smokey the Bear."

She bends to pick up my duffel then grasps my elbow and aims me toward the barracks. “Come on. You look like hell.”

“I feel even worse,” I mutter.

“You still on weekend leave through tomorrow?” I only nod. She tugs harder to hasten our footsteps toward the barracks. “Cool. So am I. I just didn’t have anywhere to go. Let me grab some stuff and we’ll find a hotel somewhere. You can fill me in when we get there. *After,*” she emphasizes, “a few good shots of tequila.”

“It’s only eight o’clock in the morning!” I huff.

“It’s always five o’clock somewhere.” She taps her military watch and studies the face before her eyes light up and she grins mischievously. “Ah, Paris! By the time we get checked out, checked in, settled, and changed, we should be right on time. We’ve got two hours.”

My room at the Hampton has two queens. I never did check out this morning. There is nothing to lose; no reason to hide anymore. I’ll be gone in a few weeks. *He hates liars.* May as well share that little piece of paradise with someone I like. Might even show her the *Twilight Club* tonight. Corbin is single. Who knows? Maybe Britt and he will hit it off.

“If you don’t mind sharing a room, two queens, I already have one for us.”

“No shit?” she squeals as she opens the door to the barracks, and we head to our spaces. “Sounds like heaven to me. Where is this place?”

The barracks doors open and in walk half a dozen of our unit. I inch my head side-to-side slowly and whisper, “It’s a surprise. Bring a dress.”

She surreptitiously shows me the strap of a bikini. “Will I need?” I nod. “Good. I’m packing two. Grandma Moses probably wore less than what that black thing of yours covers.” She stuffs a few more items into her duffel and zips it shut.

"Ready?"

"Where are you guys going?" Shana asks when she sees Britt throw her duffel strap over her shoulder, then points her finger at me. "And I have a few questions for you, lady."

Britt doesn't hesitate. "Prayer retreat. Two days. Pretty heavy duty. We're late. You guys want to join us?"

"A prayer retreat?" Shana curls her lip. Resounding grumbles of "I'll pass" come from different points of the room as my heart races. Britt needs her head examined. If any of them had wanted to join us, I would be spending my weekend here.

Britt shrugs casually. "Your loss."

"I want to know about Savannah hugging the hands-off sexy Silas. You're not supposed to play with officers," she snarks.

I'm at my limit. I just watched two of the men I love most walk away, headed for the depths of hell, one who I've already lost because he hates me, and the other I'm scared to death of losing due to the line of danger he's put himself in.

"Silas Mitchell is my brother," I tell her. "He came to tell me goodbye before heading out to fight the Antelope Canyon fire."

"Savannah." My name is but a gasp from across the room. Not sure who it came from until Constance says, "I'm so sorry."

Shana narrows her eyes. "What about Roger?"

Hearing her say his first name as if they have a history flares a pang of jealousy I know isn't justified, but I feel it just the same. "Captain Bellamy is *not* my brother," I deadpan, then turn to a closely observing Britt. "You ready?"

"Let's roll, sister." She tips her chin and glares at Shana before heading for the door.

"Savannah," Constance calls out. As I turn back, she holds her hands up in a praying position. I nod in gratitude and let the door close behind me.

Grasping Britt's arm on the way to the gates, I sneer. "Prayer retreat? That's blasphemy, you idiot! And two lies! Both about God, no less!"

"No it's not!" she snaps. "We are retreating, you just haven't told me where yet. I'm not looking to get laid. And if you think I'm not praying for your brother, you're crazy." She snaps her fingers hard and points toward the sky. "When I hit my knees this weekend, it's gonna be in prayer only. Deal?"

I burst into tears at her sentiment. I know she means every word. She slides her free arm over my shoulder. "Come on, soldier. Show me this double queen retreat and then you can tell me what the hell is going on between you and Captain Bellamy. I saw the way he looked at you."

"Yeah," I mutter as we approach the security gate. "He hates me."

"Not from what I saw. He's pissed, maybe hurt. But hate doesn't look like that."

We both reach for our creds and present them to the guard. He checks them against the computerized reader and glances at me. "According to records, you just came back."

Releasing the sigh I should have kept on reserve, I nod. "I forgot a few things. Came back to get them."

"Gonna have to search your bag," he grunts.

I hand it over without hesitation and watch as he and another security guard help themselves to the contents; dumping them out on the table. He smirks as he spots two pieces of rather *special* lingerie I had packed for the weekend and forgotten to remove. He holds them up and examines them closely, stuffs them back into the duffel, then grins cockily as he slides my duffel across the table. "Those must be what you forgot. You ladies have fun together."

Britt smiles coyly and winks. "Oh, we will." She hooks her arm in mine and pulls me out of the guard shack. "Come on, babe. Let's go."

"I'm going to murder you," I growl.

She giggles. "Wait until after the weekend. I need the scoop, and Lance Corporal Dickhead back there needs a little fantasy for his shower time. Now, give me an address so I can call for a ride."

"How have I never heard of this place?" Britt spins on the sidewalk and takes in our surroundings after we've gone to our room, changed clothes, and decided a little walk through the downtown area would be a nice way to start the day. "We've been driving to Killeen for entertainment. It's no wonder we couldn't get you to go with us."

"It is kinda nice, isn't it?" I blink back tears as I walk down memory lane rather than storefront shop like Britt is doing. She hasn't inquired yet, instead giving me a chance to gather my thoughts and recuperate from my trainwreck of a morning.

"Oh look!" she exclaims and points to a small white building across the street. "Let's get the important stuff done first. Then you can breathe and I won't be struck by lightning."

Half an hour later we leave the church; knees put to good use, and a plane full of Hotshots properly prayed for – a couple possibly more fervently than the others.

"Feel better?" Britt asks, leading us in the direction of the inviting scent of fresh coffee and baked goods.

"Yeah." I nod, swiping the old and fresh supply of tears from my cheeks. "Thanks for coming with me."

"No thanks needed. Let's get something in our stomachs. I want to hit that dress boutique before we go back to the hotel, then we'll hit the pool and you can talk if you want . . ." she tilts her head and shrugs one shoulder, ". . . or not if you don't."

"Where did I find a friend like you?"

"I found you. It was the day I walked into the clinic for my under-boob rash. That asshole Fitzpatrick told me to use Gold Bond powder and get over it." She nudges my arm. "You brought me some cream and left it under my pillow with a note that read, and I quote, 'If men had boobs, they'd appreciate them for more than just sucking on the nipples. Apply twice a day, no tight bra. Should clear up quickly. Do not use for more than seven days'."

"How did you know that was me?"

"Nobody else in that clinic is a former combat medic, much less female CM. You got lady balls. They wouldn't dare go up against Fitz."

I shrug. "I didn't go up against him; just went around him. Wasn't exactly narcotics. It was rash cream with a touch of steroid in it for Pete's sake. He hands it out like ice cream for jock itch."

"That asshole!" she growls. "So balls mean more than boobs?"

"No." I shake my head. "He just can't empathize."

"He's a dick!"

"That too." I laugh and pull open the door to the bakery. "You ready for coffee and a donut?"

We spend the afternoon around the pool – me in the shade, Britt in the sun, the Styrofoam cooler containing hard ciders between us; dwindling in number as time passes. She's heard the story: prologue, chapters, and soon to be epilogue with my departure. The edited version; details would be a violation.

"He approached you, Savannah," Britt insists. "There is not a female on base that would turn him down – short of the married ones – and even those are questionable."

"Doesn't make it hurt any less."

"He looked like he was hurting a bit too."

"He was pissed!" I throw back at her. "He hates me, Britt. And if Silas finds out, he will too."

"Oh please," she drawls and rolls her eyes. "It was pretty easy to see your brother worships the ground you walk on. I'd ask you to set me up with him, but I have a feeling that is exactly why you never let anyone know you two are siblings."

"And you would be correct," I say dryly.

She pats my leg. "It's alright, sweetie. If I had a brother that looked like that, I would tell everyone he's gay. Root out the true friends from the horny ones. Now tell me, what are the dresses for?" she asks, exchanging an empty container for a full one.

"The Twilight Club."

"Oohh," she squeals, popping the cider open. "Sounds mysterious. BDSM or regular kink?"

My head whips toward her as my face scrunches. "You twit! It's a classy piano bar that serves dinner."

She studies my face before the sweetest smile decorates hers. "He really does love you."

Did love me, Britt. Did.

Chapter 18

Roger

Thirty-seven of us on this plane – fourteen belong to me. The *Woodlands Crew* is my exclusive responsibility. Those aren't necessarily *the* rules – they're *my* rules. We've trained as a team; one unit that eats, breathes, shits, and works together.

Yet, I've got this idiot at the front of the plane trying to rearrange and dictate new rules before we even have boots on the ground. The supervisor: Timmon Oujiri.

"We have two separate burns going at the current time. They've determined arson," he informs us. "The winds are from the south. "You'll be divided into teams when we get there and reassess."

"The Woodlands Crew is mine," I announce loudly before standing from my seat to reinforce my statement. It's not a challenge, it's a fact. "We're already a team and where one goes, we all go. You will not be splitting up my men."

"I'm the supe for this unit." He narrows his eyes then checks his clipboard, enunciating my name, "*Bellamy*. Placement is my call."

"I'm the *Captain* of fourteen of these soldiers. Placement may be your call – division is not an option, *Oujiri*. This is not my first rodeo. There is no justification for dividing a team that has trained together. We *will* be staying together."

Taking my seat once again, Silas chuckles next to me. "Damn, I'm glad you're on my side. That guy is a dick."

"Hey," a guy in the seat behind us leans into the open space between ours and utters, "any chance I could get on your team?"

"You Army?"

"No." He sticks his hand through the opening between the seats to shake ours. "Fire Station 72 outta Waco for six years. Name's Chauncy Steffen. I'm no rookie, but I think I'd feel a whole lot safer with you guys than that asshole."

"Stick close," I say with a small nod. "I'll see what I can do."

"So what's the story with your little sister?" I've waited until we got settled – not wanting to seem too interested, too anxious, and definitely not too invested – before I inquired. "You said she was a combat medic. Been through hell and back?"

"Afghanistan," Silas says discreetly, checking for eager listeners around us. Finding none, he continues, "Her unit took a helluva hit and in the process, so did she."

"Hit? With what? Her body is . . ." Stopping short of *perfect* when I realize my massive blunder, I clear my throat fast and hard. "I-I mean, she doesn't look like she's been hurt."

He's so deep in thought, he remains oblivious – and I remain the unknown asshole who violated his sister. "They were on foot patrol. Didn't even see it comin'. One of the guys in her unit lost his leg above the knee. Blew it clean off." He turns, wincing. "She was in the path of it, as well as his boot. Broke some ribs, dislocated her shoulder, gash in her head, helluva concussion. But that little shit didn't miss a beat. Got right back up and started packin' wounds like it was second nature. Crawled through the dirt and had that thigh strapped so tight with a belt to stop the bleeding they had to cut it off of him. She saved his life. Her own injuries put her in the hospital for five days after." He tucks his chin and shakes his head. "They tried to discharge her, but she refused." He grins wryly. "Got a purple heart. She sent it home with Dad. Told him purple wasn't her color."

"How do you know the details?"

"When a General's daughter is injured and he wants answers," he smirks, "he gets answers. He even questioned some of her unit himself and they sang her praises. One of them asked for her hand in marriage." He chuckles softly. "Dad gave the poor bastard a one-time pass due to the IV drip of drugs he was on. Peaches isn't so much *a* daddy's girl as she *is* Daddy's girl. Make sense?"

I let that roll around in my head two or three times until it finally clicks. "She's independent."

He laughs. "That is an understatement. She's stubborn as hell too. But she's got a heart so big, I fear somebody's gonna break it someday. Dad and I are both gonna be in prison for first degree."

I'm that somebody, Silas. And someday has come and gone. I broke her heart. Hell, I broke her. I couldn't hate her if I spent the rest of my life trying.

"Why did they want to discharge her?" I ask, aiming us back to the original subject.

"It would have been an honorable one. Her CO thought the mental and emotional anguish, as well as possible long term effects from her concussion might impede her capabilities." He snorts. "We've seen guys get out on a whole lot less."

I recall our first night in the hotel. *"The noises".* At least now I have a clue where they were coming from. Nightmares, maybe? Who of us don't have them? She didn't move once she nestled into me. She never does . . . rather didn't. I told her I hate liars. I ended us. Who's going to help her sleep now?

"So, what happened?"

"She refused the discharge." His head tilts with a one shoulder shrug. "Told them she was not going to give up the GI bill education they promised. She said she had an obligation to fulfill, just like they did. They told her it was still hers, but like I said, she is stubborn. She didn't need it; mom and dad would have paid for college but she didn't want that. So the Army stationed her at Hood to finish out her time in the clinic. A couple weeks to go and she's on her way home."

Another lie. She was leaving . . . leaving me. Was she ever going to tell me? What the hell, Savvy? But I did tell her I couldn't promise her forever.

"You look a little distraught, Roger." Silas smirks. "Ah, feeling guilty for being a dick to her, aren't you? I told you she wasn't like the others. Don't worry. If she's still around when we get back, you can apologize. Peaches is pretty forgiving. It's a wonder she still speaks to me."

"What's with Peaches?"

"She was conceived in Georgia where Dad was stationed at the time, so they named her Savannah, after the city." He smiles devilishly. "I told her she was an *oops* baby due to a broken condom when mom and dad had a drunken quickie off base in the peach state on peach schnapps."

I stare at him, my jaw unhinged. "You're a real asshole."

He rolls his eyes. "Oh please, tell me you didn't tease your little sister."

"I never made her think she was an accident." I fight the urge to punch him on behalf of my little eighth wonder. "You need your head examined. Who does that shit?"

He scrunches his face and looks to the ceiling of the plane. "It's probably best I don't tell you the story about convincing her the hungry monkey at the zoo feasted on little redheads."

"You didn't," I spit in anger.

"Best lesson in my life. Grounded for six months by my dad via a computer screen. I never realized how much my little sister looked up to me until I saw how terrified I'd made her that day." His eyes mist over as he acquiesces, "I still haven't fully forgiven myself for that one. But I spent my last seven years at home trying to make up for it. I can sing a helluva lot of songs from Disney classics, and we've remained close ever since."

"And yet you call her Peaches."

He snickers and tilts a hand back and forth. "That came later. It was my underhanded way of makin' her think real hard before drinkin' and havin' sex. They lived too close to the base." He knocks his elbow against my arm. "You know how horny these damn soldiers are. I didn't need her getting knocked up and ruining her life. It's not like I was gonna be around to protect her. It made things easy. One word to put the fear of God, and pregnancy, in her."

"Peaches," I deadpan.

He pats himself on the shoulder and grins cockily. "A lot to be said for subtlety. It's also less embarrassing than yelling across the compound, 'Don't be having sex tonight!'"

I stare at him, slowly shaking my head. "My sister would have murdered you."

"You ever gonna introduce us?"

My eyes narrow as my teeth grind and a low growl leaves my throat, "Peaches."

"Say no more." He laughs then flashes me a side-eye. "See how well it works?"

Chapter 19

Savannah

"Cute piano player," Britt whispers, taking in the ambiance of the *Twilight Club.* The club is at medium capacity as it's still early. There are open seats at the piano bar, but the usual two at the end of the regular bar are vacant, and look extremely inviting. Conversation so close to a working musician seems rude . . . and distracting.

Britt is in a striking red dress with heels to match that she bought on our excursion today. My plan was to wear the black one with nude heels that I had once again borrowed from her. Key word: *was*. She virtually threw an emerald green one at me in the store and insisted I try it on. Can't say I regret it. I'd come to hate green with the daily wear of fatigues. This was a reminder not all green is the same.

"Leave the piano man alone. You said you weren't getting laid and your knees served one purpose this weekend," I whisper back.

"I'm not and they do," she returns. "I can still take note. I'm not blind. Check out that dexterity. I'll bet he's good with his hands. Now that I know this place is here, you can bet your butt I'm coming back. We can have your going away party . . . scratch that. I don't want anybody to know about this place. This is my secret. Where do you want to sit?"

"Over at the bar. We can talk and eat there."

"Looks good to me." She follows as I lead the way, but must have fallen behind when I hear her say, "What was that?" I turn in time to see her hand around the throat of a man at a table of suits – her knuckles white, his head tipped back, eyes bulging. "Not hookers, dickhead. Soldiers. And you'd better apologize before I rip your tonsils out. Now would be a good time if you want to breathe again."

He sputters and coughs through her tight grip on his throat, "S-s-sorry."

She releases her grip with an extra push for good measure, but he catches the edge of the table to avoid falling backward. She glares at the others in the group. "Anybody else at this table trying to compensate for having a tiny dick?"

A combination of wide eyes and raised hands come from the other three while each voice a meek, "No."

"Good." She tips her chin. "Be sure to give your unfortunate wives my deepest sympathies." Once by my side, she chuckles. "Nothing like working up a good appetite. You ready to eat?"

"Yup." I giggle. "Now that your fangs are out, did you still want yours cooked?"

"No more than medium rare. I didn't get to taste his blood."

I don't for a moment doubt she means it. Britt is like a big sister – the friend I didn't know I needed, the charger to my weak battery, and the tether to keep me from falling off the edge. Four years older than I am and loyal as a golden retriever.

As if on autopilot, I aim for the two barstools Roger and I have always occupied every time we come here. Corbin is at the other end of the bar serving patrons, so his sidekick makes his way to our end. "What can I get you ladies?"

"I got this, Todd." Corbin appears with two menus and a smile. "You can take the other end."

Todd sighs and grumbles, "Of course I can."

As I prepare to introduce my friend to Corbin, he takes the lead, "Where's your soldier tonight?"

My heart scrapes rock bottom. Britt had actually managed to give me an intermission today. Break my thoughts into segments rather than let me spend the entire day wallowing in loss and apprehension. "Antelope Canyon fire. He left this morning." I direct my thumb at my companion. "This is Brittany Su . . ."

"Well aware." His dazzling smile is aimed at my friend as he winks. "Still spreadin' the love wherever you go, aren't you, Sunny? That guy must not have pissed you off too much. You only cut off his air supply long enough to scare the piss out of him."

Britt's glower is one I would not want aimed at me as she speaks his name with a strong mixture of loathing and what sounds like . . . sexual tension. "Major Reeves."

"Not anymore, Sunshine. I'm retired."

"And look at you," she singsongs. "Here you are, in a bar, on a Saturday night, serving drinks to us lowly enlisted."

"I own half this bar." His voice is so low he could put

grizzlies to shame. "I retired from the military; not from life."

"Did you put your dick out of commission too?"

His eyes flash with a hint of mischief. "That soldier will never be out of commission, sweetheart."

This is obviously a party for two. "I think I'm going to powder . . ."

"No you're not!" Britt snaps and squeezes my bicep. "We are going to stay right where we are, and you," she points her finger at Corbin, "are going to send Todd back over to take care of us." She smiles slyly. "I want someone who can service me properly."

The sudden heated glare between the two of them would make the most seasoned porn star blush. "Todd!" Corbin calls down the way to his sidekick without breaking eye contact. "Call Dan to help out and get over here to take the ladies' orders."

As Corbin storms off, Todd steps up. "Have you ladies decided?"

"I'll have . . ."

"Get her a Jameson while she waits. Two if she needs them." Corbin's harsh order comes from behind me as he spins Britt's barstool, picks her up by the waist, and throws her over his shoulder – her protests weaker than one would expect from the maneater I know her to be. He grins puckishly at me. "Order an appetizer. Might be a while. I'll have her back in time for dinner, which is on the house tonight." They disappear down a hallway, followed by the slamming of a door.

"What's down that hallway?" I ask a grinning Todd.

"Corbin's office." He shakes his head in understanding. "He's never taken a woman in there so far as I know. Your friend is perfectly safe."

"I wasn't worried about my friend." I smirk and pick up the

menu, studying the appetizers. “Be sure to keep some extra bar rags handy, though. She gets a little sloppy sometimes, and blood splatters clean up better when they’re fresh. Don’t worry about the body; she knows where to hide them.” I set the menu down on the bar and look up to a wide-eyed Todd. “I’ll take an order of fried pickles, please.”

Approximately half an hour later, a slightly disheveled Britt returns from the hallway, sans one Corbin Reeves, and takes her place next to me. As she reaches for one of the slices of fried delight on the plate, I slap her hand away. “No dice. You’ve obviously already had your pickle.”

“But I’m hungry,” she whines. “I worked up an appetite.”

“So, apparently you weren’t on your knees,” I deadpan.

“No!” she snaps. “I told you those were reserved.”

“But you still got laid.”

“Technically, no I didn’t.” She reaches for a fried pickle and pops it in her mouth before I can object. “The term *laid* implies you were on your back.”

Eyeing her expectantly, I wait for her to elaborate.

She bobs her eyebrows. “He took me up against the wall.”

Dropping my forehead onto the heel of my palm, I mumble, “Can we order dinner?”

“Hey,” she says, brushing her hand over my shoulder. “I did not mean for this to happen. I came with you this weekend to try and help. If I had known he was here, we would have been eating pizza and watching a movie in the hotel room. Corbin Reeves has always been my greatest weakness.” She tips her glass to her lips and drains the entire contents. “As well as my greatest risk. What do you say we get the hell outta here and order takeout?”

We rise from our barstools in unison as Todd shows up with a bag in his hand and sets it on the bar. “Loaded with burgers, fries, and two slices of cheesecake." He leans in to whisper, "There's a fifth of Jameson in there wrapped up tight. Your ride is the black Audi out front, and will deliver you back to the hotel. Corbin's only request is that you please stay safely inside your room once you start drinking."

The fire in Britt's eyes is nothing short of inferno level as she starts to protest, "Where the hell does he get off . . ."

"Because he cares, ma'am." Todd nods sharply and walks to the other end of the bar, leaving us to take it or leave it.

We take it, out the front door, into the waiting Audi, back to the hotel, and eat our dinner and kill a few brain cells with Mr. Jameson so we can sleep tonight.

In the process, I also develop a newfound connection to Britt: *common mistakes.* Hers was Major Corbin Reeves. Mine was Captain Roger Bellamy. Not that either one of us would take them back. After all, we learn from our mistakes, don't we?

Chapter 20

Roger

Six days later

"Hold it!" I signal and yell to my crew as we're digging another line at the lower edge of the canyon – the intent to keep the fire from spreading any further south. There are thirty men working this line, half of them the Woodlands Crew. "The wind just got hotter than Satan's balls. It shouldn't be. Anybody smell that?"

"That's accelerant!" Silas hollers as he sniffs the air. A few others have removed their masks to do the same. "Petroleum?"

"I smell it too!" Conroy shouts.

"The wind is carrying it!" I scout the area to the south – the drop off obscuring the view down into the canyon – my stomach roiling as dawning hits. The saying is 'where there's smoke there's fire'. Yeah, well when you're working with arson, when there's smell, there's soon to be fire. The smoke and flames will be climbing over that crest any minute. The fuckers are causing a merge and we're about to get caught in the middle. Oujiri is nowhere in sight, so I radio him at the same time I'm running up the line to reach my entire crew.

"We gotta move! Now! To the east!" I order to every ear in hearing range. It's like a chain reaction – word will make its way up the line. The lake is to the east; the only water source in the area. The only safety from what's to come. I run to the middle of the line of men to ensure I have my total head count and veer them in the right direction, with the added head of Chauncy who doesn't hesitate to join us. The rest from the next crew will follow.

That sonofabitch! I watch as my men take instructions without question and charge east toward the lake, while the remaining men from the other crew whip their heads back and forth in confusion, as Oujiri *radios* his orders to their foreman to head west. He isn't even on the site and he's contradicting advisory measures!

"Roger, there's nowhere to go if they head west!" Silas screams. "The north and south fires will merge at that end too! There's no water source. What the fuck is he thinking?! We can't let them go off to their deaths!"

"We've got a new fire coming up behind us right now!" I point to the south ridge – smoke starting to rise – knowing it's only a matter of time. A *short* matter of time, as the winds have increased. "That's kerosene you're smelling! It may as well be a fucking bomb! I've told them, but I can't order that crew, Mitchell." I grab the sleeve of his turnout and aim him in the right direction. "Get your ass headed east!"

"I gotta try!" He yanks out of my hold and starts to run toward the erroneously directed firefighters. "That's fuckin' suicide!"

"I'll get him!" Conroy yells as he runs past me. "Dumbass."

Before I run after them, I look over my shoulder to ensure the others are following orders, and see Chauncy standing by. "What are you waiting for?"

"I ain't going anywhere until you guys go! We're in this together!"

The hideous sound that cracks through the air will haunt me for the rest of my days. It's not lightning, nor thunder. I would welcome those. No, this is the sound of aftermath. The aftermath of strong winds weakening timber at its base until it's no longer strong enough to stand tall. There is no stopping it, no predetermining where it will land. But somehow, in my gut, I just know.

"Mitchell!" My shriek echoes throughout the canyon as smoke from the south rises from below and flames dance at the edge of the ridge. "No!!"

I race to where my two men lie on the ground, crushed under the weight of the tree – Chauncy by my side. "Lift it! Lift it!" I scream, grabbing the heavy trunk and tossing it off the two motionless bodies beneath. Stripping off my gloves, I roll Silas onto his back and feel for a pulse in his neck. "I got a pulse! Can you carry Conroy?"

More of my crew have circled back to help once they saw what has happened. Smoke fills the air from the south and the flames are gaining ground. "We got 'em, Cap," one says, and tries to take Silas from me while another helps Chauncy with Conroy.

"I got him!" I holler as I sling Silas over my shoulder. "Help Chauncy. Let's go. Go! Go! Go!"

The lake is at least a half mile or more away. We have no

stretchers – no time to check for specific injuries before we carry their limp bodies to safety. A soldier runs on each side of me while one shares the load of Conroy's weight with Chauncy and two more run on each side of them. The group ahead ensures the clearest path possible. I do believe every one of my men returned to help, but I don't have the headspace to count. Right now, what matters most is getting them to the water, the low profile shelters built around the periphery, and taking care of Silas and Conroy.

Once at the lake and near the shelters by the water's edge, some of my men help me lower Silas slowly and carefully to the ground while others do the same for Chauncy with Conroy. Silas' skin pallor is gray, there's blood seeping from the corner of his blue lips, and his body is motionless.

"Wake up!" I scream, ripping the front of his turnout open to remove it. "Don't you fuckin' die on me, Mitchell! Savvy needs you!" The turnout splits down the middle as I tear it open. "Oh God." The sound of retching nearby only solidifies my resolve not to. The blood coating the entire front of his body doesn't hide the end of the pickax protruding from just under his rib cage in the middle of his chest.

"No, no!" My guttural plea is shouted to a God I'm questioning the existence of right now, or a universe that has no idea what it's lost. He was trying to save others. He was only trying to help.

I look beyond my best friend to see Chauncy knelt over Conroy. His eyes say it all as they meet mine, but he adds a minute shake of his head – letting me know we lost him too. I know my men are watching me, waiting for guidance, direction. The soldier in me retreats as I've never felt so fucking small, so human, so helpless. My body folds in on itself, wracked with uncontrollable sobs. My best friend is gone due to my failure and his compassion. Conroy is gone due to his camaraderie. I've lost the only woman I've ever loved due to . . .

I failed them all.
Is this what it's like to feel empty?

Chapter 21

Savannah

"Sergeant Savannah Mitchell?"

I turn from the cabinet I'm stocking with fresh bandages to see two MPs standing in the doorway – Dr. Fitzpatrick behind them. "That's me. Can I help you?"

"We're here to escort you to the Commander's office, ma'am," one informs me. "Would you come with us, please?"

Under normal circumstances, it wouldn't be mine to question why. But this is different. The air feels thick and heavy; constricting my lungs from taking my next breath. "Do you know why?"

"We're just the escorts, ma'am," the second one says, his expression giving nothing away. "Please come with us."

I walk with them across the base, the sound of our boots crunching on the ground growing more irritating with every step, as others stop to watch us. It's when I see the chaplain pause at the entry to Command quarters – the undeniable pity in his eyes as he turns – that the ground meets my knees as they crumple and my heart shatters. *Silas.*

"Oh, God. No, no."

"I've got her, boys." The ever familiar sound of my dad's strong, though slightly broken voice as he somehow picks me up and cradles me to his chest is the last thing I remember, until I wake up in someone's quarters, my mom adjusting a wet cloth over my forehead.

"It's not a nightmare this time, is it?" I whisper, studying my mom's swollen, red-rimmed eyes.

She shakes her head and sniffles, tears slowly descending her cheeks that she doesn't even try to wipe away. "No, sweetheart. Not the dream kind."

Sitting up quickly, I pull her into a hug. "How?"

"Your father's on that right now. All we've gotten so far is they got caught between two fires. Something called a merge."

"Oh God!" My hand flies to my mouth. "He burned to death?"

"No, no, no." She brushes my hair away from my face. "His Captain got them out of the way of the fire, but something happened and . . ."

"Is Roger okay?"

At the same time my mom asks, "Who?" my dad appears and questions, "You're on a first name basis with your brother's Captain?"

Always the General.

My eyes cast downward as I rub the back of my neck, pretending to work out a kink – you know, any old port in a storm to avoid eye contact with my father. "Si had introduced us right before they left. That's what stuck, I guess."

As I look back up, my dad's scrupulous gaze nearly burns a hole in my conscience. "He's injured, but with time and treatment he'll be okay. The men I've spoken to think pretty highly of him. Sounds like he did his damnedest," his voice cracks, ". . .to save your brother."

"They were best friends," I utter.

Tears well in his eyes before he swipes a hard hand across his cheeks as if to hide them and he steels himself once again. "We'll talk about it another day. In the meantime, your CO wants your final paperwork signed to release you a couple weeks early." As I raise my hand to protest, his comes up even faster. "No more, Savannah. By the time your family leave is over, you'd have a matter of days left. It's time you came home and went to school."

"And you did what, Dad. . ." I snap ". . .pulled strings to make that happen?" I climb off the bunk and stand tall, shoulders squared, my chin tipped as if taller stature may prove my point. "I am a grown woman. I have an end date to my contract that I plan to fulfill."

"You have a purple heart that proves you've done your service, young lady!"

My voice is even and cool as I state my case. "Yet I still bleed red just like everyone else, Dad."

Never in my life have I attempted to stare down my father, but I do right now. He's the authority – the voice of reason. The shoulders I sat on when I couldn't see over the crowd. The hand I held when I was little. The guy who couldn't hide his wink when he saluted me for the first time. I love this man wholeheartedly. He has been my rock my entire life. But this is not about his authority nor is it about honoring his wishes. This is about me, my battle, my independence. I see the pain in his eyes, but damnit I have mine too! We're both lost, and maybe in time we can help each other. *But for just this little while, Dad, I don't want to be your little girl.* I have my own path to walk, and if I ever want to stand on my own two feet, now would be that time.

"Dirk." It's not until my mom's soft whisper of his name and hand on his arm that he concedes, closing his eyes and heaving a deep sigh.

He spins toward the door and grumbles, "I'll go let your CO know things have changed. Get ready to go home to memorialize your brother."

Once the door has closed and I'm sure he's gone, I look to my mom. "Thanks."

She simply lifts a stern brow. "I never said I agree, Savannah. But I hope you realize what it took for your dad to give in."

"I do."

She rolls her eyes as she hooks her arm through mine to lead me out the door. "Good Lord, child. Give the man a few years before he has to hear you say *those* two words. Now, let's go get your things."

Britt sits on my bunk in our quarters and jumps up when we enter. She bursts into tears and rushes to pull me into a hug. "Oh God! You're still here. I was afraid I'd missed you! I am so sorry." Her tears cause another flood of my own. A large number of our unit enters in a rush, arms out, eyes watering, and expressions of sympathy from every one of them. My mother receives heartfelt condolences and hugs from each of them as well, as I pack the few items I'll need for ten days.

"I want to you to send me the info for the funeral as soon as you have it," Britt says discreetly as she helps me pack my things. "I plan on being there for you. I have some leave available. The sooner I put in for it, the better."

"You don't have to do that."

She holds my duffel in her firm grip and sets her eyes on mine. "I know I don't *have* to. I *want* to. Promise me."

"Promise." I hesitate before taking it. "Britt, do you have any idea what happened to Roger?"

She unzips the duffel and pretends to look inside as she dips her head low and whispers, "Word has it he carried Silas over his shoulder a mile to safety. Didn't even know he was injured until he tried to stand. That's all I've got." She hugs me one more time. "You will get through this. Call me."

Chapter 22

Roger

"It took 96 staples and sutures to repair your shoulder, Captain Bellamy," the doctor says calmly as the overhead fluorescent lights in the room come into better focus, making my head pound.

"Get me outta this bed." I fist the cotton weave blanket and toss it to the side. As soon as I try to swing my legs off the mattress, the searing pain shoots through my ass all the way to my ankles. "Fuck!"

"You have three ruptured disks in your spine," he continues as if he hasn't heard me. "I'm afraid you're not going anywhere for a while. Your CO is on his way. We can discuss treatment, or transport, if ortho approves it."

"Where the fuck am I!? What did you do to me?!" I demand, though even the strain from yelling hurts.

"You're in the hospital in Page, Arizona. You were brought here for your injuries as we're the closest to Antelope Canyon."

Antelope Canyon. Silas. Conroy.

"How the hell did *I* get injured?"

A male nurse at the side of the bed adjusting an IV snort laughs. "Last I heard, lifting tree trunks is not a recommended replacement for weights in a gym."

The thud of his body hitting the wall just feet away is quite unexpected, but no one moves as a scrubs-covered Chauncy pins him against it. "Get the fuck outta here before you need a surgeon to fix your face after I rearrange it." He shoves him toward the door then turns to the nonplussed doctor. "You need better people."

The doc nods. "He'll be reprimanded."

"He better be replaced," Chauncy grunts. "Fix the IV and leave us alone to wait for his CO."

"What happened, Chaunce?" I ask once the door is closed.

"It'll come back to you. Probably bite you in the ass at the worst possible time." He lets out a sigh and stares into space. "You were running on adrenaline, Roger. Gives us super strength sometimes. Doesn't mean the body's built for it." He looks at me and grimaces. "I barely had a chance to touch that tree trunk and you had it moved already."

I clench my fists in frustration. "Not that it did any good."

"Wrong place, wrong time. You tried. There was nothing you could do. You got all your other men to safety."

I wince with the pain as I try to adjust my position in bed with one arm. "What happened to my shoulder?"

Grimacing, his eyes shift to the left and I wait for the lie. "Can't say. There was so much shit goin' on. It's a wonder any of us made it through."

"Where are my men?"

"Safe and sound. They sent them back to the base in Texas from what I understand. I'm not Army, remember?"

"You stuck around?"

His lips tip as he shrugs. "You saved my ass."

The longer we speak, the more memories flood in. *Silas. Conroy. The tree falling. The failure. East versus west.*

"What happened to the other crews?"

He looks me straight in the eyes, arches a brow and inclines his chin. "They shoulda listened to you. I'm damn glad I did."

"Sonofabitch," I utter, recalling Oujiri ordering them to go west. "How many?"

He rubs the back of his neck and his eyes cast toward the floor. "Twelve the last I heard."

My stomach roils. *Totally avoidable.* "How long have I been here?"

"Day and a half. They brought us in night before last."

Throwing the blanket back with my good arm, I attempt movement once more. "I gotta get outta here, Chaunce. I got a funeral to attend. I don't even know where Conroy was from. I can send condolences to his family. But Silas and I were both from up north in Scottsdale. I am not missing his."

"You can barely move, Roger! How in the hell do you plan to do that?"

"I'll belly crawl if I have to," I grind through painful deep breaths as I slide my legs off the bed. "You're dressed in scrubs. Find me a fucking wheelchair and get me out of here."

He glances down at the hospital attire he's in as if he'd

forgotten and shrugs. "I'm on it."

Half an hour later, Chauncy has stolen another pair of scrubs for me, collected my belongings from the locker in my room, removed my IV, hoisted my ass into a wheelchair, covered me with a blanket, peeked out into the hallway to assure the coast is clear, and we are on our way to the exit doors four floors down. *It pays to have a firefighter on your side.*

"Now what?" he inquires once at the end of the parking lot, after racing up the lane like he's driving the damn Indy 500. It's hotter than sweaty balls out, but the guy has put in full effort.

"Call a rental car company."

"Uh, Roger, kinda need a phone to do that."

I tear open the white plastic hospital bag with my belongings – aka dog tags, wallet, crusty clothes, Hotshot tag ID, and watch – from the locker. "Where the hell is my phone!?"

He shoots me a wry look. "Probably right next to mine in that fuckin' canyon."

Pinching the bridge of my nose, I bow my head and take a few deep breaths. I'm resourceful; been in worse spots. Opening my wallet, I'm happy to find my bank card, some cash, and all of my ID. "You got your wallet?"

"Lucky me," he says, pulling it out of his scrubs pocket. "Not much else though."

The click of feminine heels falls close by and the head of a blonde captures my attention. Not because she's pretty – she is – but because she's usable. I haven't noticed pretty since I had gorgeous. Drop dead gorgeous with green eyes, auburn hair, and a body built for me. Only me.

"You look so familiar." I fake a smile as if I'm fascinated. "No, you're so much prettier than what I remember. It can't possibly be you."

She stops walking, tilts her head and smiles. "It could be

me."

I inherited them! It's not my fault she falls for handsome.

"You do have the face of an angel. But I didn't get your name the first time."

"It's Tara," she says sweetly. "Have you been hurt?"

I nod, grimacing. "I was, and we've been waiting for a Lyft, which obviously isn't showing up. I had to call from the hospital phone because mine got lost in the accident. I need to get to the mobile phone store to get mine replaced. It would be such a pain to go all the way back in. You wouldn't happen to have one we could borrow for a minute, would you?"

"Of course," she says, reaching into her bag.

"Tell you what," I pull a few twenties from my wallet, "if you'll order the Lyft from the app, I'll pay you cash for the charge with a nice tip, and maybe they'll actually show up this time. I got a feeling that's why the driver didn't want to take it. I couldn't order it from the app."

"Well, that makes sense." She shakes her head. "You can't really blame them though. Business is business."

Yes, and I could have called a taxi – who would know where the damn phone store is, if I had wanted to chance getting caught by asking for a phone inside the hospital. As I said . . . blonde.

She orders the Lyft via the app—an SUV to accommodate the wheelchair—and I pay her generously for her troubles.

"I didn't get your name," she says once the transaction is complete. "Or your number."

"Where are my manners?" I extend my good hand to shake hers. "Timmon Oujiri." I recite the number for Hotshot headquarters and tell her, "Give me a couple days to get settled and feeling better." I wink. "I look forward to seeing you again, Tara."

"Can't wait, Timmon." She smiles and returns my wink as

the Lyft pulls up to the curb.

"You can be a real asshole," Chauncy whispers with a laugh after we're loaded and have taken off in the Lyft.

"I can be resourceful, Chaunce."

"Damn, Roger," he huffs. "She was good lookin'."

I smirk. "You wanna go back and diddle her?"

He scrunches his nose. "Hell no!"

"Then let's go get the phones and I'll drop you at the airport after we get a rental car."

"Like hell you will!" He protests, leaving no room for argument. "Scottsdale is five and a half hours away. There is no way you can drive that alone. I'll be drivin', you will be *passengering*, and I will be attending the services as well. I liked Silas." He stares out the window, his voice breaking as he finishes, "I was there. I watched that fuckin' tree come down. I carried Conroy. I watched you break. I have never seen a team like yours. We're good in Waco, work well together, but you guys were outstanding. I ain't joinin' the Army, but I'd give anything to be on a team like that."

Damn! He nailed it. And if not for Chauncy Steffen, I would still be stuck in that hospital and would never be able to attend my best friend's funeral.

"You drive, I ride," I tell him as the Lyft pulls up in front of the cell phone store.

"Cool." He grins under watery eyes. "Now, which one of us pays for the stolen wheelchair?"

"I'll make you a deal." He lifts a curious brow at my proposal. "You cop me some crutches and a back brace, I'll cover the wheelchair."

He nods once. "Deal."

Chapter 23

Savannah

My poor mom. The harder she tries, the harder she cries. My dad her pillar of strength as he holds her close and does his best to soothe her torn and tattered heart. The way it should be.

Clearer circumstances have surfaced over the last few days. Mistakes were made. The arsonists have been arrested. The fires are now under control. But in the end, the results are the same. Nineteen firefighters lost. Two of them from the Woodlands Crew – because they were trying to save others.

Doesn't make me less bitter. My brother was *my* hero. The

rest of the world wasn't entitled to have him as theirs. They didn't love him like I did. They didn't need him like I do. They'll never miss him like I will. Who's going to call me Peaches?

I can't decide if I'm sad or mad. Sad that he's gone or mad at him for not considering those who loved him most when he took that stupid, risky job. I can't seem to cry. Am I so overwhelmed that I've become numb? I want to scream, but I'm surrounded by people – constantly being pulled into hugs I don't want.

Man, if I thought I hated country music, it's got nothing on the organ music blasting through the church. Songs that aren't familiar – some that are. My dad takes a seat between my mom and me, so we would each have a shoulder to cry on. Protocol be damned.

Following the flag-draped casket out of the church toward the waiting hearse outside is when I see Roger. It's strange how you can feel someone's eyes fixed on you in a crowded place. Someone you never expected to see. That's when I finally find my tears. There's a whole row of military in uniform behind him – on their feet, saluting as the casket passes – Britt at the end nearest to me.

The 21-gun salute at the cemetery sends a jolt through my body with each blast of the howitzers. The folded flag is handed to my mom and she hugs it to her chest. The formalities are over and the crowd is starting to thin – on their way to the reception. Why do we have receptions after funerals? Baptisms, weddings, bar mitzvahs I can understand. But funerals? I am so peopled out, it's ridiculous. Who in the hell can eat?

"Let's go, sweetheart." Dad gently takes my elbow to veer me toward the waiting limo. "People will be waiting."

"No. I'm not ready," I protest with a whisper, staring at the casket that sits on the lowering device while the attendants wait for us to leave. Silas will be put in his final resting place and there will be no one here to see him off. It doesn't feel right. He always saw me to my classroom door and made sure I got in before he left. He waited for me every day after school to get on the bus. On the bases we didn't ride the bus, we walked together.

I look up at my father, tears in my eyes. "He saw to it I got where I needed to be safely every day. I'm only doing the same for him one last time. Go. I'll get a Lyft."

"Sir," Britt's soft voice comes from behind us, "I'll wait with her. She won't be alone."

Dad gives us a curt nod. "Try not to be too long."

Britt and I observe the attendants lower the casket into the ground slowly and carefully, then remove the straps. "Sometimes loved ones add the first shovel of dirt on top," one attendant says as he holds out the tool. "It's a bit like closing the door for them here and telling them it's okay to open a new one on the other side."

Taking the shovel from him and stepping over to the pile of dirt, I scoop up a large amount and slowly tip it into the grave. "Godspeed, Silas. I will miss you." I swear I feel his familiar tap on my nose before I hand the shovel back to the attendant. "Thank you."

"Pull in here first," Britt tells the Lyft driver as we approach a liquor store. "I'll make the trip more than worth your while."

"What are you doing?"

"Keep your panties on." She opens the door and climbs out swiftly. "I'll be right back." Minutes later she returns with a brown paper bag in hand and slides the driver a note. "Let's go."

The driver takes off in the opposite direction of where we are supposed to be heading. I point my thumb toward the rear window. "Britt, the reception is back that way."

"Well aware," she says as she pulls four small sample bottles of Glenlivet from the bag to show me. "Therapy for you and a proper toast to your brother."

"This looks good," Britt tells the driver about a mile into the entrance to the McDowell Mountain hiking paths. She hands him two twenties and points her finger. "I've got your number. You are to wait right here. This won't take long."

He chuckles. "I've got you covered. I ain't going anywhere."

"Hiking! I'm in heels, you twit!" I holler at an identically shoed Britt as soon as we're out of the car. She changed out of her uniform into a dress in the backseat; shameless and talented hussy that she is. She was fast, but not shy about it. Due to the fact the driver didn't veer off the road on the way, he's either a faithful partner or gay.

"Oh hush." She leads me approximately forty feet away from the car and opens the bag, extracts two bottles of the Glenlivet; handing one to me. "Open it and chug. Hurry up, we don't have long. I'm sure the General is already checking his watch."

"You said toast!"

"I said therapy and toast. This is the therapy portion." She unscrews the cap on her bottle. "Open it and chug."

Only because I trust her, I follow orders. *Damn, that burns!*

"Now scream," she says calmly. My brow crinkles in puzzlement as I stare at her. "All these people telling you they know how you feel gets old, doesn't it? How sorry they are. They have no idea what's going on inside of you. You're mad at Silas, but you can't say it out loud. You're in love for the first time in your life with a man you can't have. You want the Army, but you don't want the Army. You've got parents that are going to be clinging to you like Glad Wrap and you want to run away, but you're conflicted due to loyalty. You're suffocating right now. Scream. Let it out. You know you want to." She arches a brow and inclines her chin. "Just...do...it."

Throughout her impromptu speech, I hadn't noticed my breaths quickening, my muscles tightening, my fists clenching. She hit home. Turning my back to her, I stare out over the canyon. I thought this last year was the worst I could go through, but the last four days have proven me so wrong. The bloodcurdling scream comes from the depths of my soul as I aim it toward the sky.

"Not good enough soldier. Do it again!" Britt orders from behind me. So I do and my muscles slowly begin to loosen. She joins me at my side and takes my hand in hers. "Now, one together because you've been the best fucking friend I've ever had, and I'm going to miss the hell out of you." She throws our joined hands in the air and together we let out an incoherent bellow of frustration, followed by tears and a hug that melts my heart. I am going to miss her too.

She takes my shoulders in firm hands. "Feel better?" I nod. "Cool. Time for the toast. Before the General sends out the troops."

Trading the empties for the other two bottles of Glenlivet from the bag, she hands one to me and unscrews the lid on hers. Holding it up in a cheers, she looks to the sky and smiles. "Silas Mitchell, you were a man amongst men. Hearing about you through your little sister is enough to make me wish I'd had a brother like you. I know you'll be watching over her from above."

Holding her bottle patiently, she waits for my words as I hold my own little bottle up. "I will miss you, big brother. If I ever have a little boy, you will have a namesake. Thank you for everything."

We tip our little bottles in unison to the sky then throw them back, draining them.

I slap my chest, releasing a slight cough. "You couldn't find

Jameson?"

"Be happy I didn't buy tequila to spare your breath. Just don't breathe on daddy. Might want to pop a piece of chewing gum. Get in the car."

When we return to the Lyft, the driver stands outside the car and holds the twenties out to hand them back to Britt. "I saw the obituary yesterday. I was an Army brat, too. It was at Garrison in Virginia that Silas handled a bully for me in junior high. Kid never touched me again. There is not a snowball's chance in hell I could charge for this ride." He opens the back door and looks to me. "Your brother was one of a kind. Tell me where we're going, ladies."

Chapter 24

Roger

"Who in the hell throws a fucking reception for a funeral at a country club?" I grumble to Chauncy, as I fumble on the crutches set high enough to keep my back stretched while I walk. The same crutches that also happen to be digging into my armpits so deep they're rubbing the skin raw. Every step feels like knives in my ass and the back brace helps minimally. Ibuprofen is my drug of choice – sort of. Kinda hard to dial up for narcotics from a doc you ran out on.

The hotel bed isn't exactly orthopedic luxury, but my little sister Ruthie found me a back brace with stiff supports in it. Sworn to secrecy to my parents about my presence in town—

I'll see them before I leave—I still saw her in the church with what must have been some college friends. I swear half of rural America is here.

"It's probably the only place big enough to hold all these people," Chauncy mutters back. "Apparently, Silas was the town's mascot. Just shut up and pay your respects, dumbass."

"I already did. At the church."

"The General specifically asked that you make an appearance here." He side-eyes me. "If you could call that asking. I'm not sure the man has ever requested anything in his life. Just tell me it had nothing to do with the redheaded daughter you couldn't take your eyes off of."

Continuing to scan the crowd, as I've done since we got here, I utter, "She's not even here. She left the cemetery with another soldier."

"Well aware, Roger. I watched it too. You wouldn't leave until she did. Is there a story there? Maybe an unfinished chapter?"

"Only the last page, Chaunce." I lift my brow and tilt my head. "I believe it's called The End."

He grimaces. "Ouch. Please tell me you don't plan to rip that poor woman's heart out on a day like today. I'll kick your ass myself. You'll need that wheelchair and I ain't gonna go get it for you."

"It's already over." My jaw tics as I clench my teeth when I see her and the now civvies-attired woman from the cemetery walk in the door.

Chaunce must note my reaction because he follows my gaze and inquires, "And why are we here?"

"To pay our respects to Silas," I grumble.

"Then let's do it right. Funerals are for the living, Roger." He lifts one shoulder and lets it drop. "Silas isn't going to know you were here, but his loved ones will. Ask yourself how he would want you to treat them. *That* is how you pay him respect." He nods toward the General, who is headed our way. "Incoming."

"Captain Bellamy," General Mitchell addresses me with a stern clip and an outstretched hand. I'm not in uniform so don't really expect a salute. How he knows who I am is beyond me, but I reach for his hand to shake it. As I do, I swear another abrasion in my armpit bleeds and I grit my teeth.

"Sir, I'm very sorry for your loss. Silas was a good man." I feel the burn behind my eyes and know if I blink, the damn saltwater is going to flow.

"Your men have told me what happened." He draws a shaky breath. "What you did for my son. The service is awarding Silas a purple heart. I'd like to see to it you get one as well."

He may as well have punched me in the chest.

"With all due respect, *Sir*, do. not. do. that." My words are gut reaction and harsh. The saltwater is threatening to run down my cheeks. "I came to express my condolences. I'll be on my way." The harder the crutches dig into my armpits as I make my way toward the door, the more fitting the punishment seems. I should have tried harder. I should have knocked Silas on his ass and dragged him to the east. It should have been me.

Before I can shove the door open, the familiar fast thuds of military shoes sound behind me. His suspicious tone tells me all I need to know. "You're not going to tell my *daughter* goodbye? *Savannah?* You don't think she deserves better?"

I bow my head, take a deep breath in, and blow it out slowly. "She deserves so much better. I hope she finds it, sir."

My CO greets me in the parking lot as Chauncy and I reach the car – though *greets* is a bit of a stretch. "Captain Bellamy." My name sounds like a taste of vinegar to his tongue and feels like sandpaper to my ears.

I turn slowly with the aid of my crutches, wincing with the pain. "Sir."

His jaw is set firm, eyes icy beneath a set brow. "Technically, you are AWOL, soldier." He draws a deep breath, chest inflating as those icy eyes roll. "Morally, it's exactly what I would have expected from you. You've got three days to get your ass back on base. Report to me first thing Monday morning."

"Yes, sir." As he turns to make his way back in the building, I call out after him, "Sir, would you happen to know if staff sergeant Conroy's services have taken place yet, and where they are?"

"Cheyenne, Wyoming, tomorrow morning, eleven hundred hours." *How in the hell could I forget where he was from?* His back to me, he offers, "We fly out this evening from Tucson at eighteen hundred hours. Would you like to accompany the rest of your men, Bellamy?"

"Commander Owens, sir, this is Chauncy Steffen. He's a firefighter from Waco. The man who carried Conroy." He finally turns around, acknowledging my seemingly newfound ride or die, before making his way back.

He takes Chauncy's hand in a firm grip. "Thank you. The Army owes you, son. Pack your bags and you can join us. We'll return you to Waco as well."

"I'd appreciate that, sir," Chauncy replies.

Glancing back to the doors one last time, I see her standing outside them, watching. Rich auburn hair that I will never run my fingers through again. Lips I can still taste, but will never again savor. Jewel green eyes and a voice that will haunt my dreams for the rest of my life. A heart that beat in time with mine. The first and last woman I will ever trust with it. She doesn't just deserve better – she deserves the best. And I'm not him. My little eighth wonder. Why she risked so much to be with me will forever remain a mystery.

Stealing one last moment to file this vision away with all the rest, I pull my shades from my shirt pocket, slide them on, and gingerly turn on the crutches to lower myself into the car. "Let's roll, Chaunce."

After stopping to see my folks, getting my ass chewed – lovingly – by mom and dad for not seeing them sooner, packing up at the hotel, returning the car to the rental company in Scottsdale, and having Dad drop us at the airfield in Tucson, we're on our way to Cheyenne, Wyoming with the entire company from the Woodlands Crew as well as a few others from the base.

"I've gotten all the info I can from the rest of your crew," Commander Owens says after he's booted Chauncy out of the seat next to me, "but I haven't gotten jackshit from you, Bellamy. It's what happens when you go AWOL. Give me your version."

Starting at the beginning, I give him the full story from day one. The only part he hadn't heard yet was the direct communication between Oujiri and me when the fire started to the south of us . . . or so I thought.

"Oujiri reported you told him to order the men to the west."

My head whips to the left in his direction but before I can respond, Chauncy, who has been keenly listening in the seat in front of us, nearly leaps out of it and yells, "That's a fuckin' lie! I was right there! Roger told him the only water was to the east! That asshole was nowhere to be found!"

Owens holds up a hand. "Hold on. This is what we're trying to get to the bottom of." He looks to me. "All of your men have stated you ordered everyone to the east. They couldn't hear what you told Oujiri because all hell was breaking loose, and they were taking orders from you." He steels his eyes on mine. "That for which they will be forever grateful, and have volunteered to go before the board on your behalf."

"My behalf for what!?"

"There were a lot of men lost, Roger. Oujiri's trying to cover his ass."

Chauncy does leave his seat this time and hovers over the Commander. "You give me five minutes with that lyin' prick and he won't have an ass to cover. I'll beat it into the ground for him. I was on the crew that was ordered to the west. If I hadn't trusted Roger, I'd be dead." His voice cracks as a sob breaks through. "It's why Silas and Conroy are dead! They ran back tryin' to save 'em and we couldn't stop 'em before that tree fell!" He plops back into his seat and leans forward, elbows on his knees, hands in his hair yanking hard. "Pointin' fingers. Boards and committees. Jesus, what is wrong with people they can't even let men die with dignity!"

Conroy's funeral isn't as large as Silas's was, but it's not too shabby. He was popular in his hometown. The boy next door, judging by the number of young women in attendance and tears shed by the same. I didn't dress in military garb, not that I had it with me, but more so that Chauncy wouldn't feel out of place. We've been a team for days. That, and it was hard enough to get dressed with a back brace and walk with crutches. The plane ride wasn't exactly conducive to disk rupture, but then riding in the car for hours on end hadn't been my smartest move either.

The most important thing is knowing we've been able to honor our comrades and lay them to rest.

"You are to report to Darnall Med Center as soon as we land," Owens orders once I'm seated on the plane back to Fort Hood. "Arrangements have been made for your ride." He tips his chin at Chauncy next to me. "You will be escorted back to Waco yet this evening. Thank you once again for your service, Mr. Steffen. Should you decide to enlist . . ." he cocks a brow, ". . . how old are you?"

Chauncy chuckles nervously. "Thank you, sir, but I'm happy with my job as a firefighter. Might be reconsiderin' the Hotshots as well, unless you can guarantee me Roger as a supervisor."

Owens shakes his head. "Not my area, son. Best of luck to you."

"I respect you guys," Chaunce mutters after he's left. "I really do. But I just wasn't cut out for the service. I can handle three days at a time livin' in the firehouse with a bunch of guys fartin', belchin', and bitchin'. But day in and day out for years to come?" He shudders dramatically. "Life's too damn short. I like to hunt, fish, and fuck." He grins cockily. "And I wanna do it while I'm young enough to enjoy it."

"How old are you?"

"Twenty six. How old are you?"

"Twenty nine." I study the back of the seat in front of me. "Ten years to go."

"In it for the long haul, huh? You ever get down to Waco? A little weekend leave now and then?"

Recalling Silas's story of his last weekend spent there with the twins, I chuckle. "I've heard it gets pretty crazy."

"It certainly can. You got my number," he says with a sly grin. "The ladies down there would love you. They start the fires, we put 'em out."

Chapter 26

Roger

"Diligent physical therapy three times a week here," Dr. Graves doles out discharge instructions like a recipe, "and light exercises you can do on your own at the base. Absolutely no lifting, no straining, no exercise outside of what the therapist gives you to do. You're off active duty until further notice."

"What the hell am I supposed to do!?" I bark. "Sit on my ass otherwise?"

"What part of my instructions did you not understand, Captain Bellamy?" he asks with a stern glare. "You've been in traction for a week. We've done epidurals. We'll do a follow-up MRI next week to see what progress we've made. Leaving the hospital in Page AMA wasn't your wisest decision, but we can't see any real difference from your scans there. The specific back brace the physical therapist ordered for you is on backorder. I'll have it sent to Fort Hood and they'll show you how to wear it properly. Works out well, as I want that shoulder wound rechecked in a couple days anyway. Follow up at the clinic there."

For the first time since waking up in Page, the possibility of less than a hundred percent recovery is scaring the shit out of me. "What happens if this doesn't work?"

"Honestly?"

"No, doc," I sneer. "I want you to blow smoke up my ass."

"Possible surgery, diskectomies, fusions. We've come a long way with treatment. But I'm not going to *blow smoke up your ass*, Bellamy. I've seen a lot of careers end over injuries such as yours. I've seen a lot end on less. If you want this, you'd better be ready to work for it."

My fists clench in frustration. I'd do it all again for the sake of my best friend, but a better outcome – his and mine – would have made it so much more worth it. "Fuck!"

"Might want to check with PT first, but I would recommend only on your back and nothing too rough, Bellamy," he says cockily. "Make her do the work. I'll see you next week."

Two days later I receive notice the clinic has my brace. No appointment time specified, no designated doctor to my case. This ought to be fun. Standing and lying down are the most comfortable positions and who knows how long I'll have to wait.

"Ah," the check-in clerk says as she looks at the computer screen. "Dr. Fitzpatrick has the order for that and he's really backed up right now. Let me see who else can do that for you."

An assistant calls my name from the entrance to the

exam rooms forty-five minutes later, and I follow down the hallway . . . slowly. "Room four. Dr. Fitzpatrick isn't available, but we have others who can do this for you." Once in the room, she blissfully – aka ignorantly – says, "You can take a seat on the table."

"I'll stand."

She licks her lips slowly then bites her lower one before batting her eyelashes. "Need help getting your shirt off, Captain Bellamy?"

Glancing at the name tag on her uniform, I spit her name through a clenched jaw, "Sergeant Shana Jones, go get the doctor before I report you for inappropriate behavior with a senior officer. Now."

She cowers like a scolded puppy and scampers for the door. "Yes, sir."

"Do not come back in this room." I lean against the exam table for support and dig the heels of my palms into my eyeballs. *That shit gets so old.*

Voices on the other side of the door capture my attention when I hear the grumble of one Sgt. Jones, "Good luck, that guy's a prick." *And my position on base has been verified once more. I don't look at nor fuck enlisted personnel. At least not knowingly.*

The door starts to open and a male voice speaks loudly from the hallway. "It's labeled well top and bottom. It's a matter of correct positioning. The stays in the back are what's most important for bracing. Just show him proper placement and teach him how to adjust the tightness for stability."

"In or outside the clothing?"

I freeze at the sound of her voice. I thought she was already gone. I've dreamed about her every night since the funeral. Not nightmares; dreams. I held her, kissed her, heard her laugh. She's the only thing that's kept me sane throughout any of this.

The only reason I could sleep – because that's where I would find her.

My little eighth wonder.

"His choice. Probably best on the outside to avoid skin abrasion. Don't forget to check that shoulder wound. Any problems, come and get me."

The door opens and she enters, chin tucked as she studies the brace in her hands as if it's a puzzle. *I deserve it. I walked away from her. No condolences, no apologies, no goodbye.*

"Savvy," I whisper, her name tasting better than the finest bourbon that's ever touched my tongue.

"Captain Bellamy," she addresses me as if we've never met. "I understand physical therapy ordered this specific orthopedic brace. If you'll just . . ."

"You should check my shoulder first." I match her tone with an order. *Outside the clothing, my ass.* Two can play this game. I know her weaknesses – my naked body being one of them. Half naked is better than nothing, and undressing each other was one of our favorite things to do. Well, ripping each other's clothes off might be a better description. I'm still leaned against the exam table, so I spread my legs farther apart so she'll need to step between them. "I need help getting my shirt off."

She scowls. "It's a button down." *There's my spitfire. Come to me, Savvy.*

"Your point?"

"Oh, for pity's sake." She rolls her eyes and slaps the brace down on the table. Reaching from the side, she attempts to unbutton my shirt but it's awkward – not to mention her hands are shaky. I'm also losing my patience. That and I want to see the spark in her eyes, watch them dilate.

I grasp both of her hands in one of mine. "Stand between

my legs, Savannah. We're professionals." As she places one leg over my thigh to step between my legs, I raise it just high enough to make contact. Pain shoots through my ass cheek with the movement, but it's so worth it. The heat, her tiny whimper. As if she can't help herself she lingers for a moment before moving. By the time she's between my legs, my third one is growing quickly. Hard as a rock and missing her desperately.

"You've got a T-shirt on!" she huffs when she pulls the hem of my shirt out of my pants. *Sassy, impatient. So reminiscent of undeniable urges.*

My lips tip in a crooked grin. "Would it make it easier for you if I dropped my pants?"

"Don't you dare!" she sneers, stripping my shirt off my shoulders, none too gently, I might add. She yanks hard on the material of my T-shirt, stretching it until it gives way suddenly, causing her to lose her grip and her hand to fly up and clip my nose. She sucks in a sharp breath. "Did I hurt you?"

Talk about a punch to the gut. How do I answer that? Yeah, but I can forgive you? Yeah, but I inflicted more pain on you? I love you too much to let it matter? I broke you and I don't know how to fix it?

Grasping the back of my T-shirt over my head, I pull it up and off. "Let's start with the shoulder, shall we?"

"Can you turn around for me?"

"No." I lean forward, my feet solid on the floor, one hand bracing the table edge, the other on her hip for seeming stability, but in truth just so I can touch her, breathe her in, pretend. "Check it from this angle, please. It's more comfortable."

Chapter 27

Savannah

"Let's do it without the shirt first and see how it feels." He smirks. "If memory serves, bareback worked quite well the first time. If it's too uncomfortable, you can help me get dressed and we'll do it with clothes on."

That smirk. He knows what he's doing. Yes, Roger, I remember riding your back – your bare back.

I hold the back brace out and prompt him to take it. "The metal stays go in the back." I don't know why I say it. You'd have to have an IQ of 20 to not know that.

"Wrap it around me, Savvy." His whisper is so low and sexy,

I swear I feel his breath on my skin from feet away. "You know how." He reaches beyond the brace in my hands and clasps my wrists, pulling me close. "Show me. Wrap it around my back, just like you've always done with your legs. Then every time I put it on, I'll think of you."

Tears well in my eyes and before I can stop them, a few slip down my cheeks. "In a good way, I hope."

He gently swipes the tears with his thumbs and whispers, "The best way."

Half an hour later, we've been through all the steps: putting it on, taking it off – on again over his T-shirt and under his uniform shirt, washing instructions, etc. Now he's dressed to go.

"I thought your time was up here. When did things change?"

"They didn't change." I shake my head. "I still had a couple weeks to go."

"When do you leave?"

"I sign out for the final time on Friday. Some of us are going into Killeen for a send-off. Staying the night and then I fly out on Saturday."

"Cancel it," he says sharply, then shakes his head. "Not the send-off, the flight. I'll buy you another ticket."

"Why would . . ."

"One more night, Savannah," he pleads. "Give me a chance to say goodbye."

"You said you hated me."

"I said I hate liars." He reaches out to brush away another tear. "I've had a lot of time to think about it. Everything you did was based on omission, *just* Savannah. You put your career in jeopardy; not mine. I think Silas would have forgiven me, in time. Hell, maybe even approved if he found out how I felt about you. The only one you put at risk was yourself, and I have no idea why." I start to open my mouth to explain, but he places a finger over it. "I don't want to know. All I want is to say goodbye, my way. Can you give me that much?"

One more night may give us both a chance to heal. Maybe in the end he'll forgive me. I don't want to say goodbye, but if forgiveness is all I can hope for, I'll take it.

My voice is so weak, I barely hear myself. "I can do that."

"Room 312," he says with a hint of a smile. "Just like always. I'll be checking in on Friday so whenever you get there on Saturday is good. I'll get you back to Killeen for a flight home on Sunday."

Harker Heights. I wonder who's going to take my place once I'm gone.

As I reach for the doorknob and twist, his hand comes around from behind me to block the door from opening. His free hand moves my hair away from my neck, gathering it in his fist, tipping my head back and turning it so the angle makes a perfect fit for his mouth on mine. The kiss is restrained so as not to leave my lips swollen, but needy in its own right.

"Saturday, Savannah," he murmurs against my mouth. "Please don't let me down."

"Cheers!" Eight hands raise in a toast; a variation of beers and whiskeys to see me off. Fruity concoctions won't be found at this table. We are ladies, but we're hardcore. Fruit is for eating. Liquor is for drinking.

"So, what now?" Constance asks after shooting down the bourbon and ordering a fourth.

"Going back to school," I reply with more confidence than I feel at the moment.

Her eyebrows shoot skyward, but she struggles to hold

them up as she blinks slowly. "What for?"

Britt grins wryly and answers sardonically, "To get even smarter?"

I nudge her with my elbow. She really has low tolerance. "OR tech. I like the medical work."

Constance waggles her brows. "Oohh, good idea. Sexy doctors all over the place. I'll bet those surgeons are good with their hands."

Britt leans toward me and singsongs a low mutter, "Not as good as captains in the Army."

I shoot her a stink-eye. "You would know."

"Mine was a major," she rolls her eyes, ". . . pain in the ass."

"You ever going back to Harker Heights?" I whisper.

"You mean am I a glutton for punishment?" I nod. "Better do it while I can. My next assignment's in Georgia. Fort Benning."

"What! When?"

She holds up her index and middle fingers. "Two months. I figure that oughta get me some pretty good sex before I leave. Corbin is nothing if not efficient."

"Britt," I whine, then toss back the remaining amber liquid in my tumbler. "You're going to be way on the other side of the country. How am I going to visit you?"

She tilts her head and arches a brow. "Did you really plan on coming back to this neck of the woods?"

Thinking of Roger, I scrunch my nose. He was pretty clear. '*One last night*'. "We've still got texts and emails."

"Yeah, we do." She nods slowly, then drops her chin to her chest and shakes her head. "God, I hate the Army sometimes."

Chapter 28

Roger

"You look a little stiff, my friend." Corbin sets the tumbler of Jameson in front of me on the bar after I've gingerly sat my ass on the stool. "Heard about the disaster at Antelope. Sorry about your buddy." He nods at my drink. "First two are on the house. One for you, one for him. Drink yours first. We'll toast to him together on the second."

"Thanks." I take my time with the first one, relishing the first drop of alcohol to touch my lips since weeks before the fire. Between training and pain killers, alcohol has been off limits. "I actually lost two, Corbin." I hold my hand up to stop him from pouring more into a second tumbler. "We can toast to both with one drink."

"So," he drawls, leaning his elbows on the bar once the toast is over, "you wanna tell me about your little redhead? *Sergeant* Savannah?"

My jaw tics. "How in the hell do you know about that?"

His brow rises, questioning me, "Her soldier friend, the one who attended the funeral with her?" I nod, though I don't know who the woman was. "She told me about it. Brittanny Sunn was my mistake. The difference between you and me is I was well aware of my misconduct. Thirteen years her senior, not to mention her senior officer."

"You were knowingly fucking an enlisted!?"

He glares and spits through a clenched jaw, "A little louder, Bellamy. I don't think the kitchen help or the customers at the piano bar heard you."

"Sorry," I mumble, ashamed at my lack of discretion. "I did not expect that."

"I wasn't expecting her." He wipes the bar top down with swift motions. "She was a lapse in my judgment . . . and restraint. My first and last. Unfortunately, had I known what a sarcastic, sassy, smart-mouthed, little shit could do to me, I would have tied my dick up before I ever touched her."

"She get you in trouble?"

"Pfft." He rolls his eyes. "Sunny's as discreet as they come. I was the idiot."

"What did you do?"

His self-deprecating chuckle is unmissable as he studies the pennies embedded in the resin-coated bar top. "I fell in love with her. She was in love with the Army. Still is. Always stick with seasoned civilian pussy, Bellamy. No rank, no rules, and no competition."

Lifting my palms as if offering a solution, "You're out now.

No more rank or rules. You want her? Go get her. Civilians mix with military all the time."

He scowls as if the very idea is revolting. "I ain't globetrotting. Done enough of that for the Army. I'm settled. She can have Uncle Sam. I'll stick with fuckin' tourists who want the sexy bartender."

"You always were a stubborn bastard."

"Not really in this case." He shakes his head and acquiesces, "Just gotta know when to admit defeat. I'm not going to hold her back. She's too young, and just getting started. I've already closed that chapter in my life and moved on to the next."

Oh the irony. That's what I'm about to do tomorrow night.

Three soft taps on the door set my heart racing. I was sure she'd show, but I was beginning to have my doubts. It's four o'clock in the afternoon. Hotel checkouts are before eleven. Where the hell has she been? We may be over, but we haven't written *The End* yet. I need an end. Like Corbin, I need to close this chapter and move on to the next.

I open the door, speechless as I take in the perfection in front of me. She didn't hide her freckles under makeup – just the way I like it. Casual clothing consisting of blue jeans and a pink T-shirt, sandals, and a dainty watch on her wrist. Her auburn hair falls over her shoulders in soft waves. One small overnight bag in her hand.

"Thanks for coming." I open the door wide, taking the bag from her.

"I said I would."

"No duffel?"

"Airport locker. I stopped by on my way here to change my ticket to assure there were no mistakes, so I left my things in a locker for the night."

"I told you I'd buy your ticket," I remind her. "Military gets priority. I could have done it from here once I had your information."

Her chin juts a little higher, shoulders square a little more; just like the soldier she is. "I can handle my own, Roger. I may be young, but I'm quite capable."

The story of her heroic efforts, saving lives despite personal injuries, refusal of discharge, a purple heart award, echoes in my mind as I stare at my little powerhouse. She doesn't know that I know – would probably be pissed if she did. *Capable* is an understatement. She is also young, and has a whole life yet to live. So many opportunities, and I won't be a deterrent.

Steering the rest of our night in another direction, I wrap my hand in her hair and pull her close. "You're also quite beautiful," *kiss* "smart," *kiss* "loyal, compassionate," *kiss* "and the sexiest thing I've ever seen." She wraps her hands around my neck, melding into me as if we're the two pieces needed to complete a complicated puzzle.

As I lift her into my arms the same way I've often done, she quickly protests, "Where's your back brace? You can't lift!"

I simply hold her tighter and mutter against her mouth, "Wrap them around me, Savvy. You're the only thing that stops the pain. And will . . . until you leave."

Carrying her to the bed, the twinge of pain in my back is the least of my concerns. I have one last night before she's gone forever. The physical pain may very well be a driving force to overcome the emotional one I swear I will never fall for again. The epidurals are starting to work, the anti-inflammatories are helping. I won't be staying on my back. Tonight, my PT is in the form of Savannah Mitchell; turning her into a pretzel and savoring every last inch possible.

The last heartache I will ever allow myself to feel.

The last eyes I will ever gaze into, because they wouldn't be hers.

The last time I let myself fall in love, because it just hurts too damn much.

Chapter 29

Savannah

"When does your flight leave?"

It's one o'clock in the morning. I'm tucked under Roger's chin, my head on his chest, the beat of his heart slow and steady in my ear. I'm sore; the good kind. The kind that strikes a memory with every twinge. Unfortunately, the kind that only lasts a short while; maybe a day or two. If only men were affected the same way, it might make women more memorable.

"Ten-thirty," I tell him. "I need to be gone by eight."

"Back to Scottsdale?"

I nod against his chest. There's no point in elaborating, Phoenix will be my new home in few weeks. What does it matter? He'll be here. This night was for him, his chance to say goodbye, and my penance for hurting him. He pledged his love once, but promised me nothing. I'm probably only a reminder of painful loss now. Another reminder that life can change right before your eyes. One day you're here, the next you're gone. I wish we could have taught each other to live every moment like it's your last, but spend them together enjoying the ones we get.

"Please tell me you've resigned from the Hotshots." I don't think I've ever pleaded so hard for anything in my life in one statement. Flashbacks can make a job so much more dangerous. PTSD makes one vulnerable. He didn't just lose men; he lost his best friend.

He tips my chin up with two fingers. "I didn't have to. They pulled me from it."

"Permanently?" I sit up in bed, secretly hoping for affirmation, but trying to look sympathetic – his next words proving I suck at it.

"Cut the shit, Savvy," he says dryly, his lips flattened in a straight line. "I'm sure you're quite happy about it."

My mouth twists as I shrug. "I'm not unhappy about it. Just promise me."

"I promise I'm done. So you still care, huh?"

"You once asked me why you, Roger. Shut up long enough to hear me out this time." As soon as he opens his mouth to protest, my hand clamps over it. "No! It's my turn. Are you going to listen?" He nods under my hand, so I lift it, and he sits up to match my position.

"I'm listening."

"I grew up an Army brat," I start. "A daughter, a sister, somebody's friend or classmate . . . for a while, but never long lasting. I had a few dates; homecoming, prom, but I was set on a military career. I went straight from high school into the Army." I firm my brow and glare at him. "Without having had sex! I had offers, lots of them, especially once I hit the service. But there was always that one component missing." My eyes gloss over at the memory of the night I met him. "I was about to give up on it and just give in and get it over with. Even you failed initially, until you set me on my feet in front of this very hotel, and kissed me. You called me your little green-eyed eighth wonder and told me to meet you in the morning instead of trying to talk me into your bed. When I did show up to your room later, you seemed to sense what I needed, and all you did was hold me that night." I sniffle and swipe at my nose with the heel of my palm. "It was romance. The one component I'd always wanted but never experienced.

"That day in the pool, when you took my . . ." I drop my forehead into my hands and feel him reach for me. "Don't! Let me finish. You felt the need to give me your last name to make it . . . honorable, I guess? It was so sweet." I raise my head to look at him. "I wouldn't have been there if I hadn't known who you were. In the woods with a stranger? That would have been so stupid and dangerous."

I study the space between us, his fingers having worked their way to lock with mine. "Then we turned into so much more. You gave me what I didn't know I was missing, and I will never forget that. I was finally something special by someone's choosing. I wasn't just a daughter or a sister. Not a soldier, a bunkmate or a friend by proxy. I'd never been anybody's anything, until you."

He lays back on the bed, pulling me down on top of him. "You have always been special, Savannah Mitchell. Hardly a proxy. I can't imagine having wanted anyone but you."

Rolling us over so I'm underneath him, he gazes into my eyes and simply whispers, "I will miss you, my little green-eyed eighth wonder." He makes love to me like he's never done before. Slow, sweet, restrained as if savoring every last single second. When it's over, he doesn't cuddle; he holds me as if he'll never let go.

When I wake to the alarm at seven a.m., the room is lit only by the slim streak of sunlight creeping through the opening in the curtains, and the bed is void of the body I expected to be next to me. The bathroom door is open and his bag is gone.

He let me go. He left. Without goodbye.

One slow stretch, a deep breath in to capture his scent on the pillow where he slept, and I crawl out of bed. It's really over. The soldier in me wants to suck it up and move on. However, the woman I am is falling apart on the inside. I don't need tears this morning, though. I have a plane ride to get through and parents to face when I get back. I'll cry later – probably for months.

Flipping the light switch on in the bathroom, I see the note on the counter as well as sixty dollars underneath it.

The money is for the Lyft ride into Killeen. I'd never pay for sex with you; that's an honor and priceless. Live your best life, Peaches. Silas would want that for you. So do I.

>>>>>>>>>>

I flip the note over to see what's on the other side.

Just so you know, you were never my "anything", Savannah. You were my EVERYTHING.

"Then why didn't you ask me to stay, you asshole?" I sob on my way to the floor where my knees hit hard. "I'm a civilian now."

Eventually, I rise from my knees, brush my teeth, throw my hair in a messy bun, and step in the shower for a quick spritz. I hurriedly dress in leggings, T-shirt, and sandals, and toss the rest of my things in the overnight bag. Taking one last glance in the full-length mirror on my way past, I flip it the bird, leaving Harker Heights and the only man I've ever loved behind.

Chapter 30

Roger

"Desk job! Fuck no!" I holler at the three morons sitting in Dr. Graves' office. One being Graves, the other two my physiotherapist and Commander Owens. The highlights of my last MRI are on the lit panel on the wall; results of which are not in my favor.

"It's the best I can offer, Captain Bellamy," Graves says. "Your spine is too vulnerable after the diskectomy. You're lucky we only had to do one, but it leaves you at risk. You're a liability. You sure as hell don't want to end up with fusions."

"Roger," Owens shuffles some papers in my direction and taps his fingers on the desk. "It's this or medical discharge.

You've got talents we can use."

"Talents," I grunt. "While sitting on my ass all day?" I whirl toward the physiotherapist. "You recommended this?"

He glances at Graves then back to me. "No, I did not. I'm not a fan of you sitting on your ass all day, and I'm even less of a fan of you in a wheelchair. You're young. My recommendation is you take the medical discharge. Your condition takes lifetime maintenance. You can get back to near normal, provided you don't let it get ahead of you." He shoots a side-eye at Graves once more. "Sitting behind a desk is not the way to do that."

Owens stands and claps my shoulder before gathering the papers. "Take a day or two to think about it. You know where to find me."

Following him out the door, we pause in the hall. Owens crosses his arms over his chest. "I had to offer you both options. It's the Army's way. Gotta be honest, Bellamy, if I had to share an office with you, I'd go fuckin' crazy. Take the discharge. It's honorable. You get the pay, the benefits. Given enough time and therapy, there are plenty of civilian opportunities out there."

From inside the room where Graves and the physiotherapist remain, the harsh words from the PT come through loud and clear. "I think the guy has suffered enough, don't you? A pick ax to his shoulder and ruptured vertebrae trying to save his men? He'll never make it behind a desk. Let the poor bastard go home. We shouldn't have even given him the option."

My glare is burning a hole through Owens as I stare at him. "What pick ax to my shoulder? I was told they were surgical scars to repair tendon damage."

Owens gently guides me to the bench against the wall behind me. "Take a seat." He leans back against the wall and scrubs a hand over his face. "You sure you want the details? They ain't pretty, Bellamy. But if there's any chance you're doubting yourself, or it comes back to you when you least . . ."

"Just spit it out," I snap.

"Mitchell was gone the minute he hit the ground. The head of a pick ax went straight through his heart when he went down. They figure the handle probably broke off when he fell on it, or it was already broken off and somebody left it behind," he hesitates, "sticking up outta the ground. The portion that didn't get buried all the way into his chest was digging into your shoulder as you carried him. There was tendon damage. Details weren't necessary. It's how you ended up needing surgery and a shitload of staples and stitches to close it."

Flashback. The vivid scene of Silas on the ground before me, crimson stains covering his torso, the tip of the ax protruding from his chest makes my head swim. It's all coming back to me.

"Did I do more damage carrying him?" I grit through a tight jaw.

"What part of gone did you miss, Bellamy? There was nothing you could have done for him," he reiterates. "What you did do was give his family a body to bury. Your team did the same for Conroy. One last chance to see them before putting them to rest. That's a helluva lot more than seventeen other families got." He squeezes my shoulder with a firm hand. "Your men are going to miss you, but I think it's time to go home, soldier."

Chapter 31

Roger

Four months, two cases of whiskey, and looming resignation later

"He's one of my instructors," Ruthie informs me. "He works on the side and I can't think of anybody who would be able to help you more. His specialty is strengthening after back injuries. He's a genius."

Ruthie is in school to be a physiotherapist – her goal to work for an NFL team. I'm damn proud of her, but still, that's an awful lot of locker rooms to spread the word in – aka: *"Did you know Ruthie's family is mafia? Their body count could fill every cemetery in Chicago. Touching her is a death wish."* She's outgoing, feisty, and determined – most days to drive me nuts.

There are nine years between us, but the older we get the less it shows.

I smirk and let out a sarcastic chuckle. "You wouldn't be looking for extra points, would you? Got a little crush on the instructor, do you?"

"No!" she shrieks. "I'm trying to help you, jackass. Besides, he's gay!"

"Gay!?" My shock is a little more profound than I mean it to be. I have nothing against preference – it's just not my preference. "Why would you set me up with a gay trainer?"

She places a hand on her hip and arches a brow. "Afraid he might see your beef, bro? Get a little thrill or tell all the ladies you're only a strip steak versus the porterhouse they dream you are?"

"When did you get so mean? You used to be such a nice kid."

"When did you turn into an asshole?" She holds up her fist. "Call me a kid again and I will punch your lights out."

Geez, judging from the look on her face and the unbreakable stare she's challenging me with, I'm beginning to think she means it. Ooh, she's got the stare down to a science, too. To the untrained eye, it's indecipherable – the tiny flicker of the eyelids – just enough to keep the eyeballs moist. She does not cower. Good girl.

I break the stare to appease her, and the soon-to-be-bruise strikes my bicep when she throws a punch. "What the hell, Ruthie!"

She bats her eyes and smiles sweetly. "You lost. I'll call Thad and tell him he has a new customer."

My jaw hangs agape. "A stare down is not the way you win an argument!"

"Not always, but I kickbox now. I let you off easy. Six months, Roger. You might not hit a hundred percent, but you can come damn close. I will not watch you give up." Tears fill her eyes before she throws her arms around my waist. "You're my hero. I want my big brother back."

I wrap my arms around her shoulders and make a promise I'm not sure I can keep, but vow to do my damnedest, "So do I, Squirt. I'm going to do my best to find him for you. Call Thad."

I won't throw the whiskey out, but I will save it for special occasions. Maybe a silent toast to an old friend. Possibly a touch of flavor to bittersweet memories of a beautiful green-eyed redhead who haunts my dreams and turned my world upside down. Nah, better scratch that idea. I'd be drinking more than I already am. A beer here and there and enough pussy to make me forget sounds like better therapy. Grief therapy. They're both gone, and it's time to move on.

My phone rings later that evening with a Texas area code. Expecting a call from *Thad*, guilt washes over me when I see Chauncy's name appear on the screen. I never took the time to say goodbye.

"Hey, Chauncy. How goes it?"

"Kinda wonderin' why I hadn't heard from you." He sighs. "Or maybe not. Thought I'd break the ice and see how you're feeling. I got a four-day spread before my next 72-hour shift. Wondered if you might wanna check out the female population in Waco, or I could make a trip up there if you got some leave time."

"Damn, Chaunce," I say wistfully and pinch the bridge of my nose. "I'm an asshole. I should have let you know. The Army booted me out on medical discharge. I'm back home in Arizona. Not much good for anything other than physical therapy and a couple of beers."

There's a long pause before he breathes into the phone, "Well, sheeyit. I won't take it personal. Sounds like your plate's a little full."

This guy was my only friend in my time of need. He stayed when no one else could. He said I saved him, but truth is he saved me. My ride or die.

"Hey Chaunce, you said you've got four days?"

"I did say that."

"Want to spend some time in Arizona? I'll spring for your ticket."

He laughs. "I'll take a couple days in Arizona, but I'll spring for my own ticket. I'll check on flights as soon as we're done and text you the info as soon as I have it."

"It'll be good to see you, Chaunce. Sorry I didn't let you know. It's been . . ."

"No apologies needed," he interrupts. "Now, let me get off the phone and make some arrangements. You're supplyin' the beers. I'll see you soon."

The next day at ten o'clock in the morning, Chauncy is waiting in the pickup line at the Phoenix airport with a smile on his face and a duffel at his feet. His cap is on backwards; his faded jeans and WFD T-shirt indicate he's ready to relax.

"Well, I'll be damned." He laughs as he climbs in the SUV and extends his hand to shake mine. "You *can* grow facial hair. I see you're lettin' the locks grow, too. Gettin' lazy or wantin' to look like us normal people? How you doin', Rog?"

Chauncy brings a smile to my face. I did need his visit; someone who knows, understands, but reminds me life goes on. "Doing okay, Chaunce. You?"

"Eh, doin' alright," he replies cheerily. "Just lookin' for a change of scenery for a few days. I figured your ugly mug was as good as any."

"Smartass." I slide the gearshift into Drive and head out into traffic. "Got a little dilemma this afternoon. My sister set me up with some physiotherapist she knows. Says he's a genius and thinks he can whip me into shape better than anybody else. Today is a more of an evaluation, I think. You okay if I drop you at my apartment while I go see him?"

"Mind if I tag along? Maybe I can pick up a few tips or exercises."

After dropping his carry-on at my apartment and a quick lunch at a burger joint in my neighborhood, we're headed back to Phoenix to see the *genius* for a two o'clock appointment.

Upon entering the building that houses the physiotherapy gym, I study the board to find the room number, grateful to see it's on the first floor. The receptionist greets us with an exuberant smile, followed by a bite of her lip – *same old shit* – then leads us down the hall to a room at the end. "Wait in here. Thad will be with you shortly. Be sure to stop at the front desk on your way out." She winks. *Yeah, yeah, yeah.*

A swift assessment of the room reveals a combination of pull bars, a rowing machine, weight bench, etc. *What the hell, Ruthie? I could do this at home. For free!*

Speak of the devil.

Ruthie enters the room in a whoosh of excitement; breathless, wearing a sports bra and gym shorts. "Oh good, I made it in time. I wanted to sit in on this."

Chauncy's eyes light with amusement as they do a slow perusal of my little sister. He mutters low, "That scenery just got a whole lot better."

"She just turned twenty-two," I grit through a clenched jaw, enunciating every single syllable.

He smiles slyly. "That's legal. I just turned twenty-seven."

"You want to live to see twenty-eight? She's also my baby sister."

"Oh sheeyit," he utters, adding the southern drawl to emphasize not only his surprise but understanding as well, diverting his gaze quickly. "Message received."

"Are you going to introduce me, Roger?" Ruthie asks sweetly as she performs her own perusal of Chauncy.

"Not necessary, Ru. You've got school to worry about."

The door opens once more and in walks, apparently, Thad. He's about mid-forties, dressed in sweats and sneakers, iPad in hand. "Hey, Ruthie. You made it."

"Hi Thad," she greets him with a million dollar smile. I know the moment she looks my way, I've screwed up. "This is my brother, Roger, and his plus one." She narrows her eyes at me. "I haven't gotten his name . . . yet."

Thad's brows rise as he smiles at us. "Ah! Ruthie hadn't told me. Bringing your support with you is a good idea. So, you guys are a couple?"

Chauncy looks absolutely mortified as he stares at Thad. "A couple o' what?"

Part 2

Chapter 32

Savannah

Three years later

"It's a privilege to be taken under my wing, Ms. Mitchell," Dr. Evans states; his glacial blue eyes disarming. "I generally prefer my techs more experienced. I don't need tools dropped, questions asked, or hesitation when orders are given."

"They won't be," I reassure him. The guy has a reputation of being a grade-A dick. He's head of the ortho department at Banner Medical, a topnotch surgeon, and demands an A-team in his OR. Being a year out of school, you don't get to pick your poison; you drink whatever they give you. Techs get passed from OR to OR on a rotational basis, but it would appear I've been given a dose of Dr. Hemlock, and I'm paralyzed by his choosing. I've worked in his OR many times and his presence is so overpowering, I feel like a faceless robot, which actually suits me quite well. Some doctors play music in their ORs, some sing – mostly off-key – and others carry on conversations while they work. Evans has a tendency to bark orders and stay keenly focused.

He flips my file open and browses through a couple pages before he furrows his brow and looks up. "Combat medic, huh?"

"I was."

He narrows his eyes and rubs the scruff on his chin as he studies my face. "So, what happened?"

What happened? What the hell is that supposed to mean?

Tensing, I still manage to look him straight in the eyes and answer as if he's just asked what my favorite class was, "I served my time, went to school on the GI bill, and now I'm here. Though, I don't need to be under anyone's wing, Dr. Evans."

He flips another page in the file. "Purple heart recipient."

"That's not in there!" I fly out of my chair so fast, it crashes to the floor behind me. My service record had to be disclosed; my *award* did not, and I certainly didn't add it to my resume. I hate the damn thing. I'd rather burn it, but out of respect for Dad, I let him store it . . . display it. Whatever.

Tongue in cheek, he goads, "But it should be, shouldn't it?" He eyes the fallen chair behind me. "Sit down, Ms. Mitchell."

I right the chair on all four legs once more and plop into it. "Why am I here?"

"Fitz and I go back a long way." My face wrinkles in confusion. "Dr. Fitzpatrick," he clarifies. "Ft. Hood?" I nod at the clarification, though my memories of Hood are so bittersweet, I fight cringing. "I'm sorry about your brother, Savannah. When I saw your service record, I inquired. Fitz speaks highly of you. He embellished more than I needed, but once he started I couldn't get him to shut up. I've been observing you. I'm particular about my team. I want you on it."

"Only yours?" My nose crinkles and my mouth twists. "What about more experience in other procedures?"

He smirks. "You really want to deal with gallbladders and hysterectomies all day? An appendix here and there? For someone who tied off a femoral artery so tight it saved a guy's life, I would think you'd be up to something a little more challenging."

He's not wrong. I have been a little bored with routine procedures. "Can you promise to never mention my service record to anyone?"

He eyes me warily. "You got problems with PTSD?"

"No." I let out a pitiful laugh. "I'm done being a soldier, Dr. Evans. I left that behind me. I don't want to be looked at differently. No desire to be anybody's anything. I want to be *just* Savannah, the OR tech."

He nods slowly, thoughtfully, as he studies my face. "Then that's what you'll be. Monday, six o'clock. Bring your A-game."

"See you then, Dr. Evans." I rise from my chair and head for the door, eager to escape the painful reminder. The knob twists in my hand.

"Savannah," he calls softly behind me. *Damnit! I was so close.* I keep my back to him as my eyes start to water. "Like I said, Fitz embellished more than I needed to know. But I will say, whoever he was, he's an idiot."

Chapter 33

Roger

"Cranky's?" Reece suggests on our way out the door after a long-ass 72-hour shift at the firehouse. Cranky's is a quiet, clean, out-of-the-way place that caters to a finer clientele. Neither one of us is big on repeats, but – *little known secret here* – if you intentionally get their name wrong at the next unfortunate run-in, they're too insulted to cling. Win/win.

Yeah, I'm back at it. Shipshape, full force. Firefighter in the 92nd district in Phoenix. Chauncy Steffen on one side, Reece Callahan on the other. Chaunce left his home in Waco about a year ago, trading cowboy boots and tumbleweeds for desert dust and scorpions. The real kicker? We're Hotshots . . .

again. Auxiliary Hotshots, intrastate only. We take over for the regulars when they're called away to cover on interstate duty.

Thad did a helluva job – worth every penny – and I tested out at 98% six months later. Enough to qualify for a job as a firefighter; scoring higher than some with no previous history. I swear some days I feel spryer than I did before my injuries.

Fighting fires and rescue work is my grief therapy for one tragedy. Getting laid on a semi-regular basis is another form of grief therapy. To forget. Forget the woman who changed me forever. I'm a cold bastard. I don't need eyes to look into, a mouth to kiss, a flavor to savor. A warm, bendable body to satisfy a carnal desire is plenty. No sweet words, no goodbye kisses, no promises for a next time. I'm back to waking in a cold bed, party of one – only now not even a memory to wash away with the first cup of coffee. They are that forgettable. Just a few of the reasons Reece and I get along so well.

Reece and I live in the same condo building, and made fast friends from the day I started – after a colossal misunderstanding. He's fun, free and easy, and a former resident of Texas himself. Still has the southern twang that women swoon over and he loves to use it to his advantage. Though he seems to use it, and his charm, more often than Chaunce does. Chauncy has found a girlfriend (sucker) though he's hesitant to introduce her to the rest of us *animals.*

Reece didn't pry into my history the day we met. Simple questions: "Are you single? You like beer? Blondes, brunettes, or redheads?" Followed with: "Got a couple units open in my building if you haven't found a place yet. A few guys there I think you'd like. There's a two-bedroom available right down the hall from mine. Got an erotica writer in the end unit. I know the two best bars in town. One's quiet and clean. The other's a strip joint. Might want to stay away on Thursdays though. The guy is hung like an elephant. Thirteen inches and rotates it like a helicopter blade. I think he's a freak o' nature."

I simply stood before him, blinking slowly a few times, speechless, until Boonie, another firefighter slapped him on the back. "Callahan, your Texas charm needs a bit of polishing and your mouth needs a speedometer. You're scaring the shit out of him. Every word of that speech sounded like a bathhouse proposition. Might want to explain that strip joint is a titty bar except for ladies' only night on Thursdays with Hank the Hung, and the guys in your building consist of a cop, a three-time divorced hedge fund manager, and the other is the boyfriend of the erotica writer."

Reece's nose wrinkled in confusion. "Did I forget to mention that?"

"Uh, yup." I nodded slowly.

Boonie laughed and pinched Reece's cheek. "It's a good thing our boy here is so pretty and usually goes for blondes. No intellectual challenges."

"Hey!" Reece scolded. "Blondes can be smart!"

Boonie grinned wryly. "Name one."

Reece's eyes narrowed as he thought long and hard, finally flashing a smug grin. "Sabrina."

"One night stand?" Boonie surmised.

"My golden retriever." He tipped his chin proudly. "Followed orders and listened better than any woman I've ever known."

"Yeah, I'm gonna run home and get a shower first." I stretch my arms skyward, arching my back to release some tension, and let out a groan. I really do need to get laid. Should probably schedule a session with Thad as well.

"That goes without sayin'." Reese snickers. "You are kinda stinky."

I sneer. "And you're kinda . . . not funny. In case you didn't know, you don't smell any better."

"Damn highschoolers," he grumbles with the reminder. "If

they ever catch those little bastards, I'm gonna string 'em up by their tiny little balls. Stink bombs in outhouses and settin' 'em on fire. Stay in touch with Bernie. If they catch 'em, I want names. I'm gonna dunk their heads in vats of cow shit."

Bernie is the fire Marshall. There is no way he's going to give us names. He knows what we'd do. It's going to take three or more showers to wash the stink off. We've already taken two at the firehouse.

"Bernie wouldn't tell us shit," I remind him of our law abiding fire Marshall as we make our way to our respective trucks. "Now, Tanner, on the other hand, may even be willing to be a partner in crime."

He tilts his head and narrows his eyes at the prospect of help from our police officer building mate and best friend. "A case o' beer, his favorite pizza, and we skip Cranky's tonight to bribe him?"

"Make it three pizzas and add hot wings," I call over the bed of my truck as I open the door. "As soon as Wiley smells that pizza, he'll be knocking on the door."

"Yeah, but with three ex-wives," he snickers, "he's got revenge down to a science. He may come in handy."

One week, three names, and an address later, we find our revenge. Tanner stays out of it, other than to *haphazardly* mention names in conversation of some punk kids charged with damaging public property by setting outhouses on fire, as well as the make, model, and license number of the car identified by street cameras.

Fermented fish guts, a couple of well-hidden dead mice, and some rotten milk sprayed onto the seats should do it. They'll never get the smell out. I really wanted to leave a couple dead scorpions, but Reece swears they have an afterlife and in all good conscience he just couldn't do it. AKA: he's a pussy, and scared to death of them. I've never felt so young in all my life . . . nor so devious. No physical damage to the car – just odor – and an enormous loss in resale value. I consider it recompense for my T-shirt, jockeys, and socks that I had to replace.

I have adjusted. I'm back to having a purpose. Just haven't found my reason.

Chapter 34

Savannah

Having patiently waited until I'm alone, I scrub from my elbows to my fingertips after leaving the last surgery of the day. The faucet at the sink next to me begins to pour and soap is being torn open, catching me by surprise. I focus on my own task and continue my blissful ignorance of the body next to mine.

"I don't think we've formally met yet," the friendly voice greets me. "Mallory Tompkins. You like Mexican food and margaritas?"

I know exactly who she is. Nurse anesthetist. A smile for everyone but Dr. Evans. A compassion for patients like I've never seen. She doesn't talk to them from the end or head of the bed; she leans over them so they know she's there. Instead of the usual counting backwards for the nervous ones, she uses unique ways of making them comfortable. The one time I assisted in cardiac surgery, the woman instructed an older gentleman to name his grandchildren one-by-one. She had a little boy recite the alphabet before an appendectomy, a little girl sing *Let it Go* from Frozen – and sang it with her as she administered the anesthesia before a tonsillectomy. She has beautiful gray eyes that light up with a smile that even the mask can't hide.

Turning my head slowly, I nod and answer, "Yeah, I guess."

"Would you rather have a burger and fries? Liquor doesn't mix well with those." She shrugs. "I suppose we can start with shakes and move on to liquor. But I hate vanilla." She squares her eyes on me and dips her chin. "Shakes or sex."

"Um," I stammer, feeling the heat in my cheeks, unsure if this is an invite for dinner or a proposition. "Mexican is fine, and don't take this the wrong way, I'd love to have dinner with you but I'm straight."

"So am I. The harder and bigger the dick, the better." She shuts off the faucet, dries her hands, then pulls her phone from her pocket and texts. "Let's see what time Libs will be done and we can figure out the rest."

"Who's Libs?"

"Liberty Collins. Cardiac ICU. She'll complete our trio of misfits." She reads the screen when a notification pops up. "Cool. She's off in twenty. You're off tomorrow, right?"

"I'm off for the next two days." I let out a deep breath and round my shoulders in a stretch. "Actually, margaritas sound good."

"Awesome! It'll give you time to recoup," she reacts brightly. "Get ready to get snockered. Hacienda in two hours. Dress up.

Take a Lyft. We'll do a share ride for the way home . . . after we go clubbing."

My entire body seizes up with anxiety. I haven't been out since my farewell night in Texas. "Clubbing?"

"You ever been to The Tempest?"

The name alone is enough to make me suspicious, and the mischief in her eyes tells me to proceed with caution. I have no clue what The Tempest is. I order takeout food or cook my own, an occasional dinner with Mom and Dad, exercise in the complex's gym, and live on wishes that will never come true. It's been years and I can't get past the pain. I'm going to burn that note someday.

"The Tempest?"

"Trying to corrupt my OR staff again, Tompkins?" Dr. Evans' voice is harsh as he leans against the doorway, unbidden in this conversation, as neither of us were aware of his presence.

"Not trying, Dr. Evans –" Mallory says sweetly, "– succeeding." Taking my elbow, she pulls me toward the door. Her parting words have me pushing my unnecessary, oversized glasses farther onto the bridge of nose. My vision is 20/20. They're simply another shield in my world of anonymity. "We're testing her depth perception. It's ladies only night. No binoculars or tape measures needed."

His low growl is indisputable against her giggle as she drags me down the hallway. "Do you make it a goal to piss him off?" I mutter as soon as distance allows.

"Every chance I get."

Good grief! What have I gotten myself into? I stare at my laptop screen; a mistake I made once I got home. The Tempest is a strip club! Thursdays are reserved for ladies only, as the strippers are men. One in particular boasting thirteen inches!

It's no wonder we won't need binoculars.

I think I just found Britt's double.

"Holy Toledo!" Mallory exclaims when she sees me coming in the door of the restaurant. Her blonde companion turns and smiles. She's gorgeous. Heterochromia. Odd, as the colors are blue and green versus the usual brown with one or the other, but so stunning it's startling. Mallory nudges her companion and eyes my legs – bare from mid-thigh to nude heels – then tilts her head. "What do you think, Libs? I'll bet if we cut them off and have them taxidermied, we could get ten grand easy."

"Oh my God!" Her friend scolds and slaps her arm. "You would think as an anesthetist you would understand microdoses . . . of drugs and your personality!"

"She thought I was gay!" Mallory argues.

Her friend extends her hand. "Hi. Liberty Collins. I'm going to go out on a limb here and bet her initial introduction included the fact she doesn't like vanilla . . . shakes or sex."

My lips twitch as I extend my own hand to shake hers. "She did mention that. Savannah Mitchell."

She looks back to Mallory and rolls her eyes. "How close was Evans?"

Mallory giggles. "In the doorway."

My eyes fly open wide as my jaw hangs agape. "You knew he was there?"

"Always be aware of your surroundings, Savannah," she warns. "As well as who's listening to your plans. Make them think north when you're going south."

Crinkling my forehead, I ask cautiously, "So, we're not going to The Tempest?"

Liberty's face sours as if she's eaten something bitter and she shudders. "Oh God, no! The man could play T-ball with that thing!"

Mallory holds up a finger. “And not have to hold it either.” She locks her hands behind her head and swivels her hips, then suddenly juts them to the left and chants, “Hey, batter-batter, swing!”

A burst of laughter sounds from the observers standing in the lobby as the host greets us with a roll of his eyes, holding three menus in his hand, “Ladies, your table is ready.”

Chips and salsa, tacos, three margaritas, and noninvasive conversation that’s lasted for over two hours has my cheeks stretched further than they’ve been in years and my ribs sore from laughing. These ladies are so much fun. I don’t know what drew Mallory to me, what made her invite me along, but I now know what draws me to them. They’re both a strong reminder of the best friend I ever had as an adult.

Brittany Sunn.

Liberty has a boyfriend: Michael Knight, cardiothoracic surgeon.

Mallory has a *convenience*: Eric Hanson, head of radiology.

When they offered to fix me up if I was interested, I explained I already had an on again – off again in Scottsdale. Not elaborating that it had been off for years, it was once again, omission. He’s *from* Scottsdale, he’s *in* Texas. Well, if the Army hasn’t stationed him somewhere else. Say it with a smile, eyes closed as if you’re blissfully happy, and no one sees your pain, the cracks in the walls around your heart. I’ve accepted the agony of defeat; just not enough to move on.

Maybe these two can help me build my confidence back. Liberty lost the love of her life at a young age and she’s recouped. Mallory’s a little older than me and she’s not settled, but quite content. Not all hope is lost, is it?

For a man who told me he hated liars, he sure was good at it. Never his anything; I was his everything. What a crock. All he ever had to do was ask.

Chapter 35

Roger

Okay, check this one off as "huge" on my list of mistakes. Good God, does she ever shut up? Her voice grates on my nerves like nails on a chalkboard. Come to think of it, a couple of her shrieks hit the same way. Four orgasms and she's *still* awake – rambling on about how good it was. *Sorry, but I've had better. This was mechanical, as always, a way to let off steam. Grief therapy.* I was trying to be a gentleman – wait until she fell asleep, slip out in the dark of night; the used condoms tied-off and tucked away in my pocket.

The sad part? I can't even tell you what she looks like. One glance in the bar and she met the requirements: brunette, pretty, nice body, not overbearing (initially), and the offer of her place. The deal is always their place or a hotel.

My place is reserved for friends – not friendlies. The latter has a tendency to overstay their welcome, make themselves comfortable, and before you know it half your closet space and entire bathroom counter is taken over by an alien that won't go away. Just ask Tanner Carson, our resident cop and good friend who's spent the last year tolerating a she-devil that we haven't figured out how to send back to hell yet. Give us time; we're resourceful.

Oh, my other private stipulation? *Never have sex up against the wall . . . again.* That memory is untainted, and sits safely in the back of my mind. The sounds of the forest and the sight of a pink bikini going over the waterfall, the fire in her eyes after her first time. Her laughter, her forgiving nature, her sighs and moans, and lest I forget, her tears. How I wish I had been good enough for her.

The moment the brunette starts drawing circles on my chest with a sharp manicured nail and asks, "What would you like to do tomorrow?", I toss back the sheet and fly out of bed. There is no tomorrow. Hell, I barely suffered through the last two hours. The tied-off condoms are safely tucked into the pocket of my jeans in seconds. My feet slide into my shoes as I zip my fly, then yank the T-shirt over my head.

"I don't do tomorrows," I state firmly. "Thought that was clear."

"You're an asshole!" she shrieks – a mere decibel lower than her mid-orgasm level– and reaches for a glass of water on the nightstand and throws it at me. I duck in the nick of time, and it crashes against the wall versus my head.

"Well aware. You've got some anger issues, sweetheart." I smirk as I walk backwards toward the door for fear she has another item to throw. "Might want to see somebody about those."

As I reach the front door, another crash is followed by shattered glass. Damn! That sounded like a lamp. Never would have thought sex could be so dangerous. And to think I almost considered cleaning up the broken glass. Dodged a bullet on that one.

Once in my truck and on my way home, a memory strikes. The last time something was thrown at me was the pizza crust Savannah threw in the hotel room. Perfect aim, but nothing that would hurt. Me naked, her topless. The vision so clear it seems like yesterday. The way we handled little spats – her over me or under me. God, I miss her so much it's painful. I wonder who gets to love her now. Is he good to her? Is she his everything?

So much for grief therapy tonight. It seems to be backfiring more and more with each encounter – drumming up thoughts of long ago. Pretending is an art I've gotten good at. Guilt seems to be the devil on my shoulder lately, and I'd love to kick that little fucker to the can. I left her in bed – cold and alone – a note on the counter with words I didn't have the balls to say. Everything but "I love you". I didn't say those words that night, either. I couldn't. I was letting go, because she deserved better.

Seeing Reece's taillights when I pull into the parking lot of our complex, I shake the thoughts currently running through my head and force myself to grin. *Pretend.* For as carefree as he would like everyone to think he is, he's quite intuitive . . . and caring. He's also a whole lot smarter than he appears. Sex is his favorite pastime, and, like me, he does not do overnights or tomorrows.

"No breakfast?" I ask as I approach his truck.

He chuckles. "I'm up for breakfast. Just not at her place."

We end up having a middle of the night meal at a 24-hour diner. Reece, as usual, plays with his food and designs female body parts before each bite, and me ready to wring his neck before we're done. The guy is thirty-one, going on twelve, but I wouldn't trade his friendship for anything. He is smart, but his social awareness consists of eyeing a set of tits and cupping his palm, estimating how much one of them would fill.

He's also a true believer in efficiency, and has a tolerance level of zero. Two days later, he proves once again how little patience he has when it comes to idiocy. We have a car hanging over the edge of a bridge on I-17 and the tow truck with the chains to pull it back can't get through the jam of traffic due to one driver that refuses to move. Reece, in all his ingenuity, decides he's going to move it come hell or high water. And he does, quite efficiently and fast. Unfortunately, he doesn't do it without damage, to the car or himself.

Three hours later, I'm sitting in a recovery room with a whining Reece who's begging me to go find the surgical nurse he swears he knows, but can't recall from where. *Silver eyes and pillowy lips.* Yeah, it's the drugs. Has to be. Reece is a tits and ass man. Maybe it was a warning from God to change his ways while he was under. Again, probably the drugs.

As we exit the elevator onto the ground floor, I'm convinced I must have breathed in a bit of nitrous oxide while on the surgical floor when long auburn locks falling from an oversized surgical cap catches my eye, as she strips it off in her rush down the hall, then disappears around a corner.

In my distraction, I'm nearly knocked on my ass when Reece jumps out of the wheelchair post-surgical patients are required to take to the door, and refuses to ride in it through the ER. Damn his ego. Unfortunately, where ego, I go. I signed to be his watchdog for the next twenty four hours. Payback: I get to drink, he doesn't.

I'm going to need it. Hallucination. Had to be.

"I'll get him where he needs to be," I assure the transport nurse. "He's a stubborn ass."

She winks. "Let me know if he needs any help at home with sponge baths."

Forcing a chuckle, I wink back. "Will do."

Chapter 36

Savannah

My, how things change.

A month ago Liberty was engaged to be married, Mallory was winging it with the handsome head of radiology, and I'd pretty much been a spectator; a fly on the wall, so to speak. That for which I have not one ounce of remorse. Mallory had asked me to keep my ears and eyes open due to suspicion. When a fiancé is caught in a rendezvous in Vegas for 'one last time' before his vows, it's best to drop his cheating ass before the paperwork is signed. No property to divide and any items left at your place can go to charity, or out the tenth floor window.

I really wish Liberty had kept the ring, though. That baby was easily worth three tropical vacations and a month in Europe. Instead, she threw it at him when she caught him . . . in the act no less. The least she could have done was shoved it down his throat – necessitating his colleagues' services to surgically remove it. What goes in must come out. I would have loved to assist on that procedure. If not through open reduction, we'd go in through the backdoor; deeming him owner of the *diamond asshole.*

Liberty works in the ER now, having distanced herself as far away from the cheating fiancé as possible, and Mallory seems to relish his misery. I get the impression she really didn't like him. It might have something to do with the list of *doofumisms* she had created over the last year and a half to present to Liberty when the inevitable happened. The woman is intuitive.

We're all single again, though Mallory seems to have charmed a firefighter prior to his emergency surgery, and he's been pretty relentless in his pursuit. Not sure the offer of a seat on his face was the best approach, but I've seen bolder propositions.

On my way down the hall toward the employee parking lot after a long and arduous day, I'm stopped by a pretty blonde. She's in scrubs, hair in a ponytail, beautiful blue eyes, and a tentative smile. Her badge reads Physiotherapy. "You're Savannah Mitchell, aren't you?"

"Yes." Her eyes are vaguely familiar, though I can't place her. She's young, an intern according to her badge.

She smiles shyly. "I-I don't expect you to remember me. It was years ago and I never did get a chance to talk to you. You were surrounded by so many people, and I wasn't even sure what to say." She winces. "I, uh, I was at your brother's funeral. I didn't know him personally, but he was my brother's friend. He took it really hard."

Her eyes rim with tears and she sniffles. "I was so touched

when I heard about Silas nicknaming you Peaches. My brother used to call me Baby Ruth. Told me I was sweet on the outside and a bit nutty." She giggles through her tears at the memory then whispers, "I just wanted to tell you how sorry I am that you lost him."

"Thank you," I manage as my own eyes start to feel the familiar burn. "I appreciate that. I'm sorry I don't remember you. That day was . . ."

"Don't worry about it. I just had to put that out there." She lifts one shoulder and poses what seems a hopeful question, "Maybe I'll see you around some time?"

I offer a soft smile of gratitude. "Yeah, maybe."

As she starts to walk away, she spins on her heel and rushes back, extending her hand to shake mine. "I'm sorry, I should have introduced myself. I'm Ruthie Bellamy."

The hallway feels like a vacuum as the air is virtually sucked from my lungs. It's no wonder her eyes looked familiar. They're a carbon copy of her brother's. I let her take my hand, and nod weakly in acknowledgement then head for the exit, desperate to make my escape. I don't dare try to talk. The only sound I would master is a sob, but I manage to hold it in until I'm in my car, door closed, and no one can hear my heart break. Every time I think I'm getting better . . .

I want to run back in and ask her where he's stationed now. If he's okay. More importantly, and selfishly, is he in love?

Cranking up the air as soon as the engine starts, I hesitate before putting the car in gear. "Screw you, Roger," I mumble to myself as I pull out my phone and scroll to Mallory's number, then remember Liberty is working the ER tonight. This is ridiculous. I'm twenty eight years old and the only nightlife I see is on my TV screen or the inside of my eyelids as dreams interrupt my sleep. So tempting to make a trip to Georgia to see Britt, but that takes planning. I'm in the mood right now. It's time.

Closing the contacts list and placing my phone back in my bag before making any rash decisions, I ponder my choices. My independence has always been a point of pride for me. I didn't get where I am by being weak, but my feelings are due to being meek. I've fallen into a rabbit hole.

I've crawled on my hands and knees through dirt, hot sand, and broken body parts. I've scraped calluses so deep in my palms they bled, suffered sand flea bites, under-boob rash, and jock itch in my butt crack. Yes, it happens. I learned to relieve myself sans a proper bathroom. TMI? Maybe. I was never a paper pusher in a brick building, claiming to have *fought the good fight.* The kind that carried a cell phone and called home to the States a half dozen times a day. Yes, they do exist.

Yet the one thing I haven't done is take the risk of trusting someone to unbreak my heart – the lone piece that hasn't felt whole in years. A damn good orgasm delivered by something other than a nightstand buddy might be nice too.

Tomorrow night. Get some sleep first, Savannah. You look like hell anyway.

Standing in front of the full-length mirror, performing one last evaluation before I change my mind, I'm not as disappointed as I thought I might be. It's the emerald green dress Britt talked me into the night we went to The Twilight Club. Nude heels. My hair is longer than it was then; soft curls falling halfway down my back. Makeup on point and eyes shadowed perfectly to highlight the green. No glasses, as I'm not hiding tonight. My first venture out on my own in years. Google, research, and Yelp ratings helped me decide.

Pulling up the Lyft app, I order my ride, entering the address for my destination point. *Cranky's.* Odd name, but by all descriptions, it was the closest thing to The Twilight Club I'd ever seen. No piano bar in the pictures and I didn't see a resin coated bar-top with pennies buried inside, but it looked clean and classy. Maybe I can find a seat at the end of the dimly lit bar and simply observe this evening. Then again, maybe I can get lucky.

Chapter 37

Roger

"Did you notice the new blonde in the ER?" I ask Reece over the sound of the shower water.

He sputters under the spray as if he's just gotten a mouthful. Not surprising, as we're trying to purge the smell of diesel fuel, burnt rubber, and death from our systems. Okay, death isn't really an odor per se. More of a perception. Doesn't mean you don't try and scrub it off. We've worked long hours this evening; not having the luxury of clocking out when you're in the midst of administering lifesaving measures. Telling Mr. Smith his time is up because yours is too is frowned upon.

"Only you, Roger. An ER full of gurneys and bodies, and you're still scouting for pussy."

"Actually," I chuckle, "it was her ass I noticed first, but then she turned around. Have you ever seen anybody with different colored eyes? If I only looked at one at a time, it'd be like having two different women at once."

He belly laughs as he shuts off his faucet. "You've been reading Ava's books, haven't you? Is our resident erotica writer giving you fresh ideas?"

I shiver under the hot water at the thought of our mid-fifties neighbor before slamming the faucet off. Wrapping a towel around my waist, I step out and scowl. "Fuck no! I don't need books and I sure as hell ain't reading Ava's. That'd be like lessons from your mother."

"You actually look in their eyes when you're having sex?" Reece asks curiously.

His question drums up memories I've tried hard to escape. I haven't looked into a set of eyes since Savannah. Disconnect. No kisses, no intimacy; just sex. I brought it on myself – it was a joke – but I didn't expect it to hit with such impact, so I turn the question back to him. "You don't?"

He snickers. "Mine are so lost in ecstasy, they couldn't focus if they tried."

"Idiot," I grumble. "It's no wonder you can't remember their names."

"Yeah," he bobs his eyebrows, "but they always remember my dick."

The following evening we saunter into Cranky's, ready for a couple beers, a fresh view, and exercise of a different kind. The rhythmic kind – on a mattress.

Reece has been extremely resistant to get back out and into his old habits since the surgery. But after a run-in with his surgical nurse obsession at dinner tonight, the discovery that she has a boyfriend, and his chances are nil, it wasn't too hard to talk him into his first choice of old hangouts. Unfortunately, after a forgettable one-night-stand greeted him at the titty bar as if they were long lost lovers – yeah, she's a stripper – we decided Cranky's might be the better choice.

A gentle burst of laughter from my left near the end of the bar has the hair on the back of my neck standing on end. *I know that laugh. It's unique. A breath of fresh air to a dying man's lungs. I've heard it in my dreams for years.*

"Damn, a little more crowded than we're used to," Reece mutters, eyeing the busier than usual surroundings. "Not that we ever have competition, but who let the word out?" He backhands my bicep. "There's a couple o' seats at the bar over here. Better grab 'em while we can." He shoots a look to our left. "What the hell is the attraction down there?"

"Good question." I glance in the general direction he's speaking of, but only see a group sitting and/or standing at the end of the bar.

We take the two stools available and JT, the usual bartender grins as he approaches with two ice cold brews in hand. "Hey guys. Looking to wash the smoke and ash down or rub the tits and ass down?" *He knows us well.*

"Bit o' both," Reece says with a laugh before taking a long pull. His eyes draw wide over the rim of his mug before he sets it down hard and stares at the end of the bar where the music to my ears came from. "What the fuck is he doin' here? I don't screw his nurses. He shouldn't be on my playground either."

My eyes follow the path his are aimed and find exactly what I feared. She's smiling, though her light has dimmed. She's more beautiful than I remember. Her hair is longer. Those stunning green eyes are adorned with makeup, and a little glazed from the alcohol. Where are your freckles, Savvy? The ones I used to count with kisses – my favorite at the pulse point of your neck. Do you still have the constellation on your belly – the one I used to trace with my tongue?

I can't help but stare – the memories and the pull so strong I cannot look away. She must feel it, because she finally turns my way and our eyes lock. Unfortunately, it could not happen at a worse possible time, as I feel the set of silicone enhanced tits press against my back, freeze when the sharp, manicured nails slide against my scalp, and hear the sultry, irritating voice grate in my ear as she nips the lobe, "How ya doin', handsome? You up for another round?"

Oh, the pain. Not mine; hers. She looks as if I've driven a knife in her heart . . . and twisted it. Savvy never could hide her tears – not from me – and the proof lies bare as I watch a fat one roll down her cheek.

The man sitting next to her turns to see what has upset her, as the forgotten bimbo behind me presses further and whispers something in my ear. He rolls his eyes then shakes his head, but what happens next has me seeing red. Savannah grasps the front of his shirt and lays a kiss on his mouth that drives that knife right back in my heart.

"Lucky sonofabitch," Reece mutters next to me. "Why the hell would he keep me away from Mallory when he already has a woman that beautiful?"

Tearing my gaze away from the unbearable sight before me, I inquire, "Isn't that your surgeon?"

"Dr. Slice and Dice in the flesh," he says cockily, then grumbles, "Bet his dick is as little as Mr. X-Ray's."

Still bent out of shape after seeing Mallory with the radiologist at dinner earlier this evening.

Tossing back the rest of my beer, I rise from my seat – the clinger still holding onto hope behind me. "Reece, find yourself a set of doubles tonight. You've been too long without. I'm outta here."

The clinger follows me out the door uninvited. Once out in the parking lot and seeing her to her car – I am a gentleman – she runs manicured fingers up the front of my shirt. "You do remember the address, don't you?"

Gently removing her hand from my shirt, I remind her, "What I remember is not making any arrangements with you. Goodnight, Miranda."

"It's Ruby, you asshole!" she screams and stomps her foot.

See how well it works? Told ya. And Miranda? My go-to name. Tanner's ex-girlfriend. Ugly memory, uglier personality. Leaves a bad taste in your mouth.

"Huh," I say with feigned puzzlement. "Must not have been that memorable."

A few choice words later, she slides into the seat, revs the engine, and throws gravel as she spins out of the parking lot. Geez, she could have gone back inside and found another opportunity. I don't have a magic dick; he's just better than the average bear. Not that he's had much exercise lately. His last workout was the lamp thrower. After tonight, I may have to bury him in the metaphorical graveyard of guilt.

Climbing into my truck, I take a few moments to gather my bearings. *The medical field.* She followed her plan. No idea what she does, but she's out with a surgeon. Does he know what she went through? What she's lost? How hard she fought for others? How fucking brave she is? Is he good enough for her? Not that I have the right to ask . . . I certainly wasn't.

The door to Cranky's opens and out walks my beautiful girl under the arm of the surgeon. She's wobbly, and he doesn't hold her as if they're lovers. No, it's more for support. They stop and chat as if disagreeing, then she concedes and he guides her to his car and they climb in to the shiny Mercedes. *Figures.* I text:

"What's your surgeon's name?"

"Evans"

"First name"

"Carter, I think"

I roll my eyes. Never anything normal. You know, like Roger.

"Think or know? You sure it's not prick? It is what you called him."

"I called him a lot of things. It's Carter. Why? He just left. Damn! That woman was fiiiiiine."

Gritting my teeth – he has no idea just how *fiiiiine* – I send one last text: *"Get your dick wet, Reece. Fires have started down south. You never know if we're going to get called in. Better get it while you can."*

Antelope Canyon. I never thought I'd see it again. No one knows I've been there before; no one but Savannah and Chauncy. They and the fire chief are also the only ones that know I'm former Army, too. My past is my own. Sometimes it's best to let sleeping dogs lie. Becoming a Hotshot again was more a personal effort to regain everything I had lost. Everything but the girl and the entire career that had been stripped from me. The one promise I broke. I promised her I was done. Something inside me broke when I realized *we* were done. My Savvy was gone and I had lost my reason, so I needed a purpose. Men bend, women break. As I had no one to break, there was no reason not to do it again. Now, onto the information I need:

"I need an address for a Dr. Carter Evans"

"And you think I could get this for you how?"

"You're a cop. You have access. He has something he shouldn't"

"Planning a B&E?"

"No. I'm going to knock. Promise"

"What? Three taps before you beat the door down?"

"Tanner, please"

"What's the real reason?"

"Cockblocking"

"Ruthie?"

"Fuck no! I'd have to kill him"

"You plan on leaving bruises?"

"Pleading the Fifth. You'll never be tied to it"

"Is Reece with you?"

"Nope. Working alone"

"Then I'll give it to you. Reece's temper is going to land you both in jail someday. Delete this correspondence after you write it down. Here ya go . . ."

Once again, it pays to have friends in the right places.

Chapter 38

Savannah

"Oh my God!" I gasp as I attempt to pull away from the kiss I just planted on my boss's mouth. "I didn't mean to . . ."

He seals his mouth over mine for another; his hand wrapped tightly around the back of my head, fingers wound in my hair, his other hand on my cheek. But it's not lascivious, not sloppy. There's not even any tongue with it. He murmurs against my lips, "Relax, Mitchell. Make it convincing. You're not my type."

Admittedly, he's not my type either, but the man can pack a wallop with his mouth. I mean, it's a good kiss – firm and dominant – and a couple more of these and I could probably be talked into things I would have never considered. *No, Savannah! It's the alcohol talking! That and the jealousy.* I used to nip Roger's ear like that. I know exactly how it feels to rub up against his back. To feel those hard muscles. I got off doing it!

Dr. Evans breaks the kiss and leans his forehead on mine. "Take a peek and tell me if he's gone yet."

"He's gone," I say immediately, my eyes closed. "He left with that woman."

"How do you know? You haven't looked."

I shrug against his grip and he releases it. I crinkle my nose as I look into his eyes. "Sorry, Doc. You're a really good kisser, but you're not my type either. I'm always aware of my surroundings. I peeked during the lip lock."

He narrows his eyes. "Yet you let me continue kissing you."

"You told me to make it convincing."

He tilts his head in curiosity. "Is he a new idiot, or the original?"

His question takes me back to the day in his office when he disclosed his knowledge of my past. Losing my resolve the longer he studies my face, my eyes water as I admit, "The only."

"Come on." He stands and offers his elbow, and I find I'm a bit wobbly when I stand to my feet. Four Jamesons will do that. "Let's get out of here, before people start thinking I'm the one who caused those tears. You're in no shape to drive. I'll give you a ride." He places his hand on my lower back to guide me out the door, but slides it up and over my shoulder for a stronger hold when I wobble.

Once outside under the overhang, I hesitate. "I came in a Lyft. I can call for a ride. I don't drink and drive."

He pins me with a stern glare. "You're not going to drink and ride either, Mitchell. Not alone with a stranger."

"I can specify a female driver," I protest.

"You can get your ass in my car, too. I had two drinks. Sober as a saint." He wraps his arm around my shoulder again and grumbles, "What is it with you ladies and your firefighters?"

"Wait a minute!" I stop at the car door he's just opened for me. "The guy he was with. That's the firefighter you operated on, isn't he? The arm injury from the car window?"

He smirks. "You mean the one with the hot temper?"

I giggle. "The one that wanted to kiss Mallory."

His jaw tics as he arches a brow. "Get in the car, Mitchell."

"Is she your type?" I tease. "I can keep a secret."

Exasperated, he places his hand on the top of my head and presses down to urge me onto the seat. "What you *keep* best is being a pain in my ass. Get in the car. Now."

"So," he starts as he pulls out into traffic, "you want to tell me about you and the firefighter?"

"Your patient? I don't know him."

He continues after a moment, "The other guy. I recognized him from recovery. He signed the paperwork to stay with Callahan for the first 24 hours after the surgery."

"Roger's not a firefighter. He's in the Army." I shake my head. "You must have him confused with someone else. He's probably just here on leave for a while. They must know each other. His family is from Scottsdale. I met his little sister the other day. She works in the physiotherapy department."

He winces. "Uh, Savannah. That guy is a firefighter. He and Callahan are pretty popular at Banner. They work out of the 92nd district."

"Roger's a firefighter? Here, in Phoenix?"

He glances my way for only moment before setting his eyes back on the road. "That's your Army guy? I take it you didn't know."

"How long?" I ask, the drinks I had ready to make a reappearance.

He blows out a deep breath, hesitating. "At least a few years."

He should have left the note signed, 'You were never my anything'.

My breaths start as shuddered and shallow as my chest feels like it's caving in. Breathe in for four, out for five, slowly. If only I could get one deep enough. My worst nightmares never left me so broken.

Evans pulls the car to the right and comes to a sudden stop. He unbuckles my seatbelt and pulls me into hug. I break in his arms, sobbing as he rubs circles on my back, shushes me, reassures me it'll be okay.

After a long session of displaying my greatest weakness, I finally pull away, sloppily swiping my cheeks. My makeup is long gone, I'm sure. That which hasn't ruined my dress and painted my face all the way to my jawbone.

Evans tips my chin and swipes at the moisture under my eye. "I'm taking you home with me. After that episode, I don't want you to be alone."

"I don't need pitied, Dr. Evans. I'd make a pretty lousy partner."

He wrinkles his nose. "Yeah, you would. I told you before, you're not my type, and I am definitely not into pity sex. I'm much better with broken bones than I am broken hearts. But I do have three younger sisters, and I've been known to kick a few asses in my time."

I huff a pitiful laugh and he taps the tip of my nose. "Much better. I am not letting you go home to be by yourself. I have a guestroom with its own bath. It's all yours." He shakes his head slowly as he offers a sad smile. "You are too damn beautiful to be real. Those eyes could melt hearts of steel. He is such a fucking idiot."

He gently adjusts me back in the seat and buckles my belt for me. "Thank you."

"No problem." He holds up a finger and lifts a brow. "There is a caveat. You can't tell anyone I was nice. I do have an image to uphold. I'm the number two asshole in the ORs. Knight took the number one spot when he cheated on his fiancé." He buckles up, puts the car in gear, and heads back out onto the road. "Another fucking idiot."

I will not disagree with that. Liberty is a treasure. I wish I could tell her and Mallory about this, but I won't betray his trust. He was a knight in shining armor this evening. Someday he'll find a princess. If he weren't so harsh with Mallory, he just may stand a chance.

Chapter 39

Roger

I promised Tanner I wouldn't break the door down. However, after six knocks and a fast session of pounding on it, that promise is becoming harder and harder to keep. The house is located in a quiet community on the outskirts of the city; too damn big for a single guy. It's dark, but I can't see the windows to the back of the house where I'm sure the bedroom is located. Ringing the bell is an option, but it doesn't make a statement like a fist to the door does.

I know he's here; his car is in the driveway. She climbed into it – I watched her.

Finally, the latch clicks and a cocky Carter Evans stands

before me – silk pajama pants (*figures*), no shirt, and a glass of amber liquid in his hand. He casually takes a sip and smirks. "Looking for something?"

"Where is she?"

"Sleeping."

I snort sarcastically. "That was quick."

He takes another slow sip. "And yet here you are at my door. What did you do, settle for a blow job in the parking lot?"

My fists clench and I fight the urge to punch him. "She followed me out. I swear didn't touch her."

His hum is low, nodding slowly. "I suppose there's a first time for everything. Funny how guilt works, isn't it? Savannah is in my guestroom." He sneers. "I don't take advantage of vulnerability. And I'm not about to leave you in a position where you can, either. Don't you think you've done enough damage, *Captain Bellamy*?"

The mere mention of my former title not only makes my stomach churn, but also lets me know Savvy must have told him everything.

I swallow hard and let out a slow breath. "I need to make things right."

"How many years have you had to do that?" Disdain drips from his tongue. "How many women have you gone through while you took your sweet time?" He polishes off the liquor in his glass. "I've spent years watching that girl grow stronger, come into her own, gain confidence. She doesn't need you to make things right in order to ease your guilt."

"I didn't know where she was," I say slowly.

He smirks . . . again. "You found my house, and since I'm not listed, it would be interesting to find out exactly how . . ."

"I want to talk to her."

"Not tonight." He begins to close the door, but I block it with my hand.

"I love her. I've loved her for years."

"You've got a helluva way of showing it."

"Why did she kiss you?" I demand.

His lips tip as if he's on the verge of laughing. "You cannot be that fucking stupid. That, my man, is called payback for leaving her when she needed you most. It would seem the score is even now." He tilts his head and grins. "Or maybe she won."

"I didn't think I was good enough for her," I utter in an attempt to defend myself.

He snickers. "Oh, I know you're not good enough for her. Goodnight, Bellamy."

The door closes in my face with a soft click and the sound of the deadbolt follows. Standing on the porch, I stare at it; the simple barrier that separates us. So close and she's never felt so far away. I should have sought her out the moment I passed my physical. The day I realized I could be there *for* her and not be dependent *on* her. The day I let go of the guilt of Silas' death – Chauncy playing a huge role in convincing me that we all make our own decisions – that Silas' heart was a little bigger than his brain that day. Sometimes it pays off and sometimes it doesn't.

Chapter 40

Savannah

Rolling over onto my back, I squint against the sun shining in through the tiny slits in the blinds. I don't do that. I flip the blinds upwards to keep the sun, and the heat, out. Who . . . . Oh shit! My head pounds as I lift it off the pillow. This isn't my room, or my bed. It's comfy, though. And pretty, I think to myself as I glance around the room, appreciating the neutral tones with colorful paintings on the walls, and note the soft linens I'm lying in.

Oh no! Dr. Evans! The soft, worn T-shirt brushes against my nipples as I throw off the blankets and look down to see U of I across the front of the shirt. Illinois? Oh...black and gold. And

Herky. I always liked that little guy. Evans went to Iowa? Good school, cold as hell. Beer capital of the country during football season. I lift the hem quickly. Boxer shorts. I think I remember sliding the T-shirt over my head. Okay, where are my clothes?

The loud knock on the door jolts me from my thoughts. "Mitchell! Coffee's on. Don't let your breakfast get cold. Hurry up, I got shit to do today."

Wait a minute! He was nice to me last night. Keeping me company on the barstool next to mine; conversation geared toward hospital gossip and a new less invasive procedure for joint replacements. *Yawn.*

A quick glance at the clock on the nightstand reveals nine o'clock. I never sleep this late. My head starts to fill with events of the prior evening. Roger. He was there. Oh God, he looked so good. I've never seen his facial hair so full, so thick. His hair is longer, golden and sun kissed, slight curls at the nape. His eyes still so blue, that piercing gaze. He left with another woman.

"Mitchell!"

"I'm coming!" I snap with the sudden change of mood. "I can't find my clothes."

"You're not going to. I sent it to the cleaners with mine. You can find something one of my sisters left in the closet after breakfast. Hurry your ass up!"

He sent my dress to the cleaners? It had a built-in bra! All I have is built-in boobs, with nipples that have a tendency to salute when I'm nervous, angry, cold, self-conscious, or whenever they damn well please.

"Let me pee, I'll be right out." Etiquette be damned. When you gotta go, you gotta go.

A literal growl comes from the other side of the door before he grumbles, "I'm starting without you. This is why I live alone."

I don't know about that, doc. I think you live alone because a mate might murder you. A face that women may love to ride, but a temperament only a mother could love.

Opening the door slowly, I peek down the hall to ensure it's safe to come out. I need both arms to fold over my chest before stepping into the kitchen this morning.

"Have a seat. How do you take your coffee?" His back is to me as he pours two cups. Huh, guess he did wait.

"Black, please."

He sets the full mug on the table in front of me along with my phone. "Who's the General?" My brows shoot up with the lift of my chin and before I can respond, he says, "Your phone's been going off for the past half hour. Does he always scowl like that?"

"Oh shit," I whisper, more to myself than him. "That's my dad."

He smirks. "Your purse was ringing. I don't make it a habit, but after the fourth round, I figured I'd better open it and take a peek. After seeing his face on the screen, I wasn't about to answer. They were video calls and I don't care to have my body found at the bottom of a canyon somewhere."

"His bark is worse than his bite. Just give me a minute and I'll be done." I roll my eyes and pick up the phone. Four times is a bit extreme, but I'm sure he's just checking in.

"Hello, Trouble," he greets me with a smile. I knew it. Be prompt, pick up when they call because they know your schedule, and put their minds at ease because they love you.

"Morning, General," I return. "Is this about dinner tonight?"

"Actually, we were thinking about coming there. Your mother wants to . . ." He narrows his eyes. "What's that background, and why do you look like you just got out of bed?"

Oh God, I knew it. Don't flinch. Don't stammer.

"I stayed with a friend last night." *The truth, the whole truth, and nothing but the truth.* Though the way Evans is glaring at me right now tells me he's not feeling very friendly. It might be the finger gesture as he slices it across his throat as well.

"Where is she?" Dad asks. "Introduce her."

"Dirk!" my mom scolds, then appears on the screen. "We'll see you at seven tonight at your place, sweetheart. Dress up. We'll drive. Love you." She disconnects the call before Dad can get in another word and I laugh. Mom for the win.

"I can understand your dad's concern," Evans says as he sets two plates of eggs, bacon, and toast on the table, then grins, "but I like your mom. How many stars on your dad's uniform?"

I sigh. "Four."

"Damn," he breathes with a laugh. "I really like your mom this morning."

We eat in comfortable silence for a while until he says, "Bellamy was here last night. Thought I'd better let you know."

"What?"

He nods. "Yup. He thought I brought you home for nefarious purposes. Think he was trying to cockblock me."

Setting my fork down hard, I snap, "Like he has any room to talk. I watched him leave with that woman."

"He swore he didn't touch her." He sets his fork down as well and blows out a deep breath. "I'm not going to lie to you, Savannah. We had words. I'm not about to tell you what to do; not my place, not my business. You're a lot stronger than you were a few years ago. But tread carefully. Don't let your emotions overrule your senses. I saw how easily you broke last night. Bellamy and Callahan go through women like water. I would hate to see you whet his whistle only long enough to let him open those wounds again. The next time you may not heal so well." He lifts one shoulder and flashes me a puckish grin.

"Besides, I can't always be around to suck face with you to piss him off."

Oh my God! Flashback. He was *really* nice to me last night . . . after I attacked his mouth like it was my last meal. The heat rises from my neck and spreads slowly across my cheeks as I grimace. "Uh, yeah, about that."

He rises from his chair and stands beside mine. Lifting my chin with two fingers, he uses his thumb to brush something from the corner of my mouth. Grinning cockily, he says, "I'm not sure what I'm enjoying more. The flush of your cheeks or the egg on your face. Go get dressed so I can take you home." He gathers some dishes and heads for the sink. "Six in the morning, Mitchell. Hip replacement. Don't be late."

And we're back.

"Um . . ." I gather my own dishes and follow, setting them on the counter, ". . . can we never mention that kiss again?"

I feel him behind me as his body heat warms the skin on my back. His hands lock me in as they grip the counter on each side of my hips. His breath in my ear and sexy growl has a teasing lilt before he whispers, "Savannah, had that been a real kiss, you would still be in my bed. You didn't get my tongue."

The slightest trace of his tongue along my earlobe before he nips it shoots a buzz straight between my legs, causing the most embarrassing whimper to rise from my throat.

"*Exactly.*" Barely audible, but I catch it. He shoves off the counter and backs away, his voice stern as he orders, "Now, Mitchell, go get dressed before I stuff you in my car and take you home in my T-shirt. You. are. not. my. type."

Don't have to tell me twice, doc. Well, three times actually. I'm outta here.

I'll bet he doesn't discuss joint replacements with those who *are* his type.

Chapter 41

Roger

The last notice on my monitor three hours ago showed two new fires out west, on top of the current three they're fighting, with no success on the fires they're fighting down south here – in *Antelope Canyon.* Dread fills me with the thought of revisiting my nightmare of six years ago as I check my phone once again.

Chauncy takes a seat next to me in the kitchen area at the firehouse. "I see you're lookin' at the same thing I am."

"You having any seconds thoughts, Chaunce?" I ask sincerely. "You know you can back out at any time."

"Hell no," he snaps, then looks around to ensure our conversation is private. It is. "Gotta fight your demons eventually. This one's farther up the canyon than the last one was. Kinda wish them people would quit buildin' in those areas though. I think they're askin' for trouble sometimes. You want peace and quiet, go build a fuckin' cabin on a lake." He scowls. "Somewhere in the Midwest. Go fishin' in the summer, build a fire in the winter, and snuggle on a big ol' bear rug with your woman."

I laugh. "Naked?"

He nods firmly. "Ain't no other way."

"When are you going to introduce her to the rest of us?"

"When are you guys gonna quit actin' like animals?"

"So," I twist my mouth to the side, "I'm thinking maybe never?"

"Sounds about right." He tilts his head. "You havin' any second thoughts?"

"Nah." I shake my head and turn to look out the window. "Just never thought I'd have to see that place again. Talk about an old haunt."

"Maybe we'll have some good spirits there to watch over us." He slaps me on the back and stands. "In either case, I guess we're all on alert. Sounds like I might be seein' you before next shift."

Reece Callahan is officially a pussy. Correction: Reece is pussy-whipped. Turns out his little surgical nurse wasn't karma come to bite him on the ass after all. She was an obsession from his past. But that's Reece's story. And I'm officially jealous. Not that I would tell him – he doesn't have my cold, hard edges. I don't care much for the mouthy little Mallory – she's like a burst of bitters when you're expecting bourbon – but she makes him happy. Ecstatic really.

The night I left the good doctor's house was a rude awakening for me. I did leave her when she needed me most. I begged her in the clinic at Fort Hood to see me one last time and just like always, Savvy didn't let me down. I let her down though. I couldn't get out of my own way long enough to explore a path for the both of us. I didn't fight for us – I fought for me. Where in that equation can you claim to love someone? But I do. I would lay down and die for that woman, a thousand times if I thought it would matter. How can you fix what is so broken? I can't bring Silas back. I can't undo the pain I've caused her, but I can stop inflicting any more. I can stay away, let her be what Evans said – stronger, more confident.

And that is why, as the time draws nearer to being called away to Antelope Canyon, I make a stop at Cranky's to find some quick relief before I leave for the depths of hell. No liquor. A simple club soda and a warm body will do. Ten minutes later, I'm back in my truck and . . . on my way home. Worst idea ever. Stuck in a time warp since the lamp thrower and recurrent thoughts of Savannah, my demons are rearing their ugly heads as if we're inseparable.

Had I known he would be on the plane, I would have thrown him off just before the doors closed. Total lie. I would have waited until we were in the air. As it is, we're in the midst of a stare down that would burn holes through the walls if it veered off of each other. *Oujiri.*

Chauncy twists in his seat, ire and hatred flaring in his eyes as he gives me a *what the fuck?* look. We, along with the entire crew gave testimony of the events of that day. I simply move my head with a subtle twitch so as not to draw attention to himself. *We will not be separated.* He knows it, I know it, but Reece has no idea what or who we're dealing with.

"Where the hell is Timmons?" Reece inquires discreetly about our usual supervisor.

I ignore his question as the announcement from the asshole at the front of the plane coasts its way down the aisle. *Arson*. They've upped the hazard level and are sending us farther south to dig lines. My stomach roils as Chauncy and I exchange wary glances. Déjà vu.

"You guys got any questions?" Oujiri's eyes are set on mine, as if daring me to challenge him.

"Yeah." I mince no words as I glare back. "Tell me you learned something from six years ago." He knows better than to answer – to tempt me – to give me a reason to go to prison. I may not have a crew of my own to lead, but I have two partners on this plane with me, and I have every intention of ensuring they get home safe and sound. As Oujiri turns to sit down in his seat, I move my lips so Chauncy can read them while tempering my voice so Reece can hear it, "We stay together."

Chaunce utters, "Damn right we do," as Reece mock salutes and adds, "Roger that."

Knowing the level of interpretation is worlds apart between these two yet the severity of it is one and the same – we've all got each other's six – I simply roll my eyes at Reece. "It's no wonder she calls you moron."

The other level of severity? Reece is sappily in love, Chauncy is head over heels with a woman we have yet to meet, and I really am not ready to die.

Chapter 42

Savannah

Mallory can't seem to stop checking her phone between nibbles of her taco and tiny sips of her watered down margarita, as the ice has melted. We're out to dinner after a long week of OR and ER duty, and discussing final details of Liberty's upcoming wedding to the man who stole her heart years ago, and kept it bound tightly in a little white box with a promise she made.

For the happy-go-lucky *[insert smartass]* person I know Mallory to be, she's been hyper-focused this past week in and out of the OR, rushing to go home as soon as her job is done.

"What has you running out of work so fast every day?" I ask

her after she's set her phone down once more.

"I'm watching the news," she answers straightaway as if it's something we should all be doing. I, myself, haven't turned the TV on in days. I know what's on it. *Antelope Canyon.* The place where dreams – and brothers – go to die.

"Mal's boyfriend is fighting the wildfires down south," Liberty explains then grimaces. "She's worried." *Yeah, I would be too.*

"Boyfriend?" I ask, surprised. "And he's a Hotshot? Have I been living under a rock? Who's the lucky guy?"

Liberty smirks. "Weren't you in the OR the day the sexy firefighter was brought in? The one who offered to whisper dirty things in her ear if she . . ."

Giggling at the grapevine gossip and the sacred secret that apparently Mallory *is* Evans' type, I ask, "The one who offered you a seat on his face?"

Liberty gasps. "You didn't tell me that!"

I clear my throat as silence befalls our group under Mallory's glare. I hold up a finger. "Just one question. Did you take him up on his offer?"

She tips her chin indignantly. "Ladies never tell."

Liberty rolls her eyes. "Oh please. If you were a lady, we'd never have asked."

The banter is over for me as a deep sense of apprehension starts to build. Mallory's boyfriend is the same man who was sitting with Roger at Cranky's. A firefighter. According to Evans, they both are.

No. He wouldn't. He promised me he was done with the Hotshots. But it was the Army who took that job away. Did his injuries heal enough to go back to it? It's still a broken promise. A Hotshot is a Hotshot. And Antelope Canyon? It's the place where nightmares are created.

Liberty's phone rings and the smile that lights her face when she sees who's calling dies within seconds after she answers. "Lucas wants us to wait for him here," she says as she sets the phone back down.

"Did he say why?" an anxious Mallory inquires. "Libs?" she inquires again when she doesn't answer.

Ten minutes later, we find out why. Liberty's fiancé is holding Mallory by the shoulders, explaining that her boyfriend was caught in a merge and they've lost him and the others, aka, they're dead. I observe as Liberty catches a broken Mallory in her arms and does her best to console her.

Caught in a merge. Oh the horrors. Six years ago. All those men, yet if they had just listened to one . . . Silas and Conroy would still be alive.

"Libby, I still have to get to Roger's sister," Lucas explains. "I came here first because I knew Mallory had you. I need to wait with Ruthie until her family gets here from Scottsdale."

"Ruthie?" I demand. "Ruthie Bellamy?"

"Yeah," he says hesitantly. "You know her?"

The soldier I struggled to leave behind years ago appears as if she left the field this morning. I refuse to believe Roger is dead without proof. I would feel it. Army or not, he's a leader. He may be *lost,* but it's temporary and only to the ones looking for him. It took a day to find them last time. He always knows the landscape before going into it. Plan your exit before entering. And he'd never leave anyone behind. *Even if they were already gone.*

"Not as well as I know her brother," I snap back. "Did they specifically say lost or recovered?"

His jaw is set tight as he reluctantly answers, "They reported lost, as in gone."

Suddenly sober, but knowing she's the only one of us who

could pass a breathalyzer test at the moment, I ask my teary friend, "Mallory, you sober enough to drive?"

Misunderstanding my intentions, Lucas snaps, "I'll take care of Ruthie. It's my job."

"I wasn't offering." I glare through narrowed eyes. "I'm going to find her dumbass brother. Roger's one of the best Hotshots in the country. He's not dead, but I may kill him myself when I find him." I tug on Mallory's arm to lead her toward the curb to catch the shared ride we always order when we drink. "Lyft is three minutes away. We can take my car or yours. Let's roll. Liberty, you coming?"

"Where the hell are you going!?" Lucas demands.

"Mallory and I are going to ground zero. We'll make sure Liberty gets home safe first." I spin back and point a hard finger into Lucas' chest. "Tell Ruthie *Peaches* says hello and you'd better only inform her that her brother is *missing*." I lower my voice so only he hears. "Do *not* tell that poor girl he's dead. The first time was bad enough. Got it?" We leave a shocked Lucas staring at us as we climb into the Lyft.

"Does somebody want to tell me what is going on? And who the hell is Peaches?" Liberty asks once seated and buckled in.

"I'd like to know, too," a teary-eyed Mallory adds.

I'm too busy on my phone to go into details, so I'll give them Cliffs notes while I can. "I'm the product of a broken condom and too much liquor on the Army base in the state of Georgia. Mom and Dad thought it was cute." I flash them both a practiced grin before answering the call. "Hey, General. Can you help your girl out?"

Lost in a state of confusion – located between the borders of *Areyounuts* and *Whatthefuck* – Mallory has been too busy following directives and trying to figure out where this person in the car with her came from, and doesn't ask questions.

Admittedly, once my camouflage pants and boots went on, it felt like a true mission.

Finding the General at the base was easy – all six feet, two inches of him standing at the guard shack awaiting our arrival. I'd never asked him for much – maybe a Barbie doll house and a new bike – but this is life and death. He hadn't asked; just told me to show up. That is the General – my dad – the man I've always looked up to, and the reason we are now in a helicopter on our way to Antelope Canyon. Make no mistake. He didn't do it with a smile, but he did do it for his daughter.

Mallory casts me questionable looks from her side of the deck whenever she's not staring at Granger, our search and rescue Shepherd strapped between us, for fear he's going to make a meal of her. At 98 pounds, he is convincingly terrorizing, but I could lie down with the dog at any given time and use him for a pillow if need be. I've participated in his training and quite frankly, besides my father, found him to be the most reliable male in my life. If I could transplant his brains, heart, and personality into a human two-legged model with a little less hair, a lot less drool, he could make a good mate for life.

Chapter 43

Roger

They say the olfactory sense is the strongest for drumming up memories. A good ol' stroll down flashback lane brought on by a whiff of an ex-girlfriend's perfume, grandma's pie, locker room sweat after a football game. But one particular odor that only reminds you of death will take you back to a place you never want to be again. And that's where I am as the smell of kerosene permeates my nostrils.

He didn't have the lower quadrant inspected . . . again!

Three wide hot stripes of flames behind us race toward the riverbank. Unfortunately, the dry river bank, as fallen timber have blocked the flow. There are nine of us working this line, the flames aimed at the space between our team of three and the next.

"Hit the riverbed!" I scream. "They're gonna merge!"

Chauncy's howl of pain as he goes down has both Reece and me haphazardly lifting him by his arms and throwing them over our shoulders as we virtually drag him along with us. We can fix broken bones; we can't revive the dead.

The river flows in this direction – when there's water. It only makes sense there has to be shelter somewhere; some caverns hidden amongst the canyon walls. I swear my boots are melting with every step I take, anticipating the heat from the flames gaining ground. You'd think the sweat from my ass would douse a few, but no such luck. Chauncy lost his helmet and mask with the fall. His head hangs forward as Reece and I move in sync to find shelter.

"Up there!" I yell when I see the shadowed opening in the red rock. My hope is that it's not a mirage. As soon as my boots hit damper ground beneath them, my hopes rise. It's a water cavern; has to be. This was our only hope. Deep inside, the smoke shouldn't enter; it rises. Drinkable water if we need it, not to mention – it doesn't fucking burn!

Once inside, the air is cleaner and cooler. The water depth increases the farther in we dare. The walls are flat; no ledges. Once hip deep, we stop. We're in far enough to be safe-*er*, cool enough to be tolerable, and we're not looking to swim.

"Chaunce," I breathe hard and lift his chin. He's out. No way. I am not doing this. "Wake up! Don't you dare die on me! I am not singing Amazing Grace at another funeral for one of you fuckers!" My voice is panicked and Reece watches with rapt interest, but as he opens his mouth to speak, I order, "Strip off his turnout."

We each take a sleeve and remove the heavy coat. Gently holding his shoulders, we dunk him neck deep in the cool water and bring him up quickly. Shock value. He sputters with the temperature change and gasps. Reece places his oxygen mask on Chaunce's face and turns the valve on the small portable tank inside his own turnout. "He'll be alright, Rog. He's comin' around," he reassures me, then turns to our partner. "Slow breaths, Chaunce. It ain't your day to die."

"It ain't anybody's day to die," I mumble and lean back against the wall, wondering where the other six men are. Looking around the spacious cave, the pit in my stomach widens. There's more than enough room. Where did they go? Where the fuck did they go?

It's dark in here. Our headlamps are the only source of light, so we alternate between Reece's and mine to save on battery life. Chauncy's is melted, I'm sure, somewhere out there. No communication. Should they ever catch these fuckers, this time will be retribution of the horror movie kind. The last ones are still sitting in prison; three squares, a bed to sleep in, sunrises and sunsets to see every day that nineteen others don't get. Hardly punishment.

"How did you know this was here?" Reece asks.

Leaning my head back on the hard red rock, I let out a deep breath. "We had nowhere else to go. I don't have a fucking clue."

A weak Chauncy turns his head toward me and slides the mask off his face. He attempts to chuckle, but coughs then grunts in pain before reminding me of our previous conversation in the firehouse kitchen. "Felt like a *spirited* run to me." He lifts a brow and mutters, "It's only the ghosts that haunt you if you let 'em." He winces. "How's your back? I think I broke my leg. It hurts like a bitch."

Reece is keenly watching us, taking in the conversation with interest. "You two have history, don't you?"

Desperate to change the subject and get back to a plan to get us the hell out of here, I wink at Reece. "I've never cheated on you, honey. It's been only you since the day we met, I swear."

My goal was to catch him off guard – shut him up – but every once in a while, Reece brings his game to the table. Just one of the reasons we mix so well. He looks to Chaunce and shakes his head. "You can have him back. Mallory's blow jobs are so much better."

How the hell do you argue with that? Reece for the win.

Hours later we feel the vibrations as the ground starts to rumble under our feet and the pool of water develops ripples. My initial thought is an earthquake, until I see the twigs start to slowly flow on top of the water into the entrance of the cavern.

"Motherfucker! We gotta move, now!"

We each slide an arm under Chauncy's shoulders and he howls in pain with the lift of his body. "Sorry, Chaunce," I tell him as we rush toward the entrance, both of our headlamps lighting our way; the high beam on the earthmover up ahead indicating I was right. That sonofabitch didn't even look for us first. In the process of moving dirt to douse the embers, he's shifting the fallen timber, which will eventually release river water to flow downstream . . . at a deadly speed . . . into the cave. We'll all be dead men.

"Do what you gotta do," Chauncy groans. "Just get us the hell outta here."

"Go toward the light!" I yell at Reece in an attempt to give him a target and keep us moving forward without swaying, causing further injury to our partner.

The machinery's engines whir to a grinding halt, and a bright light is suddenly aimed on the entrance to the cave, blinding us and causing our footsteps to falter when we see the half wall of broken limbs blocking the entrance.

"Roger, get your ass out here!" *Music.* It may be in the form of the loudest trumpet I've ever heard, but I know I heard it.

"Reece!" Another shout follows. "Where are you?"

Loud barking echoes off the walls of the cave as a sorely disappointed, and apparently disoriented Reece looks over Chauncy's shoulder at me. "We died, didn't we?" It is the most pathetic I've ever heard my friend sound. This must be what love has done to him.

"Yup," I say, keeping it casual. "Now, let's go toward the light."

His feet stay frozen in their spot. "I thought there would be angels."

"You ain't dead, Reece, and that ain't heaven." I snort. "Pretty sure we ain't going to the same place anyway. Your angel's out there. Though I think my demons have come back to haunt me."

Chapter 44

Savannah

“Girls!” Dad latches onto a bicep on each of us and tugs us away from the chaos taking place on the riverbed. “Let these men do their job. It’s too dangerous down there. Don’t get in their way.”

“Dad!” I protest and give my best effort at yanking my arm away, but the man has an iron grip, and somehow or other he knows how to do it without causing pain. It’s a dad thing. Protective. “I’m quite capable of . . .”

“Get Granger outta here!” The desperate shout comes from the area they’re working furiously to open at the mouth of the cave as a roar comes from farther up the canyon.

The dozer moves closer to the bank of the dry river bed and lowers the bucket as far down as possible over the edge. We are mere bystanders – observers – at this point. Helpless. Hoping, praying, pleading. Unbeknownst to Mallory, I've been in this position before. Six years ago, praying for both my brother and the man who's trapped down there. The little white church in Harker Heights; Brittany Sunn by my side. I reach around my dad's waist for Mallory's hand and he finally releases his grip on our arms. We stand together in silence, hands locked in a death grip, and from a distance watch a group of men race to the bucket just in time to be lifted in the air before the rush of water and splintered timber covers the riverbed below them.

Dad places his arm around my shoulder and cradles my head to his chest. I feel his mouth on the top of my head when he kisses the crown and whispers, "He did it, Sweetie. Maybe this will help."

The reunion between Reece and Mallory is sweet. Someday I'll get their story.

Roger is a little slower to make his way toward the Jeeps where we stand; the high beams shining on his soaked uniform. He's filthy. The mud, ash and soot only make those blue eyes lighter. The dirty hair falling onto his forehead only makes him sexier. The fact that he's standing on two feet and not lying in a casket takes me back to the time when one of them was, and terrified me that eventually he would be. And with that thought, the fact he broke his promise to me, and I know he's okay, I take charge in lieu of waiting.

"You irresponsible, selfish, bullheaded, arrogant ass!" I scream as I stomp my way to him.

He smirks. He actually smirks! Hands in his pockets, he tilts his head the tiniest bit to the right when I reach him. "Tell me how you really feel, Peaches."

"If I told you how I really feel," I take a step closer and tip my chin, "my dad would wash my mouth out with soap."

My old, cocky Roger reappears as a sinister chuckle leaves his throat and he winks. "Oh, Sweetheart. Your dad has much better reasons to wash your mouth out with soap."

I step closer, edging toe-to-toe and watch as his hands leave his pockets, fisting at his sides, battling restraint. His voice low and pleading as he says, "Don't do this, Savannah. Keep your distance."

"Or what, Roger? What are you going to do?" I reach out and run a teasing finger through the now thick beard I've wanted to touch since that night at Cranky's. "Kiss me? Hold me like you used to?" My eyes meet his and I all but beg with my last question, "Fall in love with me again?"

"Not again, Savvy." He looks agonized as he confesses, "I never stopped."

There is no meeting him in the middle. He has my hair fisted, my head tilted, and his mouth on mine before my next breath. Just like he used to do. There is no give and take – we just are. We were always this way. Each of us knowing what the other one needed.

The hollers for Granger ring out and we separate mere seconds before the dog reaches us and tackles Roger to the ground. A wise man who's worked with military service dogs knows not wrestle with them; you submit. Apparently, Roger is aware.

"Granger, nein!" I scold and tug at his collar to pull him off a fuming Roger. "Es ist okay, junge!" *(It's okay, boy)* I tell my favorite four-legged friend, who obviously felt I was in danger and was doing his job.

Roger's on his feet in no time and scowls. "German commands? Really, Savvy?"

Holding the collar, though it is tempting to let go, I glare at him. How ungrateful. I nearly growl on behalf of his rescuer, "Don't start with me, you stubborn ass. He saved your life. You haven't even thanked him yet."

I shouldn't have snapped at him. He doesn't know the dog led us to the cave. The stress and emotional strain we've all been under for hours has taken its toll. My bet is he isn't aware they were reported dead. That the asshole Oujiri had ordered earthmovers to start covering hot embers; hence the river water washing down into the cave they were stuck in. That I had already punched that asshole when I got here, out of simple frustration and hatred from six years ago.

"Bellamy!" Dad bellows on his way toward us. "We need to have a discussion." *Oh God! Just once, Dad, let me handle my own.*

"Dad," I warn through a clamped jaw. "I don't need you to . . ."

"Savannah Leigh," he snaps harshly, as if I'm one of his soldiers.

"Not here, Dad." I match his steely glare then roll my eyes – you know, stopping short of sticking my tongue out at him, like a child.

He can snap all he wants, but I'm learning how to win these wars, as an adult. I respect the man tremendously, but I do not need my hand held.

The EMS workers approach with a gurney loaded with the third man rescued from the cave and Reece and Roger join them.

"Where are you taking him?" Reece asks one of the medics.

"The hospital in Page. It's the closest."

A strained chuckle comes from the injured firefighter as he looks to Roger. "Sounds familiar, don't it?"

I can't hear the remainder of the exchange between him and the EMS workers, but I can see the tension build in Roger's shoulders.

"You'll be all right, Chaunce," Roger reassures him as he

gently squeezes his shoulder. "I'll see you back in the city." He steps away and charges toward the Jeeps. "Once they let me out of jail."

Headlights beam brightly as a third Jeep pulls up and Oujiri slides out, cocky as can be. His lip is swollen from my punch to his face earlier, but it only makes me think I didn't hit him hard enough.

"Good call, Savvy," he credits me as if I should be grateful for the praise. Roger bristles at his use of the name he gifted me with. "Glad to see you boys made it out. That merge caught us off guard. Bellamy and Callahan, you both need to be checked out at the hospital for injuries."

Roger meets him before he can make it to us, his voice so low and full of hatred it would scare Satan himself. "The only one gonna need a hospital is you, and that's only if you don't need a morgue. You incompetent motherfucker!" Fist meet face, over and over as Roger tackles him to the ground.

Reece and my father head in their direction to stop the brawl, or so I thought, but Dad holds Reece back. "Let him be. He needs this."

He may need it, but he doesn't need to go to jail for murder. "Roger, please," I plead as I yank on the back of his shirt to pull him off. "He's not worth it. You can't bring Silas back."

Something must work, because the pummeling stops but he doesn't rise off of him. "You will never be in the field again. I will see to it myself. Kerosene. You never even fucking checked and you knew it was arson! Two men dead today and how many injured, Oujiri? We should have never been where you put us. Just like we should have never been where you put us six years ago. This one's for Silas, you asshole!" His right fist rears back and comes forward with a force so hard it knocks Oujiri unconscious.

He rises to his feet then looks to my dad, his voice cracking,

"I shouldn't have said that in front of you. My apologies, sir. I need to go check in. Thanks for your help."

"Roger," I plead as I grasp the front of his shirt and attempt to block his path. "Don't do this again. Don't shut down on me."

He gently, but firmly removes my hands from his shirt, eyes set on my dad as if I'm not even there. "I'm sure you'll see to it Savannah gets home safe and sound." He nods toward a groaning Oujiri when he stirs on the ground. "Might want to call a bus for him. Looks like he tripped over something."

Dad takes me in his arms and holds me tightly as I fall apart . . . again. I may not need my hand held, but a hug never hurt. Maybe I can't win this war after all – with or without his help – as an adult or that same lost creature left behind at the Hampton Inn in Harker Heights so many years ago.

At least he's alive. I'm only dead on the inside.

Chapter 45

Roger

Firing up the Jeep that Oujiri drove, I whip it around in the direction back toward the camp. Rage is all I feel. Of course, he made it through. Two men die and others are injured, but that asshole once again comes through unscathed. We came so damn close. If it hadn't been for. . . Oh shit! Why is Savvy here? General Mitchell?

"Reece!" I yell back before taking off. "I've got two empty seats. If you want a ride, better get in now." I could offer three, but fear that Savannah may see it as an invitation. Offering two opens one for Reece's mouthpiece. I'm soaked to the skin, filthy, and in need of dry clothes. I'm also in desperate need of a shower, but it's not top priority right now. I simply need to get the hell out of here. The combination of location, more deaths, memories of Silas and Conroy, Oujiri's fuck up, and Savannah has my head spinning so fast it hurts.

She was so close I couldn't help myself. I swore I wouldn't hurt her again; that I would stay away and let her fly. It took mere minutes! Minutes from kissing her as if she were the air for a dying man's lungs to handing her back to her father as if she were too good to be paired with the likes of me. She is, and I need to remember that.

My bubble of determination and thoughts is burst when Reece climbs in the Jeep and I take off – at an unreasonable speed.

"Where's the fire, dumbass? Slow down!" he yells, buckling the seatbelt I hadn't been patient enough to wait for. "We damn near died once today. That was enough."

I slam on the brakes and pull to a stop. Putting my head in my hands, I hold back the fresh fury. "Nobody had to die, Reece. He should have never been on this job. He didn't have the bottom quarter checked. It's where we got fucked . . . again."

"Again?"

Realizing my error, I put the Jeep in gear and answer with a simple, "Yup."

He lets it go and instead asks, "You wanna talk about the redhead?"

"Nope."

"If you change your mind, I'm here."

"Appreciate it," I tell him, switching to third gear. "But you're not the kind of therapy I need." That one statement causes me to ponder my choices: have my head examined, visit Cranky's, or own up to my mistakes and be a better man.

The guys at camp headquarters are busy slapping our backs

and handing us waters when all I want to do is get into dry clothes. When the chief looks at us with disbelief and says, "Damn, it's good to see you guys alive. When Oujiri reported you were amongst . . ."

Reece and I both drop the water bottles as I gasp. "Tell me you haven't notified our families."

As the chief's eyebrows furrow, we both yell in unison, "Give me a satellite phone!"

Two phone calls home later, an emotional Reece looks for my reaction. "Ruthie and your folks okay?"

Pinching the bridge of my nose and holding back a laugh that I cannot make rhyme or reason of, I mutter, "Of course she did."

After explaining to Ruthie the three of us from our station got out safely, she broke down and cried hysterically, then explained that *Peaches* ordered Tanner to report us *missing versus lost.* "I knew it! Silas was watching over you! Where did they take your station mate?"

"We have seats on the chopper," the General announces to the manager at camp headquarters as soon as our phone calls are over then looks to us. "We'll take them back with us."

"I can arrange my own . . ."

He squares me with a look my own father never had to use. "I said we have seats available. I highly recommend you use one, Mr. Bellamy."

Not offering . . . highly recommending. Yup, that's General Mitchell.

I nod in reluctant compliance as we head for our tent to change and empty our footlockers. Reece eyes the cot where Chauncy keeps his. "Think we should take Chaunce's with us? I'd hate to see him lose anything."

At the same time I agree, we share a look of horror. "Oh shit.

They would have contacted his family," Reece voices. "You got a number for him?"

"Nope, but I know somebody who will."

Five minutes later, I end the call with our own fire chief. He'll take care of the Steffen family and we are on our way home. A week of leave and a physical, as is the usual after Hotshot duty, and now with the loss of life – psych evaluations. I won't share my homicidal ideations; Oujiri's been on my list for six years.

Seated on the chopper according to assignment, aka General Mitchell's orders, Reece and I are on benches in the back with the soldiers who accompanied them, while Savannah and Mallory are seated in the two rear seats with the mutt in between them. I see her intermittent tears; the ones she surreptitiously swipes at when the dog isn't trying to spit wash them away with his tongue. If I could get to her seat, I'd even take sloppy seconds of dog spit to swipe them with my own tongue. Make them all go away. Kiss those freckles again.

"Just waiting to see what charges Oujiri presses for me beating the shit out of him," I utter to Reece.

Reece's face sours. "What are you talkin' about? You didn't touch Oujiri. He took a tumble down a hill. Got pretty busted up, too. Shitloads of witnesses."

"What?"

His eyes glint with mischief and he nods sharply. "That's what the General said. And if the General saw it that way, everybody else saw it that way." He tilts his head and his lips tip. "Funny how that works, isn't it?"

My gaze slides toward the front of the chopper where the General sits in the passenger seat. Deep creases around his eyes where there used to be slight ones years ago. He's been through hell. Silas never spoke a bad word about his dad. High regard, ultimate respect that was earned and not demanded. They were close.

"I would imagine he wanted to get in a few punches himself," I mutter, the words meant for myself, but Reece doesn't miss a thing.

"Another one you have history with, I take it." It's a statement, not a question. "Anything to do with the beautiful redheaded daughter?"

I run dirty hands through my hair and yank at the roots. "If only it were that simple, Reece. We all suffered loss. Can't seem to find our way back."

"Can't find your way back, or can't get out of your own way?" He lifts a brow as if posing a question I need to ask myself. He places a hand on my shoulder and squeezes. "Figure out what your obstacle is. If it's daddy, you better gear up and fight for what you want. If it's your own stubborn ass, move it over and make room for her. Mallory told me if not for Savannah, we'd be dead men."

"What are you talking about?"

"The minute Tanner showed up to deliver the bad news, Savannah put the wheels in motion. Got daddy invested, a helicopter, the search and rescue dog, and these soldiers to help out," he hesitates, "because she refused to believe you were dead." He holds up and finger and shoots me a cocky smile. "Oh, she does plan on murdering you herself, so I'd keep one eye open."

"Huh?"

He laughs and holds up a hand. "Don't shoot me, I'm just the messenger."

Stunned, I watch my little eighth wonder out of the corner of my eye. She came to my rescue, even after what I did. *Not a one-time thing; a once in a lifetime thing.* My words that night in the hotel. I can try harder. I can be better. I would be willing to do whatever it takes. Fuck Evans and his opinions. I'm not good enough for her, but what man who truly loves his woman feels he is? How many times did I tell Reece those doctors are no better than us when he was pining after the surgical nurse?

Chapter 46

Savannah

"It's going to be okay, Trouble," Dad reassures me as he gives me a hug goodbye at the guard shack once back on the military base. "We've been down this road before. I know a few soldiers around here that would definitely be interested."

"Not funny, Dad." I sniffle against his chest. "I was an Army brat and a soldier myself. Not looking to be an Army wife. Thank you for everything. I love you."

He ruffles my hair lovingly, kisses the top of my head, and chuckles. "Love you too, kiddo. Call your mom, she misses you."

The somber mood changes when Mallory and Roger start to argue after he's announced he will call for a ride in lieu of riding with us back to the hangar where Reece's truck sits. Her voice rises with a threat to his testicles no sane man would take lightly. "You've got two choices, Buster, and a Lyft is not one of them. Plant your ass in the backseat of my car or end up in my OR where I'll remove them without anesthesia. Five seconds to choose. Five…four…three…two…"

Roger grumbles as he heads for her car, "That explains what happened to his. Where did you put them?"

Reece and I laugh when Mallory sasses as she smiles, "I let him keep his. They're too pretty and I like playing with them."

I love my friend's quick wit. She is Brittany Sunn on steroids.

When Reece politely asks for the front seat so he can 'ride next to his girl', Roger grouses from the back, "Are you sure she doesn't keep them in her back pocket so she can squeeze them at will?"

I slide into the backseat on the driver's side and lean forward, the need to thank and compliment my friend simultaneously is strong as I whisper in her ear, "When I grow up I want to be just like you."

Strong hands yank me back and to the other side of the seat. Roger buries his hand in my hair while his other grasps my chin. There's admiration in his eyes and a plea in his deep timbre as he demands, "You are all grown up, and don't you ever fucking change." His mouth crashes to mine, desperate and needy, and a groan of pleasure vibrates in his throat as a tiny whimper leaves mine.

"Everybody buckled up?" Mallory chimes from the front.

"Just drive, Mallory," Roger mumbles against my mouth.

"Alrighty then," she teases, because, you know – last word and all. "Safety is not the top priority. I can turn up the music if you like. Do you prefer classic rock, jazz, or blues? Just don't make a mess on my seats."

"Jesus Christ," Roger mutters as I giggle against his lips, then breaks our mouths apart. "Put your belt on, baby." He looks toward the front. "Reece, mind if I borrow your truck? I'll make sure Savvy gets home."

Reece turns in his seat. "You know the code," he arches a brow, "and your way. Try to stay out of it this time. Fob is in the console."

Roger responds with a subtle nod. Pretty sure there was a hidden meaning of some sort in there, but I'll be damned if I know what it was.

An hour later, we've picked up Reece's truck at the hangar and pulled out onto the highway. "What's your address?"

Butterflies start to take flight in my stomach. He really is taking me home . . . to drop me off. Trying to keep the bite out of my tone, I ask, "You're taking me home?"

His eyes don't leave the road ahead. "That seems the sensible thing to do."

"The sensible thing," I repeat with a huff then give him the address. "You can just drop me off out front."

"That's the plan," he says as he punches in the address to the GPS on the console. "I'm too dirty to come in. Pack some things, enough for a couple days. You're going to break my condo cherry."

"I – I'm what?"

"I've never had a woman in my condo, Savvy." His eyes flit to mine for only a moment then back to the road. "Just like I'd never shared my secret place in Harker Heights." He holds his hand out, palm up, offering it to me and I take it. "Some things aren't meant to be shared with just anyone."

I stare at him from my side of the cab. '*Some things aren't meant to be shared with just anyone.'* Preaching to the choir, Roger.

"Did you ever go back after us?"

He shakes his head. "It wouldn't have been the same. The waterfalls, Harker Heights, Twilight Club, Hampton Inn. Those were all us. I was a mess, Savannah. They did surgery on my back and it left me too damaged for Army standards. It was a desk job or discharge. I took the discharge. My little sister got me set up with a physiotherapist here. Kicked my ass, but he knew what he was doing. Got me back to where I was able to work fulltime."

"Ruthie," I say with a smile.

"You know her?"

"Not really. She introduced herself one day at the hospital. She recognized me from the funeral. Told me her brother was a good friend of Silas' and shared a story about nicknames. Wanted to give her condolences because she didn't get to that day. She's a sweet girl."

He furrows his brow as if in thought then murmurs, "Peaches."

"I had to send a message to give her hope." I blow out a deep breath. "It was all I had. I know what it's like to lose all hope," my voice cracks, "but I also knew I would feel it if you were gone. I knew in my heart of hearts you weren't dead."

"And then you showed up to rescue me. Thank you, by the way. I'd be dead right now if it weren't for you." He lifts my knuckles to his mouth and drops kisses to each one. "Still want to murder me?"

Tears roll down my cheeks, my hand still in his, as I turn to see my building up ahead. "Jury is still out."

He chuckles softly. "Should I sleep with one eye open?"

"Probably safer if you just sleep on your belly."

He pulls into the lot of the complex and finds the nearest parking space, maneuvering the truck like a pro. He unbuckles both of our seatbelts and reaches across the console, meeting me in the middle. His nose brushes against the side of mine. "I thought you liked playing with mine."

I narrow my eyes. "My grip has gotten a lot stronger than it used to be. You might not enjoy it."

He laughs against my mouth then kisses me. "You can squeeze my balls as hard as you want, baby. I deserve it. Now, go get a bag packed."

Somewhat confident he won't lie to me, doubt still rears its ugly head. Some things take a long time to heal. "Are you going to be here when I get back?"

He closes his eyes, and a deep sigh of guilt follows as he presses his forehead to mine. "I deserve that too." He pulls away and opens his door. "Let's go. Hope you got air freshener for your condo. Damn, I need a shower."

Chapter 47

Roger

Why should she trust me? I left her alone and lonely in that hotel years ago. Some cash for her ride and a note with the lamest excuse in the world. Had I told her the truth, I would have been the burden, she would have never left; never been where she is today. She is so damn strong, but I see the vulnerability and residual pain. I've got a long road ahead of me. A path to widen enough for two and get out of my own fucking way when I stray toward the middle. Walk beside her; not in front, not behind. Protect her like a grizzly, but don't act like an ape.

Google books: How to be a good boyfriend for dummies

Boyfriend, hell. I'm going to marry this woman. I can suffer through visits with the in-laws . . . maybe. Holidays. If we trade off with my folks, that's only every other . . .

"This is me," Savannah slides her key into the deadbolt lock. Damn! Maybe we should have gone to my place and picked up an overnight bag there. The lady has style. It feels like home the moment you walk in the door. Not frilly. It's warm – inviting. Overstuffed furniture that I could sink into, put my feet up. Big throw pillows versus those dinky decorative ones that get stuck under your ass when you least expect it. A wall mount TV big enough for football games. A fluffy rug in front of the fireplace that would be perfect for two naked bodies to . . .

Oh shit! What have I done?

Savannah walks out of the bedroom with an overnight bag slung over her shoulder. "Ready?" The mortified, panic stricken look on my face must be obvious because she stops dead in her tracks. "What is it?"

"Savvy, I fucked up. I gotta go." I run a quick hand through my hair and try to catch the breath stuck in my throat. "It's not you, baby, I swear. This is my fault. I left my ride or die behind to fend for himself."

She stares at me, as if I've lost my mind. "Your ride or die?"

"Chauncy," I state clearly though she has no idea who I'm talking about. "I've got to go back to the hospital in Page. He didn't leave me when no one else could stay. He's the reason I made it to," I stop short and grimace, "Silas's funeral. If not for Chaunce, I would have had nobody. He stole a wheelchair and got me scrubs, and crutches, and found the phone store, a rental car, and drove me to . . ."

"Then what are we waiting for?" She snatches her keys from the counter and crinkles her nose. "You do need a shower first. Let's go to your place and get you a shower and some clothes as well. We'll probably be a couple days." She looks down at what she's wearing. "Damnit, I could use a shower myself. I just figured I'd get one at your . . ."

My jaw hangs agape as I listen to her speak. "We?"

She rolls her eyes. "You think I'm going to let you drive? How many hours have you been awake? You're not going to do him any good if you fall asleep at the wheel and crash."

"Y – you're going with me?"

"Would you rather have my dad take you?"

O-kay, that was shiver inducing. "Let's go." I follow her out the door and wait for her to lock it before we take off toward the elevator.

"Wait a minute!" She stops before we step on. "You should call the hospital first and make sure they didn't transfer him up here. That would be quite a wasted trip."

The woman has brains, beauty, and *balls of steel*. "You're right." We stand in the hall as I google the hospital, call general information, and get put through hoops. I lie about my identity – aka I'm his chief at the station – and am eventually informed he's in surgery. *He ain't going anywhere, unless I kidnap him. Role reversal, but been there; done that.*

Savannah showers at my place while I shower at Reece's, and drop off the keys to his truck. Having scrubbed myself thoroughly in record time, I had high hopes of catching her in a towel – maybe some skimpy undies – but instead, she is fully dressed, her wet hair up in a messy bun, and she is ready to roll. I guess it's true: You can take the girl out of the military, but you can't take the military out of the girl. The woman is efficient. One good thing? No makeup. I get Savvy and her freckles, every single one of them. I'm going to name them this time – with every kiss, with every touch of my tongue, with every . . .

"Did you pack a bag?"

Reaching for the duffel I'd placed by the sofa, I throw it over my shoulder. "Got it right here."

She holds her hand out. "Okay, give me your keys. You can take care of the GPS. Let's go."

My forehead creases as I pat the fob in my pocket. It's not your everyday kind of vehicle and I'm extremely reticent to let just anyone drive it. I insisted Ruthie prove herself behind the wheel before I was willing to leave it as a backup vehicle for her. "Savvy, my truck is pretty big."

She shoots me a wry look. "So is your ego. Not to mention something else I remember handling just fine. Now, give me your keys."

Crooking a finger, I whisper, "Come here."

"Why?"

"Because I really need to kiss you."

She stands her ground, the way she always used to. Chin tipped in challenge, shoulders squared, that same fire in her eyes I fell in love with so long ago. "Then you need to come to me."

Three steps is all it takes and it's almost too many. Anywhere Savvy is that I'm not seems too far away. I know we need to leave, but Chaunce isn't going to begrudge me two minutes for the taste I've been craving for years. The taste that tells me I'm forgiven. The taste that tells me she's mine.

"I will always come to you, Savannah. Whether you need me, want me, or simply have an itch that needs scratched. Leaving you was the hardest thing I've ever had to do. I didn't leave you because I wanted to. I left because it was best for you."

"You broke your promise. You said you were done with the Hotshots."

Not wanting to split hairs or pick a fight, and we don't have time to even skim the surface of the last six years, I choose the one basic answer I hope she'll understand. "I needed a purpose, because I had lost my reason."

Her tone is laced with bitterness as she huffs, "The Army."

"No, Savannah." I palm her cheeks and bring my mouth so close to hers I can almost taste her. "You."

If time were ours, I'd make love to her for the rest of the day, prove how much I've missed her, how empty my life has been without her. But as it stands I have a debt to repay; a moral obligation to fulfill. So, I pour everything I have into the kiss. My heart, my soul, every ounce of pain and guilt I have felt since the day I walked out on her. And just like Savvy always did, she soothes that ache.

"I loved you then as *just* Savannah, my little eighth wonder," I murmur against her mouth before taking one last taste, "but I love you even more as *my* Savvy."

"I never stopped loving you, either." I don't doubt she means it and I feel the comfort all the way to my bones, but I find a whole new admiration for my sassy little spitfire when she squares me with a look of self-confidence I've never seen before and informs me, "But I'm still driving to Page. Now give me your keys."

Chapter 48

Savannah

The trip took a little over four hours. Not bad for an estimated five and a half hour drive. Good thing Roger slept for over half of it. I've learned how to talk my way out of tickets over the years, but somehow I'm not sure he would appreciate my tactics. So much cheaper to bat your lashes, smile, and flash a bare left ring finger than it is to pay outrageous fines. Don't judge! It was only once or twice, maybe twenty times on the outside. That's a lot of car payments! However, the roads were clear today – of traffic and officials.

"Hey." I brush my fingers over the soft beard that covers his cheeks and chin. "We're here. Time to go see your ride or die."

He's groggy, but wakes easily and takes in the surroundings before swiping a hand down his face then shakes his head. Checking his watch, he does a double take. "How in the hell did you get us here so fast?"

Lifting one shoulder, I shoot him a look of pure innocence. "I drove."

There's a sudden fire in his eyes as he unbuckles his belt and reaches over the console, wraps his hand in my messy bun and pulls me close. His brow lifts as he speaks through a clenched jaw. "Like a bat outta hell, apparently. My truck is not built for the Indy 500."

"Neither am I," I whisper cockily. "I hope you plan on taking your time."

He gazes into my eyes, searching, seeking answers he'll find if he studies them long enough. "I plan on taking a lifetime." He seals his mouth over mine just like he used to when we planned on seeing each other again in two weeks. The kind of kisses that held desire, dreams, and hope. "I will spend a lifetime making it up to you, Savannah."

"How about we start fresh and see where it goes?" I want to put every hope and dream I have in this, but hope is for fools and dreams are for little girls. I do love him, but I loved him then too. I haven't been in a relationship since him. What do we really know about each other?

He grips the back of my head firmly as if to make his point clear. "I already know where it's going. I simply need to convince you." As I open my mouth to add what probably wouldn't be worth two cents, he kisses me once more then says, "Let's go see Chauncy."

The post-op orthopedic floor on fourth is quiet but for the subtle beeps of machines here and there and hushed laughter and conversation between the nurses. Room 4102 is located near the nurses' station and the door is slightly ajar. Roger taps lightly and pokes his head inside then opens the door to step in, but waits for me to go first.

A smile lights his face initially, until the female brushing her fingers through the patient's hair and kissing his cheek looks up.

"Ru?" His voice is sharp, a mix of shock and anger, and I watch as a nasty streak of red ascends from the bottom of his neck toward his jawline.

At the same time Ruthie smiles and cheerily says, "Hey, bro, glad you're okay", the patient gifts him with a dopey grin and a deep southern accent, "Hey, Rog. No time like the present, I guess. You wouldn't kick a man when he's down, would ya?"

His lower leg is casted. But his thigh is heavily wrapped as well and he's in a traction unit. My best guess is a double fracture. Ouch.

Roger stands frozen, glaring, nostrils flared, as Ruthie looks at the two of us and waves her finger between her brother and me, and grins brightly. "Hi, Savannah. You know the goon?"

While three of us find it humorous; one is fuming.

"Sugar," Chauncy coughs and groans with his pained laugh, "not sure now is the time. He looks a little pissed. We should probably break him in slowly."

Ruthie runs her fingers through his hair again and kisses his forehead. "I'm sorry, honey. Do you need more pain meds?"

"Oh yeah," Roger says threateningly, a wicked gleam in his eyes. "He is definitely going to need those pain meds." He fixes his glare on Chauncy. "My little sister?!"

Oh, how the years of being protected and memories of being referred to as 'little sister' wash over me. If only I could hear it again. But Silas and I did learn to respect each other's boundaries, eventually. Would he have approved of us? Ever? I'd like to think so.

"She is not your *little* sister!" I scold and wrap my fingers around his bicep, applying a goodly amount of pressure. "She is your *younger* sister. And correct me if I'm wrong, he is your ride or die. Seems to me she could do a lot worse."

His bicep relaxes under my grip and his face softens as he turns, his whisper meant only for me, "See why I need you around?"

"Oohh," Ruthie singsongs. "I like her, bro. I think I just found my new bestie." She tilts her head and squints, as if examining something. "Well, look at that. The red streak of anger is already fading. She must have you under some kind of magic spell."

Chauncy chuckles and lightly coughs. "Darlin', he's been under that spell for years." He moves his tired, glazed eyes to Roger. "'Bout time you pulled your head outta your ass." He nods weakly at me. "Good to see ya, Savannah."

"Have we met?" I ask him, confused as I cannot place the man.

"Not formal-like." He grimaces. "But these are better conditions."

I recognize him now; the man beside Roger at the reception for the funeral, shaking the CO's hand by the car before the two of them left. I'm sure someday I'll get the story of his role in the events; how he could stay while others couldn't.

I walk to the side of the bed on wobbly legs as tears sting my eyes. Extending my hand to shake his, my voice shaky as I tell him, "Thank you for getting him where he needed to be."

He glances past me at Roger and a sad smile tips his lips. "It was a joint effort."

Roger's sigh of concession is heavy as he groans. "Fine, you can date my sister."

"Oh my God!" Ruthie giggles and buries her head in

Chauncy's shoulder.

"Ruthie." Chauncy's drawn out pained moan is partnered with a wince. "I'm only injured temporarily. Let's not give the man reason to make it permanent."

Roger's eyes narrow. "What am I missing?"

Having been a little sister for many years, I'm aware we are known to push our brothers' buttons, but Ruthie seems to enjoy it more than most. Her tenacity is admirable, however . . . "I'm taking Chauncy home with me. He's going to need a lot of care and rehab." Her mischievous grin and wink takes it over the edge. "And a *lot* of sponge baths."

I'm pushing Roger out of the room backwards, bear-hugging him around the waist, as the vibrations rumble through his chest. Once out the door, we're met by the whitecoat-wearing doctor who's obviously come to check on his patient.

He studies Roger and tilts his head back and forth, eyes narrowed as if trying to solve a puzzle. "Ah, come back to steal a wheelchair or the patient?"

Roger scowls. "I reimbursed the hospital for that wheelchair."

The doctor folds his arms over his chest. "You can't reimburse us for the patient, Captain Bellsy. He's immobile, which means you can't have him. You got us in enough trouble the last time with your CO."

"It's *Bellamy*," Roger enunciates. "I hadn't planned on stealing him. I came for moral support."

He smirks. "Isn't that what his wife is for?"

"His what!?"

I swear there is steam shooting from Roger's ears, and daggers from his eyes as I yank hard on his arm and pull him down the hall as fast as I can, scolding with a whisper, "Keep your voice down. My bet is it's a ploy and the only way Ruthie could get in to see him. Now calm down before you have a stroke."

We wait in the hall as Roger paces and grumbles to himself until the doctor exits the room, followed by Ruthie, and watch as they glance in our direction. Ruthie rolls her eyes, the doctor grins, and they part ways.

Ruthie approaches and holds her arms out, waving her fingers inward. "Bring it on in, bro. I'm glad you're okay too."

Roger inclines his chin and arches his brow. "Depends. Am I hugging Ruthie Bellamy or *Mrs. Steffen*?"

I step forward and take his place in her arms and hug her. None too quietly, I defend him, "You should probably cut him some slack. The only sleep he's had is a small portion of the trip back down here in the truck and he's a little grouchy."

She pulls away from me and stares at her brother, eyes misting with tears. "You drove back down here? From home? Why?"

Chapter 49

Roger

"Why?" Ruthie's eyes fill with tears as she stares at me.

"I owed him." I'm not going to elaborate; not with Ruthie. There is so much more to the story and I haven't had a chance to tell Savannah yet, and I feel I owe it to her first.

"He's always said he owes you," Ruthie responds as if confused. "It's why he wanted things on the DL until, well . . ."

"We work as a team, Ru. We all owe each other in one way or another. You still haven't told me, is it Bellamy or Steffen?"

She growls in frustration before glancing back at the nurses' station. "Do you really think I'd do that to you or Dad?

I prefer my groom alive, not to mention working parts for the honeymoon, thank you. I had to lie to get information," she whispers. "They wouldn't have let me in if I had said girlfriend. His family is flying in from Waco. They'll be here in a couple hours."

Reminded of my sassy redhead's scolding moments ago, I meet her eyes only to be gifted a smug expression and an added, "Told you." *Wiseass.*

I roll my eyes before looking back to Ruthie. "Does his family know about the two of you?"

"Of course they do." She tips her chin. "His mother loves me. Can't wait for blonde, blue-eyed grandbabies."

"What about your dreams of working for the NFL?"

Her face glows brighter than stadium lights on game night as she smiles. "Did I forget to tell you? The Cardinals offered me a position upon graduation in April."

"You got the job?"

She giggles when I pick her up and twirl her in a circle as I breathe an enormous sigh of relief. Her dream come true. All my scheming of threatening 300-pound linemen comes to an end. They're Chauncy's problem now. I can pass on a few tips and tricks – help him out when he needs it – but the responsibility will not lie solely on my shoulders. And Reece's family is all men, filthy rich, and live in Texas. I'll bet they have connections with the Cowboys. *Teamwork.* Why hadn't I thought of that before?

Setting her back on her feet, I grip her shoulders. "Just tell me he's good to you."

I should have seen it coming. Ruthie may have a sensitive side – she's sweet, caring, and the first to step up if you're in need. But given the opportunity to utilize her smartassery and put you in your place, she is a pro; proving it as she rolls her eyes and moans. "Provided you don't ask for details, I can verify he is fan-freeeeaking-tastic."

There are two hands on each of my arms, their sad attempts at holding me back futile, shoes sliding on the floor beneath them like socks as I head for his room. "I'm gonna kill him."

Reentering the room, probably ten fingernail divots leaking blood from my skin, I stop and assess the situation. She could do worse, a lot worse. Hell, she really couldn't do much better. I'm tired, on edge. I think I've slept two hours in the last two days. Being here drums up hellish memories I've fought for years to let go of.

"Give me a minute with Chauncy," I tell the two clingers who haven't dared let go of me.

"Think I'll stay," Ruthie snarls and grips my arm harder. "I prefer him alive."

"It's okay, darlin'," Chauncy says weakly. "He may want my balls in a vise, but I don't think he's gonna put me in a grave."

Ruthie looks to me, a searing glare as she points a hard finger to my chest. "Quit being an ass, bro, or I will kick yours to kingdom come."

Savannah stands on her tiptoes and whispers in my ear, "And I will be right beside her to make sure she doesn't miss. I was somebody's little sister too, and somehow I think he would have approved . . . eventually." She drops a soft kiss on my cheek. "I love you, despite your stubbornness."

The door closes behind me and I stand studying the face of the man who stayed by my side when I needed him most. What do I say? Who am I to talk, to judge? Chauncy hasn't been out with us in forever; a virtual ghost at Cranky's for who knows how long. I can't actually recall him leaving with any women.

"I'm in love with her, Rog," he admits. "Ruthie is everything good in this world. She's better'n any damn therapist to take away the nightmares. Keeps me on my toes. Makes me a better man."

"Why didn't you tell me?"

He lifts a knowing brow. "Would you have approved?"

"Hell no."

"Rightfully so," he agrees calmly. "But if you're lookin' for me to ever be good enough for her, plan on spendin' a lifetime lookin'. I'll never be good enough for Ruthie. No man will. But you are lookin' at one who's willin' to do his best to make her happy."

"What really made you move to Phoenix?"

His mouth twitches on one side and he eyes the ceiling. "A change in scenery."

Recalling the first time they met in the physio clinic and their mutual reactions, my suspicion grows. "Who made the first move?"

He raises a weak finger in the air and shakes his head. "Now that is a well-kept secret." *Ruthie.*

My jaw tics. "How long?"

He glances at his crotch and a dopey grin swallows his face. "Haven't measured it since junior high, but my best guess is at least seven inches." He moans with the pain his lone laugh causes by his not so funny – well, maybe a little funny – joke.

It's the drugs, I tell myself at the long ago memory of a laughing Silas regaling me with the story of the overprotective General. *"One of them asked for her hand in marriage, but he gave the poor bastard a pass due to the IV drugs."*

"You asshole." Yeah, that was a pass.

"We good, Rog?" he asks, extending his hand to grasp mine.

I clutch his hand in mine in a fisted hold of brotherhood. "We're good, Chaunce." My forehead creases as I consider the risks involved on my sister's behalf. "Just tell me you're done with the Hotshots."

He chuckles and releases another slight cough. "In keepin' with the desire to hold onto my balls as well as your sister, I am officially retirin' from the Hotshots."

"You and me both, brother."

"Silas would approve, you know," he says softly.

"What?"

His eyes dart toward the door. "You and Savannah. You're a good man, Roger. The only one who can't seem to see it is you. She loves you. Don't fuck it up."

My exasperated groan matches the tugging of my hair as I yank it hard. "My greatest fear is I will, Chaunce."

He grins. "You can bet you will, probably a hundred times in the next week. I said you're a good man; not a perfect one. But she knows that. Now go feed the women and let me sleep for a while. I don't think Ruthie's eaten since yesterday."

"You really love her, don't you?"

A cocky smile tips his lips on one side. "More'n my Harley Roadster."

"Dumbass," I grunt, knowing his passion for the "donor cycle" he rides.

"I bought that bike two weeks before comin' to visit you the first time," he reminisces and smiles. "Named her Ruthie." He arches a weak brow. "Coincidence? I think not. Go get my girl so I can kiss her before you leave."

"We'll be back later, Chaunce. I'm gonna stick around for a couple days, but I gotta get some sleep."

Before I get the door open, he calls after me, "Hey Rog, I'm gonna marry her."

Nodding slowly, my back to him, "Yeah, I kinda figured that out."

"But only after she's settled in her new job. Don't want to

clip her wings."

"Get rid of the bike, Chaunce." I take a deep breath and blow it out slowly. "It ain't the riders; it's the drivers that don't pay attention. We've cleaned up enough of those messes, don't you think? Get a big-ass pickup like the rest of us."

"Already in the works," he reassures me. "We're gettin' a big-ass SUV, though. Need the seats for all those beautiful babies we're gonna make."

I spin slowly, my jaw slack beneath the glare I shoot him. He shrugs a single shoulder. "What? No football players are gonna hit on my pregnant wife."

My eyes narrow as I ponder the ridiculous, though ingenious idea. "Well played."

He gives me a thumbs up and a cocky grin.

It's the drugs, has to be.

Chapter 50

Savannah

"I booked two hotel rooms for us," I inform Roger as the door closes behind Ruthie on her way to tell Chauncy we're going to get something to eat.

"Two?!" He looks as if I've slapped him. "You don't want to stay with me? Savvy, I know I can be a bit bullhead . . ."

I place my hand over his mouth to stop his rant. "One for us, one for your sister. We'll bring her back here after we eat. She's waiting for Chauncy's family to arrive, so she wants to come back here when we're done."

He breathes a sigh of relief and wraps his arms around my

shoulders, squeezing so tightly he makes it hard to breathe. "You scared the shit out of me. It's been so long, Savannah. I don't want to be away from you."

"You need some food and some sleep," I mutter against his shirt.

Lifting my chin with two gentle fingers, dark circles under tired eyes, he whispers, "What I need is you."

In the midst of the soft kiss he's planting on my mouth, the door to Chauncy's room swings open and Ruthie's teasing voice makes its way toward her target. "You ready to be cockblocked, bro?"

He leans his forehead on mine in conjunction with a pitiful groan. "Please tell me you did not book adjoining rooms."

An hour and a half later, bellies full, we walk Ruthie back up to the fourth floor to see her safely to Chauncy's room. The agreement is she text to let me know she's arrived at the hotel safely, and by Roger's *orders*, not too late this evening. I chose a hotel with a valet service, so she won't be walking through a dark parking lot. Roger? He doesn't let just anyone drive his truck. We'll be walking.

Chatter comes from inside the room as we approach, and Ruthie timidly cracks the door open. "There's my angel," Chauncy's groggy southern drawl comes from within. "Did you finally get somethin' to eat?"

"Ruthie!" a female voice rings out to greet her. "My ray o' sunshine."

Poking my head in next, I smile at the scene before me as Roger pulls back on my hand, keeping us in the hallway. "We are not staying long," he warns with a whisper. "I've already been told I can't steal the patient and we'll be back tomorrow."

I turn so no one in the room can see my scowl. "Are you always this antisocial?"

"I'm feeling very social, baby," he murmurs into the crook of my neck, pinches my butt cheek, then enunciates, "for a party of two."

Me too, but I'm trying to be polite.

"Did ya bring the hero with ya?" an unfamiliar male voice asks from inside the room.

Roger stiffens and nearly stumbles backward. I spin fast to try to catch him, but he's already taken the steps to back away and balance himself. The shadows of pain that cross his eyes make my heart ache. He can't get past it. He's here – same place – same circumstances. PTSD and guilt rearing their ugly heads in unison. A double dose of misery; half that dose standing in front of him.

This is why he left me. He didn't abandon me; he let me go, to live my best life. What he thought Silas would have wanted. But what has he done with his? Reece's words make sense now. "You know your way, try and stay out of it this time".

Grasping his cheeks firmly, some of his soft locks in my fingers gripped tightly for extra hold. "Look at me. The only one that blames you is you. The only one still holding onto the past is you. And the only one who couldn't love you more than they do is me." Salty tears find their way to my chin. "You wrecked me once, Roger, intentionally or not. I don't know if I could survive a second time. You need to choose what to let go of. The past, or me?"

He squeezes his eyes closed as if in pain, the crease between his brows deepening. I want to smooth it with my fingertips; take it away. "I'm nobody's hero, Savannah."

"You're mine." I loosen the pressure on his cheeks and run my fingers through his beard instead. "You showed me what it was like to be wanted. You taught me how to love so deeply, so thoroughly, and so hard that I haven't been able to find that since you."

One might think I've crushed him with my words as guilt washes over his features. "Some would consider that ruining you."

"Then I guess if you still want me, you'll have to settle for the spoils."

"Spoils?" His tone is scolding as he wraps his hand around my neck and brings me close. "You're the fucking prize, Savannah. The one I didn't fight for, the one I don't deserve."

"Let it go, Roger, or I'll be the one you don't win." I fight back the tears as I broach the painful subject we've never touched upon. "I understand now why you did what you did. But here's the part you need to work on for yourself. Silas is a precious memory, not a ghost. And he would kick your ass if he knew how you were remembering him. You saved thirteen other men that day. We don't get to pick and choose who lives or dies.

"You were a hero that day to so many. You were mine before then for a whole different reason. But if my presence is only going to serve as a reminder of one that didn't make it, then I have no place in your life, because you're never going to heal."

He squeezes the back of my neck firmly. "You're the only one that makes me feel, Savannah. I've been numb for so long, convinced the only woman I ever loved hated me. I begged for one more night with you, to love you one last time, so I could end a chapter and open another. The minute I closed that door, I realized I had closed the whole damn book." He brushes his nose against mine, his lips so close. "Write a new one with me. Page one: The day Roger stopped being an asshole."

His mouth is on mine before I can agree – or disagree – not that I would. But then it wasn't really a question. The kiss is passionate, greedy, demanding, all Roger.

"We'll start with a prologue," I murmur against his mouth. "You might need some training."

That concentrated crease forms between his eyebrows

again. "Just tell me we'll never write The End."

"You guys do know somebody's probably recording and will sell this on the internet later as soft porn." Ruthie's quiet teasing comes from the open doorway. "It's also rude to make people wait. Get your butts in here."

"Be nice," I utter a stern order in his ear.

"If I have to," he concedes with a sigh. "I really am tired . . . and horny."

"So you want to sleep first and then . . ."

His glare is enough to seal my lips closed, but they still tip in a slight grin as I take his elbow and we walk into the room to test his patience, and tolerance, and ultimate limits.

Chapter 51

Roger

Relieved to hear Chauncy's parents will see my little sister back to the hotel, as they are staying at the same place, I couldn't get out of there fast enough. Duties fulfilled: aka check on Chaunce, meet the eventual in-laws by extension, not murder my station partner for keeping such a secret, and feed that said secret, my sights were aimed on a hotel room with one shower, one bed, one woman, and no more interruptions.

Tossing the overnight bags ahead of us into the suite I upgraded us to, I'm a bit more careful with her purse; sliding it off her shoulder onto the floor . . . somewhere. The door slams behind us and I flip the extra latch for security, take her hand in mine and lead us toward the bathroom.

"In a hurry?" she huffs behind me, though her resistance is minimal.

"You have no idea."

I had upgraded the room for a reason. A simple tub with a shower curtain are barely accommodations for a man my size. I wanted something special, something more. A chance to do it better, do it right. If she wants a prologue, I'll give her one. We're starting over. We may not be able to forget the past, but we can skip a few chapters, leave them in the rearview mirror. Not all of it was bad.

Turning the shower on so the water has plenty of time to heat, I strip my T-shirt off and toss it to the side. She leans on the counter, watching as I squat down in front of her, tap an ankle so she'll lift it to allow me to remove her sandal, then repeat it for the other side. Reaching for the button on her jeans, I slowly lift my gaze, asking for permission. She nods and brushes the tips of her fingers through my hair. I haven't felt tingles since the last time she did it. *Years*. I slide her jeans with her panties down and off – multitasking – and lean into her. Skin like silk, the scent I could never forget, the taste I could never get enough of. Cold shower be damned. I bury my face in one of my favorite places. Let the prologue begin.

"Ro-roger," she breathes hard as her thighs quiver. Her hands in my hair, she pulls and pushes, unsure if she wants more or can't take anymore. Nothing's changed; still my spitfire. My green-eyed, eighth wonder. My everything.

Dropping slow kisses across her midriff, I rise from my knees and lift her tank top up and off as I do. Still the constellation on her belly, still my favorite freckle at her pulse point. Her front-close bra unlatches easily, but before I can lower the shoulder straps, she's frantically working the buckle on my belt and has my jeans to my thighs in seconds flat.

Taking her hands in mine, I arch a brow and toe off my shoes and socks. "Who's in a hurry now, Savannah?"

Frustrated, she stares at me. "I thought you said you were horny."

"It would seem I'm not alone." I lower the straps of her bra, drop my jerseys, and kick off my jeans. I take her hand and lead her to the enormous walk-in shower; hopes high the hotel doesn't ration the hot water and we haven't depleted the stores. Better not; I paid a fucking fortune for this suite.

The water is still hot, shooting from three heads; two overhead, one on the wall. I'm more tuned into the sound than I am the water itself. The memory. The day she took my heart and never gave it back. This shower isn't for soaping up, getting clean. It's for starting over. Second chances. A replay of the beginning to be done better. I'll take her back to the falls again someday, but that particular trip takes planning.

After warming under the hot spray, needy moans and kisses of intent, I back her up to the wall of the shower. "You sure you want this?" I ask, teasing as I rub myself against her welcoming heat.

"Roger, please," she whimpers, lifting one leg to wrap around my hip.

"Wrap them both around me, Savvy."

She complies without hesitation as I boost her up, both hands under firm ass cheeks. I know what she's expecting; a deep dive at the speed of light. It may have ended well back then, but it didn't start well. I enter her slowly, a couple inches, then withdraw and do it again, a little deeper this time. She opens her eyes, pleading for more. So I oblige, then withdraw once again.

"*Bellamy*," I whisper. "Roger Bellamy. I am that guy and I can promise you more. I should have done it right the first time." I push all the way in, slowly, gently, and relish the way she moans with the sensation.

She doesn't close her eyes, but rather gazes into mine. This moment in time will go to my grave with me when tears well and a sad smile tips her lips as she whispers back, "Mitchell. Savannah Mitchell." It's forgiveness, acceptance, understanding. For both of us.

"Keep your eyes open, Savannah Mitchell," I murmur and drop a soft kiss to her mouth. "You should never forget who's going to be your last."

We move together as if we've been doing it for years. She's so responsive, just like it always was. The way she moans, whimpers, whispers my name. I'm so close to exploding when it dawns on me I hadn't even considered condoms. I'm bare, but I don't care. Nothing has ever felt so damn good. In fact, I think I drive even harder with the last few thrusts. Savvy and I would make the most beautiful babies.

"You're gonna marry me, Savannah," I tell her as I catch my breath.

"Is that so?"

"Mmhmm."

"Do I get a say in this?"

"Absolutely. You get to say, 'I do' as soon as the preacher asks, 'Do you take this man for better or for worse?'" I shrug. "Can't guarantee the ratio, baby, but I'll give it my best shot."

She giggles. "Maybe we'll save that subtitle from page one. You're really in need of training."

I brush a damp wisp of hair away from her face. "And you're so fucking beautiful, it hurts. I love you, Savannah Mitchell. My best memory of us has always been Harker Heights. This waterfall may only have been from the showerhead, but I guarantee there was no danger of your bikini bottoms going over the edge this time."

Narrowing her eyes, she challenges my memory. "What color was my bikini?"

I grin. "Hot pink. A shade or two lighter than the color of your cheeks when you screamed my name." I nuzzle her neck and slide my tongue over my favorite freckle at the pulse point. "The scream that's replayed in my dreams for years. My little green-eyed, eighth wonder that turned my world upside down. I was your first, and you were my unforgettable. I want you to be my last."

"You really didn't forget."

"I told you that day I wouldn't," I whisper so softly it's only a breath against her skin. "How could I forget the first and only woman I've ever loved?"

"You were my first that day." She brushes her fingers through my scruff, sending that old familiar rush down my spine. "You've remained my *only* ever since, so I guess it's fitting you be my last."

Something about the way she says '*only*' steals my breath. She hasn't had sex in the last six years? W-what? W-why? H-how? I lost countless nights of sleep, wondering who was holding her. Who had managed to put a ring on her finger, coerced her into a lifetime of . . . An officer the General fixed her up with? A doctor that saw how special she was? A French billionaire that swept her off her feet? (*fucking Tony and his stupid song*).

The water is tepid now, adding to the wakeup call I've just been handed. Not bad for 72 sleepless hours, with the exception of two on the trip down. She's mine, and page one has just become the title of the book: "*The Day Roger Stopped Being An Asshole*".

Rinsing us off quickly, I snatch the fluffy towel from the bar and dry Savannah off first, then finish with myself. It's late – small wonder we're not both tripping over our own feet.

Stunned speechless, I lead her to the bed and throw back the blankets. Tomorrow I'll find the words. Think I'd better start with "I'm sorry."

Chapter 52

Savannah

The last time I woke in a bed with anything other than a pillow I was hugging to my body was the morning of *Antelope Canyon* and the call to duty. The same morning all of my secrets and lies were revealed a few hours later.

He was asking my forgiveness last night, but the truth is, I've never forgiven myself. It's why I've never moved on. It wasn't that I couldn't have – there were opportunities – but it would have been like letting go of my most cherished possession: the memory of us.

Roger doesn't stir as I slip out from under his arm and off the bed. Not surprising that I'm able to, as he'd been up for days before collapsing last night. I was a bit shocked with his stamina in the shower. Dark circles under his tired eyes, the deep crease between the brows, but his drive and desire were strong as ever. Tight jaw, head thrown back, and that ever familiar deep groan as he released took me back to everything I'd been missing. So worth the wait. So worth the pain.

Closing the door softly behind me after snatching the hotel robe from the end of the bed, I find the coffeemaker with a variety of pods in the kitchenette on the other side of the living room, and start the first cup. Running quick fingers through my hair while I wait, I do my best to go from bedhead to shades of morning-after look.

I had booked a simple room – king size bed, complementary breakfast – but Roger upgraded as soon as we stepped up to the reception desk. My first thought was he wanted to assure we had no adjoining room with Ruthie, but after last night, it became pretty clear he had a reason of his own for the change.

Roger's never been extremely vocal – a strong believer that actions speak louder than words – but he's never failed to get his point across. It was his way of apologizing. I chuckle softly to myself as I think of the personality similarities he and Dad share. Staunch, gruff. A doer; not a talker. Is it the Army that instills those traits? Either way, I don't think Roger would appreciate my comparison.

"What's so funny?" I jump at his grizzly, sleep laden voice in my ear as he nuzzles my neck from behind, hands on my hips, squeezing gently. There is no missing what else is behind me. That virile morning wood is up before any other body part of his. I wonder if he knows *Hank the Hung*. Get enough *gifted* players together to make a team and they could all play hands-free T-ball. 'Hey, batter-batter, swing!'

Mallory Tompkins, I hate you right now.

"Coffee?" My voice is two octaves too high as I grab the cup from the machine, and rush to evacuate that highly inappropriate thought from my brain. But the harder I try . . . *T-ball teams take six players, so how many hip thrusts would it take to . . . 'And the crowd goes wild as Roger Bellamy drives the ball into left field . . .* Stop it, Savannah! Ladies' nights out should remain just that. Though I should jot those lines down so I have something to contribute next time.

I clear my throat once, twice, thrice, until a horrendous snort precedes the giggle released into the air. Coffee sloshes onto the counter until Roger takes the cup from my hand and sets it down.

He spins me around, lifting one brow. "As a matter of fact I would like coffee. But I prefer drinking it to licking it off the counter, Savannah. Care to share the reason for that giggle?"

Glancing at the admirable package that fills his jerseys, I move my gaze back to his and scrunch my brow. "Do you know Hank the Hung?"

He smirks, as if reading my thoughts. "It's fake. A rubber, motorized prosthetic that performs at the touch of a button. Dicks don't twirl like windmills the way nipple tassels can. Why do you think he never gets close enough for any of you ladies to touch it?"

I gasp. "I would never touch it! I've never even seen it! Only heard about it."

He pulls the belt on my robe until it's untied. "What do you think a thirteen-inch dick would do to you, Savvy?"

My mouth twists as I consider the possibilities. "Probably shove my womb up into my chest cavity."

His hands grip my waist and he sets me on the countertop, before opening my robe and sliding it off my shoulders. He brushes light fingers over my breasts before pinching my nipples. "And if it twirled?"

My breaths increase with the sensation it shoots to my nether region. "Um, I'm guessing a total, uh, hyst-

hysterectomy."

"Mmhmm," he hums as he slides my hips closer to the edge of the counter, then reaches to drop his jerseys. "Are we done thinking about Hank the Hung, Savvy?"

Bringing my legs up to wrap around his hips, I squeeze tightly and pull him to me. "Who needs Hank the Hung when they've got Roger's rocket?"

"Damn straight, baby," he utters, and as he enters, I start a lame rendition of "Fly Me to the Moon". He freezes, stares, jaw set tight before I start to giggle and he gathers me in his arms. "You are so fucking perfect. Squeeze me any tighter with those giggles, sweetheart, and the only one getting off the ground this morning is me."

Chapter 53

Roger

She is perfect – so damn perfect. Everything I remember, plus. She's stronger, a little more stubborn, bolder, challenging. And it makes me smile. I need that challenge; the balance. The metaphorical kick to my ass when I need it, aka eighteen hours a day. Keep in mind, I'm sleeping at least six of twenty four.

"Since Chauncy's family is here with him now, and I know he's not alone, what would you say to heading home?"

We've showered, dressed for the day, ordered and had breakfast, and we're an hour away from checkout time, if we're not staying another night.

"Whatever you decide is fine with me." Savannah stacks the plates from breakfast and makes a neat little pile on the table. "We'd better get ready. Checkout is in an hour."

"We'll go visit for a while first and leave from the hospital. How's that?"

"Okay."

"When do you have to be back at work?"

"I called in while we were at the hospital yesterday," she explains. "Figured we might be here for a few days. I'm not due back until Thursday, so I have three more days."

"Perfect." I stand and collect the few items I haven't packed into my duffel. "So, are you staying with me or am I staying with you?"

Her mouth quirks on one side as her brows rise. "Isn't this something we should discuss?"

"Nope." I stuff the items into my duffel and zip it. Keeping my back to her, I confess, "Six years was long enough, Savannah. Right now I'm not sure I could take six days. Hell, six hours seems too much." I make my way across the room to her and take her shoulders in my hands. "I'm sorry. So damn sorry. I didn't want to be dependent on you and I sure as hell wasn't gonna hold you back. I knew that if you found out I was bordering the edge of disabled, you'd find me, try and take care of me, out of pity. It was better to make you hate me. But never in my wildest dreams did I think it would keep you from finding love somewhere else. You said I wrecked you. Well, I wrecked me too.

"I didn't look for you for fear of what I'd find; that someone else had my happiness. I used women, but only ever saw your face. I didn't go looking for love, because I'd found it once, and it was the best and worst thing I'd ever experienced. The best because I'd never felt so whole. The worst because when I lost it, I'd never felt so empty. I love you, Savannah Mitchell. Tell me we do not have an end."

Tears pour from those beautiful green eyes and her full bottom lip trembles before she leaps into my arms and sobs. "You can find words. That was beautiful."

"Oh baby," I whisper into her hair. "I should have said those words so long ago. I should have looked for you. You've always been my everything; my reason. I never stopped loving you, Savannah."

"No more Hotshots," she demands through sniffles.

"No more Hotshots."

"Then I guess I'll let you marry me." She squeezes around my neck so tightly my air supply is cut short before she pulls back and plants a kiss on my mouth that is sure to leave a bruise. Pain has never felt so good.

"You will, huh?" My smile is so big it tugs at facial muscles that haven't been worked in years.

Her nose scrunches in the most adorable way. "You'll have to run it past the General first."

Aw shit, she's right. However, I am a strategist . . . "Vegas is only one state over. Want to make a pitstop on the way home?"

She slaps my shoulder. "That was so not funny."

I give that dynamite, firm ass a smack. "It was a little funny. Let's go."

All the way to the hospital my brain is working overtime to come up with a different strategy. Buy the old man a good bottle of whiskey, wait until he's buzzed, and then ask for his daughter's hand in marriage. Oh screw it. He's got a freebie coming. I get the buzz, he gets one shot. Correction: one punch.

Eight hours later, we pull into the parking lot of my complex so I can grab some more clothes and a few items I hadn't bothered with for the trip to Page. As luck would have it, our resident idiot, Wiley Bergman, and infamous erotica writer, Ava Mynx, stand in the hall chatting as we make our way to my door. Their heads round in our direction when they hear us coming.

Ava gasps and runs toward us, clutches my cheeks in her hands and squeezes them into a pucker. "Oh thank God! You are alive. You haven't modeled for one of my books yet. Young man, this lifestyle of yours is over. If I'm going to suffer a heart attack it will be from an orgasm of epic proportion that John delivers. Not from crying over your dead body. Where's Reece? He needs a good ass chewing as well."

Savvy observes from under the arm I have over her shoulder, eyes wide with curiosity, before Ava finally acknowledges her presence. She studies her face as she tilts her head back and forth, then taps her chin in thought. "You are almost too pretty for him. Never thought I'd say that."

"Hey!" I scold and tuck Savannah a little tighter under my arm.

Wiley's burst of laughter is as irritating as usual. "How's it feel to be brought down a rung or two, big guy?"

My girl proves she's on my side, like always, as she runs a fingertip through my beard and smiles. "He makes up for it under the sheets."

Ava giggles and extends her hand. "I like you. Ava Mynx."

Savvy reciprocates with her own. "I know. Savannah Mitchell. Mallory talks about you, a lot."

Ava's eyebrows shoot skyward. "Reece's Mallory? You're friends?"

"Good friends," Savvy replies with a huge smile and exuberant nod.

A low groan comes from Wiley and he pales, revealing his lack of fondness for Mallory is about as profound as my own.

"Another bulldog?"

I shoot him a scowl of warning before proper introductions. "Savannah, you've met Ava. This here is Wiley Bergman, Liberty's future father-in-law," I arch a brow at Wiley, "and our resident idiot. Guys, this is the love of my life, Savannah Mitchell."

Ava's smile is soft as her eyes flit between the two of us. "I'd love to hear your story sometime."

I give her a wry look. "Did you plan on making it a book?"

Savannah giggles. "We could have her skip page one."

I incline my chin, eyes narrowed. "As well as all the others. She writes smut."

Ava's eyes twinkle in amusement as she winks at Savvy and whispers conspiratorially, "I think Roger's one of my closet readers."

My future wife does not help the situation at all when she flashes me a sexy smile and says, "Is that why you're so good at . . ."

"Okay, we're done here." I wrap my arm around the back of her neck and pull her with me toward my door.

Once at my door, I hear Ava whisper to Wiley, "She's the one."

I look back over my shoulder. "Yeah she is, Ava."

"Is her mother available?" Wiley asks, stupidly, of course.

Smirking at our three-time married and divorced resident idiot, I proffer, "You can call her four-star General father and ask."

Wiley wrinkles his nose. "Maybe I'll check out one of those dating apps again."

"Stay away from Tinder," I warn teasingly as I slide my key in the lock. "I think you're still listed as the guy looking for 24-

inch wood."

"I was searching for two-foot logs for a campfire, you asshole!" he screeches, flipping me the bird.

"Choose your words carefully, Wiley." I wave a hand. "See you later."

We never have let him live that down. Poor bastard still has nightmares from the dick pics he was sent. You live, you learn. The hard way. Or hard-on way in Wiley's case. Literally.

Chapter 54

Savannah

"Hey, General," I answer my dad's call on our way back to my apartment. "A little late for you to be calling. Everything okay?"

"Hello, Trouble," he returns. "Your mother and I were in town having dinner with friends and stopped by. Your car is in the lot, but you're not answering your buzzer. Are you out with friends?"

Oh shit.

"Um, sort of?" I glance at my driver as he gives me a side-eye and arches a brow – Dad's voice carries. My parents don't make a habit of dropping by unannounced, but after the last few days I'm pretty sure they're concerned.

"Tell him to stay put and we'll be there shortly," Roger orders then reaches for my hand, grins, and whispers, "I can administer CPR if need be."

"We'll be there in a few minutes, Dad," I tell him as if it were an everyday occurrence.

"Who's we?"

"See you soon." I end the call as fast as I can, bypassing an answer for his question slash demand. He'll find out soon enough. Sometimes the element of surprise can work in your favor. I know he's grateful to Roger for his efforts years ago, somewhere deep down inside maybe even likes him. But will those two things equal approval? It won't change my feelings, but it certainly would make my life easier.

Roger parks the truck after we've passed an oblivious Mom and Dad standing at the entrance to the building. Tinted windows help.

Roger leans over the console and wraps his hand in my hair, pulling me close. "He may be a stubborn ol' buzzard, but I'm not letting go of your hand, Savannah."

"Nor I yours."

He plants a lingering kiss on my mouth, then slowly pulls back as a sad smile pulls at his lips, and I swear his eyes glass over. "Because you're not *a* daddy's girl, you *are* daddy's girl."

When puzzlement paints my face, he reminisces, "That was your brother's description of you, emphasizing your independence, your strength. Our last flight together, Silas explained what happened to you in Afghanistan. Told me he knew the details by way of your father because when the General wants answers, he gets them. How you refused your father's demands that you accept an honorable discharge. Your purple heart. He was so damn proud of you, Savannah." His voice cracks. "Just one more reason I had to let you go. Put you first, so you could do you and accept that we couldn't do us. It wasn't because I didn't love you. It was because I did."

Tears run so fast they drip from my chin, but he lets them fall away and onto his skin. "I didn't fight for you before because I didn't have anything to fight with. I do now. I will be there for you, no matter what. You're stuck with me. No end, okay?"

Six years of pain and anguish, a thousand questions why, a million tears, and one enormous heartache are washed away with the knowledge his pain was as profound as mine. That he did what he did out of a sense of loyalty to my brother and an obligation to me.

"You're stuck with me, too."

He starts with a slow flick of his tongue to my jaw to collect the tears that have fallen, then peppers kisses to my cheeks and under my eyes. "Super glue," he whispers before dropping a soft kiss to my mouth. Harsh taps to the driver's side window interrupt the moment, and Roger pulls back just enough to squeeze his eyes closed and grumble, "Cockblocker. Wait here, I'll come around to get you."

Chapter 55

Roger

The General waits until I close my door, though blocks the way for me to move to the other side of my truck to open Savvy's. "Send my daughter inside with her mother."

I resist laughing. I don't *send* Savannah anywhere. I can ask her to give me a minute with her father, but about the time I try to give her an order, she's going to tell me to shove it up my ass and use her foot to put it there. So instead, I make my way to the other side of the truck, open her door, and help her down. "Hey baby, could you and your mom head up and give me a minute with your dad?"

She flashes her dad a silent warning – eyebrows lifted, green eyes narrowed – before turning back to me and pulling me down for a delicious kiss that knocks my socks off. She tips her chin at her dad and points her finger. "That better not be the last one I get from him. Do I need to pat you down, General?"

Even the hardcore General can't keep a straight face as he runs his hand from his forehead to his chin. "Is it any wonder I call you Trouble?"

"I will see you *both* upstairs in ten minutes." She pulls out her phone and sets the timer. "Time starts now. No bruises! I like his face!" She storms toward the front door where her mother waits.

My eyes track her every movement as I make my way back to the other side of the truck, smiling as I do.

"She and her mother are all I have left," General Mitchell says as we watch them disappear inside the door. "You just watched my entire world walk inside that building, Mr. Bellamy." His gaze is harsh, but I see the pain of loss behind it. The Army can instill tactics to hide your emotions, but they've never mastered the art of hiding the pain. And there is a difference.

I look him straight in the eyes and spill my truth. "Savannah is my everything, sir. I told you once she deserved so much better, but she deserves the best. Not gonna lie, I'm not sure that's me. But I can guaran-damn-tee you, I will give it my best. I'll never hurt her again."

He looks to the ground, nodding slowly, over and over, contemplatively, before lifting his eyes to mine once more. The General is gone; replaced by a father who means every word. "I know what you did for Silas, and I owe you a debt of gratitude, but it will never be at the price of my daughter. You've got one more chance, Bellamy. Savannah only has one heart. Break it again, and I'll rip yours from your chest. Are we clear?"

"Crystal." Not sure this is a good time, but if he's going to draw blood, it may as well be in the parking lot and not on Savvy's furniture. "I plan to marry her, sir."

He folds his arms over his chest, inclines his chin and arches a brow. "You make that sound like a statement, Bellamy."

Oh for God's sake! I said sir! We didn't elope! She's not pregnant . . . that I know of. In for four, out for five. Slowly. Do not roll your eyes. For the first time in years, I hear Silas' laughter and voice in my head. "Protocol, dumbass. Think fast, idiot."

"General Mitchell, sir. I'm asking for your daughter's hand in marriage."

"Have you asked her?"

Hmmm, uh, nope. If memory serves, that was a statement as well. However, she did tell me I could.

"I'm asking you first, sir. That is protocol, isn't it?" *And it wasn't a lie.*

"You done with that Hotshot shit?"

"Yes, sir, I am."

"Kids?"

Taken aback at his question, I shake my head. "No, sir. No kids."

His jaw tightens and the low growl that leaves his throat has me ready to duck for cover. "You don't plan on giving my daughter children?"

"What!? No, I mean yes! I thought you were asking if I had any!"

Silas' laughter rings in my head once again. "Maybe I should have taught you everything I know, Roger. The General only gives one pass. Time to shut up now."

"You remember my warning, keep your word, and I'll give you my stamp of approval," he says with a curt nod. *Stamp of approval?* Yup, you can take the man out of the military, but you can't take the military out of . . .

"I heard about your career with the service ending." His forehead fills with creases as he studies my face. "That couldn't have been easy."

"You know, General," I let out a short huff, "it doesn't bother me anymore. I would have never found Savvy if things hadn't worked out the way they did. Your daughter is one of a kind. I'm the lucky bastard who won her and I will never take that for granted."

He extends his hand to shake mine. "Then I guess you have a wedding to plan."

I chuckle as I shake his hand. "I'd like to ask her to marry me first, sir."

"Shall we put together a gathering of people for you to do that?"

"Nope. I know exactly how I want to do this."

Three weeks later

"Why are we going to Killeen?" Savvy inquires when she eyes the destination board above us.

"There's something I want to show you."

It's taken some footwork, a few phone calls, rearranging of schedules, and a bit of pleading with the Chief to let me do a trade-off of shifts. Once I shared my reason, he snickered and pointed to the door. "You found somebody to put up with you? Better lock her down, Bellamy. Get the hell outta here before she changes her mind."

The plane lands at ten o'clock in the morning. The Jeep is in the rental lot at the airport just as ordered, and we head down the highway toward Harker Heights. Savannah doesn't say a word as she takes in the sights around us. Not much has changed; a few more buildings, a couple of new businesses, maybe a few houses.

Her lips twitch when I park the Jeep at the Hampton Inn. "Room 312?"

"Wouldn't be the same anywhere else."

Turned out Tony was still the manager, and I had asked that he ensure the room was not just up to par, but as near to perfection as he could manage. Gotta give the guy credit, he not only managed but had chosen to surprise me with the remodel they had finished only months ago.

Not wanting to spoil any surprises, I had told Savannah to pack an overnight bag with two simple changes of clothes.

Dropping our bags in the room on the sofa, I hold out my hand. "Ready?"

Her mouth twists, amused, as she yanks her T-shirt up over her head, tosses it on the floor and places her hands on her hips. "You want more, work for it. Your delivery sucks, Roger. You haven't even kissed me."

I swallow hard, admiring the black lace pushup bra – my favorite – that has a tendency to make my palms itch and want to tear it off to get to the goodies underneath. Six years ago, we would have both been naked by now and on the bed, or up against the wall, over the end of the sofa, in the shower. If we start, we'll be here for hours. Quickie and Savvy don't belong in the same universe. The shops will be closed and while I may adore the cutoffs she wears, the club has a dress code.

Snatching her T-shirt off the floor, I turn it right side out and slip it over her head. She slides her arms through the sleeves and I straighten the hem. "I will kiss you whenever you want and whenever *I* want, after we run an errand. Let's go."

Chapter 56

Savannah

Never in this lifetime would I have imagined Roger sitting on a sofa in a boutique waiting for me to choose a dress for the evening.

"The red one," he says firmly as I step out of the dressing room in a little black number that I happen to favor.

"I like this one." I turn in front of the three-way mirror, taking in all the angles.

"The red one," he repeats, "with the silver shoes."

I crinkle my nose then look at the clerk. "Nude."

"Sorry, baby." He chuckles. "While I appreciate you naked,

the club has a dress code."

"I meant the nude heels," I huff and roll my eyes.

He shrugs. "Why? You may as well go barefoot."

"Been there, done that."

"Oh, I remember, Savannah." He winks. "Wanna leave the Jeep at the hotel, walk back, and go for a replay?"

My cheeks flush with embarrassment at the memory as Roger rises and walks to me, then tosses back at the clerk, "We'll take both dresses, as well as the shoes. Silver. . ." he waggles his eyebrows at me, ". . . and nude." My mouth hangs agape but before I can protest, he tips it closed and whispers, "Save that jaw, Savvy. You're going to need it to thank me later."

I sigh dramatically. "The sacrifices I make for you."

"You love it, and the power it gives you."

My head bobs with a happy nod and I giggle. "I really do."

We spend the evening at the Twilight Club, much like we did years ago: Corbin Reeves serving us our drinks, the same piano player providing the music. It almost feels like time has stood still, waiting for us to find our way back. Fortunately, Roger made the wise decision to drive instead of walk.

The following morning we're back in the Jeep and headed toward the falls. History repeats itself as Roger slips through the opening at the side of the *off limits* trail and we make our way up the bumpy maintenance road.

"I thought we were coming to see the falls!" I protest after the umpteenth rut and bounce of my ass on the seat. "I don't have a swimsuit!"

He reaches for my thigh and gives it a good squeeze. "You're fine. We're here for the memory, baby." The ease of his words and his touch blanket my anxiety, but there's something in his smile that keeps my guard up. I want to rip his shades off and force him to look me in the eyes, peek under his shirt sleeve and see what he's got hidden up there.

We hop out together once we've reached our destination, and stand at the pool's edge. The trees are taller, the greenery more lush. The birds are chirping loudly as the crystal clear water flows in one path, out the other; just like it did years ago.

"Strip," Roger orders as he lifts his T-shirt up and off then tosses it to the side, his shades following soon thereafter.

"What!? I don't have a suit! I told you that on the way up here!"

"Don't need one," he says casually. "There's no one around, Savannah. The only ones playing peek-a-boo are the wildlife." He squats to remove my chucks and slides them off my feet when I lift an ankle for each.

"I'm not going in there naked!"

He drops to his knee and reaches into his pocket, pulls out a small velvet box, and opens it. "You won't be. You'll be wearing this." He removes a beautiful princess solitaire from within, takes my left hand in his, and looks up. "You already told me I could, but I understand there is a formality to this." He holds the ring to the tip of my finger. "I told you I would never forget that day, *just* Savannah. I have lived and breathed every day since with thoughts and memories of you. I want to live and breathe every day for the rest of mine with you in them. You agreed when I demanded, but I need you to say yes when I ask. Savannah Mitchell, will you marry me?"

I drop to my knees – equals in everything. Our battles, our losses, our pain, our gains. Now, we finally get our happy. Through tears, I answer without hesitation, "Yes."

He slides the ring on my finger and gathers me to him, my knees off the ground so the flawless fit we've always had is molded together; his height versus mine, my chin level with his shoulder. The kiss is not rushed, not harsh, not even needy.

It's romance – Roger Bellamy style. *My favorite.*

When he breaks it, his smile is a bit cocky. "I told you, you won't be naked." He holds up my left hand to display my new ring. "You're wearing the most important part of the wardrobe." He stands with me in his arms, sets me on my feet, and pulls my tank top over my head. "Now strip."

Still in training, I remind myself. Baby steps.

I narrow my eyes. "So much for chapter one. What page are we on?"

He pops the front clasp of my bra, slides the straps off my shoulders, then reaches for the button of my cutoffs. Within seconds I'm standing naked as Roger drops his shorts to the ground.

He takes my cheeks in his palms, his gaze fixed on mine. So many emotions cast in those piercing blue eyes, but I can read every one. "We've already lived the book, Savannah. Some of those chapters I'm sure we'd both like to leave behind. We have one helluva long epilogue to write, though. Let's start here and begin our own happily ever after."

Fine. Maybe just some fine tuning. It doesn't get much better than that.

"We can do that." I take his hand in mine and we enter the clear, crisp water that feels so familiar.

He makes love to me in the exact same spot he did the first time – against the wall at the edge of the pool – not as virtual strangers, but as kindred souls who found their way back to each other. A melancholy farewell to a painful past while starting a new future at the same time.

Roger holds his lips to my forehead as our breathing returns to normal. "So, what are we going to tell our kids when they ask where daddy proposed?"

My unrestrained giggle forces his deflating erection from

its home. "How about we tell them *near* the waterfalls? We did still have our clothes on. You want kids with me?"

He trails kisses from my temple to the sweet spot behind my ear. "I want everything with you, Savvy. A life, a home, calm, chaos." He pulls back and grips the nape of my neck. "Forever."

Tears pour from a place so deep I feel it in the pit of my stomach – in a good way. I still don't know if I like kids – haven't had enough exposure to be sure – but I can't think of anyone I'd rather have them with.

"Forever it is."

"Damn right," he whispers, then captures my mouth in a bruising kiss I won't soon forget.

We say goodbye to the waterfalls; this time with a few pics of us taken by a tourist. Smiles on our faces. Roger Bellamy and Savannah Mitchell. Nothing to hide, no secrets to keep.

That evening we walk back in to the Twilight Club for one last memory, me in the red dress and silver heels, Roger in navy slacks and a dress shirt with a tie. Will wonders never cease?

Halfway through the club, a harsh pinch to my ass makes me jump and a familiar voice breathes a dramatic whisper in my ear from behind, "Hey babe. They thought we were hookers last time. Wanna give them a show tonight?"

I whirl at the sound of music to my ears and shriek, "Britt!" I don't think I've ever hugged anyone this hard as I grab my bestie into my arms and squeeze. I haven't seen her in two years. Emails, texts, and video calls are simply not the same. "What on earth are you doing here?"

"Came to see the rock . . . and show you mine at the same time." She holds up her left hand and wiggles her fingers, revealing a beautiful oval diamond.

"Oh my God!" I gasp. "Did you bring the man that goes with it?"

Corbin Reeves appears behind her and pulls her to him in a tight hold just under the rib cage. "She didn't have to. He's always here. And in two more months, Sunny's going to be here, too." He nuzzles deep into the crook of her neck. "Aren't you, baby." It's not a question, it's a plan.

"You're getting out?" I ask.

She nods and leans her head into the nuzzle. "I am. He's tired of traveling and I've finally figured out his bed is more comfortable than anything Uncle Sam offers."

Corbin grins wryly. "Yeah, it's all about my cozy linens."

"Meh," Britt shrugs, "your dick's not bad either."

"Shall we toast?" Roger says impatiently then rolls his eyes.

Corbin grins puckishly. "To my dick or the pending nuptials?"

"Depends," Roger deadpans. "Is it whiskey or water? Go pour, you idiot."

"You arranged for her to be here, didn't you?" I ask softly on our way to the bar.

He snugs his arm around my shoulder and drops a kiss to my hair. "I asked Corbin if he knew how to get a hold of her. I knew they had a history and I knew how close the two of you were."

"Thank you."

"I want to give you the world, Savannah."

"Give me you and I'll have everything I ever need."

He stops us right in the middle of the room, not a care in the world who's watching, and places my hand on his chest. "You've always had me, my little thief. You stole it the day we met and never gave it back." He brings my mouth close to his and whispers, "I'll let you keep it, because no one's treated it better than you."

Training is over. He's graduated with honors.

Chapter 57

Roger

Three weddings down, two to go – the one today my highest priority.

Tanner and Liberty won the prize on taking the longest to find each other again. Eighteen years. Who would have thought a combination of bubble gum and an undelivered *kiss* could carry such an impact on preteens?

Reece and Mallory took fourteen years. A horse ride and a stolen unforgettable *kiss*; after which the dipshit was so smitten he forgot to get her name. Never forgot the shapely ass, perky tits, silvery eyes, pillowy lips, or the taste of cotton candy, though. Social moron? Just a bit.

Corbin Reeves finally got his soldier, Brittany Sunn, after twelve years. His *off limits, enlisted* soldier. At least she was when the forbidden affair started. It wasn't a morals issue; more a rules issue. Protocol. But the heart wants what it wants, and that's the one organ the Army can't control. I should know.

The future wedding? Ruthie and Chauncy; in four months. She really couldn't do better. He adores her. He still likes to hunt and fish, but he's never mentioned *fuckin'* since that day on the plane. Wise man. He saw me through the worst days of my life, got me where I needed to be, and has asked that I be his best man.

Which brings me to today. I've served as a best man for the first three – one to go – now committed to be the best man I can be for the one about to take place, and every day thereafter for the rest of my life.

Adjusting the bowtie for the hundredth time to no avail, I slip my fingers under the collar in an attempt to stretch the material, seeking relief from what feels like a noose around my neck.

We're gathered in one of the back rooms of the church preparing for the final countdown. I am minutes away from marrying the woman of my dreams.

"Havin' a little trouble breathing, Roger?" Reece inquires with a smirk.

"Are you sure they sent the right shirt?" I pull at the material again. "Good God, my Adam's apple is going to end up in my mouth at this rate."

Corbin chuckles. "Nerves will do that to you."

"I'm not nervous, asshole! I would have run Savvy to Vegas months ago if she'd let me." I scowl and yank at the bowtie again. "If her father hadn't insisted on three hundred guests and a country club reception, it wouldn't have taken so fucking long to get this over with."

Chaunce holds out a shot of whiskey. "Best be prepared. The General is not above punchin' you, Roger. A little somethin' to numb the pain before he knocks those teeth out."

"I didn't know it was him," I spit through clenched teeth, as the memory of sneaking off to the hotel room after our engagement party leaves a bitter taste in my mouth. "I thought it was you assholes coming back to cockblock me!"

All four burst into laughter, as Reece waggles his finger. "Bet you never neglect to check the peephole again."

Tanner shakes his head and rolls his eyes. "The least you could have done was wrap a towel around it."

"Gotta admit, Rog," Chaunce nods in agreement, "showin' your future father-in-law your dilly at full staff probably wasn't your finest moment."

"Knowing his daughter was in the room probably put you a little higher on his shit list as well," Corbin adds.

"Give me that glass," I demand before I snatch it out of Chauncy's hand and throw it back. Yes, my future father-in-law got a flash of the full Monty, in all its glory, firm salute to boot.

"You're going to be sitting at every family get together from now on with your legs crossed, aren't you?" Tanner teases.

I refill the shot glass myself. "I couldn't cross my legs if I wanted to. I'd squash him."

"Well," Reece starts with a cocky grin, "if mama and the aunts start starin', you'll know daddy told them all about it."

"Aw shit," I groan as shudders run from my neck down to my toes at the very thought. "You assholes." I forego the shot glass and tip the bottle back; my collar so tight it causes me to choke.

"Oh, no you don't. You gotta be sober for your vows,"

Tanner says, reaching for the bottle, hand under my chin so it doesn't spill. "Reece, remove it. I think he's suffered enough."

Reece reaches for the back of my neck and removes a stiff object from under the collar of my shirt, the result of which decreases the pressure on my windpipe.

"That should do it," he says confidently, then straightens the back of my collar as if finished. He puts whatever he's pulled out in my palm and folds my fingers over it. "This is just a keepsake. Don't look yet," then calls toward the closed door, "Come on in, Bernie."

Our fire Marshall steps in the door, nods to one and all, and holds out a small box to me. "Hey, Roger. Congratulations."

"Uh, thanks, Bernie." Taking the unwrapped box, I tell him, "You didn't have to buy me a gift."

He shrugs. "I didn't. It's on the city. Open it."

My hand is still fisted around whatever it is Reece handed me, so I carefully maneuver opening the box. Staring at the contents, my throat tightens for reasons totally unrelated to a snug collar. My new badge and ID revealing I've been selected for the new fire Marshall position stares back at me. I've turned the job down two times in the past; comfortable in my position as a firefighter and the adrenaline rush it often gives. This is a better fit for a family man, a father, and a schedule that will allow me a lot more time with my wife. No more 72-hour shifts away from home. I was sure after two times of declining it, I had permanently screwed myself.

Lifting my gaze to Bernie, I see him smiling. "This is for real?"

"You've got three weeks, Bellamy. You start on the 26th. Don't be late." He extends his hand to shake mine. "Like I said, congratulations . . . on both fronts." He lifts a brow and smirks. "I've met your fiancé. Young and a redhead? Don't break anything on the honeymoon. I'll see you at the reception."

"You can unclench the fist now," Reece says, reminding me of the item he placed in my hand before Bernie walked in.

Opening my hand, I find a small black box, about 3x1 and an inch thick. It's no wonder I felt like I was choking.

"What the hell?" I scowl at the perpetrator. "How did you get this back there?"

Reece shrugs. "I was the one who straightened your collar for you. Shoulda been payin' attention. Just a little heads up for your future. Now open it."

Inside lies a keychain—a ball and chain keychain; the delicate inscription of my soon-to-be wife's name on the ball. Gotta hand it to him, Reece is not easily outdone. Definitely classier than the squeaky rubber testicles I gave Mallory as a gag gift—sort of. The woman is a ballbuster. What a man won't do for his friends.

Rolling the gift in the palm of my hand, I grin. "Can't think of a better place to keep my housekey. Thanks."

Chapter 58

Savannah

"You ready for this, Trouble?" Dad holds his elbow out for me to take.

"Question is," I grin up at the man I've admired my entire life, "are you?"

"Eh," he shrugs one shoulder, "...you could do worse."

If he only knew how ready I was for this. Six and a half years in the making and the only man I've ever loved is waiting for me at the altar. He's all alone as Reece and Mallory march toward him, followed by Tanner and Liberty, Chauncy and Ruthie, and bringing up the rear are Corbin and Britt.

It's not the same church we bid farewell to Silas in. There's a big difference between taking the good with the bad without choice, and mixing the good with the bad intentionally. We all have a past, present, and future. Each has its place and sometimes don't partner well. However, as I make my way down the aisle on the arm of the General, I swear I see the ethereal figure of my big brother standing by Roger's side. He's in fatigues—his classic goofy grin that he kept on reserve just for me—as he tosses me a salute and a wink, then disappears into thin air. It could be my imagination, maybe wishful thinking, but I don't think it is.

By the time we near my future husband, tears are rimming my eyes, causing Roger to take two steps forward and reach for me and the General to clear his throat loudly in warning and a reminder of protocol.

Roger's own eyes are tinged with moisture as he ignores my dad and asks, "You okay?"

I smile softly and whisper, "More than okay."

The archaic words of the minister break our gaze as he asks, "Who gives this woman in holy matrimony today?"

I fight an eye roll and the urge to utter *"Sorry, General, he's already had me"* as my dad answers, "Her mother and I do." Dad then kisses my cheek and places my hand in Roger's with a small nod and a lifted brow—aka *thank you* and *I have friends in low places and don't you forget it.*

"Family and friends, we are gathered here today to witness the joining of . . ." the minister starts.

The vows have been shared, the unity candle has been lit, the hands of all attendants have joined together in a circle around us with promises of support and camaraderie, and we are down to the final words from the minister.

"Roger and Savannah, by the power vested in me by the state of . . ."

"Hold on!" Roger stops him, his hand held up. He takes my cheeks in his palms and speaks so softly, only I can hear, "Goodbye, *just* Savannah Mitchell." The kiss is soft, tender, only the tip of his tongue against my lips. He then turns to the preacher. "Proceed."

The confused minister continues once again, "By the power vested in me by the state of Arizona, I now pronounce you husband and wife. You may kiss your bride."

Roger's thousand watt smile is the one I live for as he dips me low and mutters against my mouth, "Hello, Savannah Bellamy." Cheers erupt all around us as the long, drawn out kiss and the promise of forever takes place. "I've wanted to say that for so long."

"I've wanted to hear it for even longer."

"Well, now you get to hear it forever because we have no end, right?"

"Come on you guys! Start your march," Mallory urges from somewhere, but loud and clear as is the usual. "Tell your horny groom he has to wait. We have a reception to attend. It's time to dance."

Roger stands me upright and scouts for the bane of his existence. "So go dance."

"No one can dance until the bride and groom do. Any moron knows that," she snaps in return.

"Guess that means Reece was well aware." He grins wryly. "So, go drink instead."

She giggles. "Oh please. We started that two hours ago."

His eyes track back to me and his brows furrow. I answer the upspoken question before he can inquire, "Not me, they did."

"So, you remember what you vowed?"

I tilt my head and arch manicured brows, teasing, "The part

about taking you for better or for worse?"

He scrunches his nose. "I was thinking more the 'til death do we part promise."

"Ah," I giggle and run my hands up his chest, grasping his lapels and pulling him to me. "Behave yourself, Mr. Bellamy, keep the *better* ratio high, and I won't have to murder you in your sleep."

He laughs against my mouth before one last dip and delicious kiss. "God, I love you. Don't ever change."

Upon entering the country club, I'm reminded why I was never one of those little girls who planned her Cinderella wedding from the age of ten; building notebooks from magazine pictures and searching Pinterest for the latest trends, but after suffering through the last six months, I truly think my mom may have been a closet junkie. Vegas had started to sound really good after the first few weeks of planning.

A hundred buttons on my dress? Good grief! It would take Roger an hour to get me out of it. Oh! I get a second one to wear for the last half of the reception.

Lingerie? Thanks, but I'll choose my own. I refrain from adding he likes it best on the floor. Besides, the bridal shower supplied a lot, much to my mother's and aunts' chagrin. They really could have skipped the edible undies.

Flowers? Uh, pretty ones.

Makeup and hair? Roger likes my freckles.

A sit-down dinner! Can't we settle for burgers and fries? Maybe tacos?

Cake? Whatever happened to chocolate and vanilla?

Uh, guys, we are not seeing Hank the Hung for my bachelorette party! Do I tell them the truth or let them believe it really does twirl?

Crystal and China, and beautiful flowers topping fine linens on every table, chandeliers hang in the foyer, bottles of expensive liquor waiting to be poured by the staff dressed in black and white uniforms.

It's a long way from sand up my ass and dirt crusted fingernails. The limo ride a lot comfier than the Humvees. The colors so much prettier than camo green turned crimson.

"Ladies and gentlemen," the DJ announces after endless toasts, speeches, cheers, and a full sit-down dinner. "It's time for the bride and groom to take their place on the dancefloor."

We meet in the middle of the dancefloor as the room goes quiet. "It's not the first time, and I'm pretty sure it won't be the last," Roger warns me, "but the General is going to be pissed." I stare at him, puzzled. "A little change in plans. I chose the song, Savannah."

"Of course you did." I giggle, not knowing what to expect but sure it will be something to get the entire room out on the floor with us so as to deflect attention. However, when his hand goes up to cue the DJ and "*When I See You Smile*" by Bad English starts to play, nothing and no one else in this room exists.

When the song ends, he wraps a hand in my hair and holds my gaze. "I don't want to just see the smile, I want to be the one to put it there. Think you can put up with me seven days a week?"

"What are you talking about?"

"No more three-day shifts. You're looking at the city's newest fire Marshall."

He doesn't have to lift me off my feet, because I jump into his arms. "A normal house? With regular hours and you'll sleep with me every night?"

"Unless I'm called out for emergencies, but nothing like it has been."

I draw back from his hold and point to my beaming smile. "See that? You put it there."

"The first of many, Mrs. Bellamy," he whispers before sealing his mouth over mine. "Damn, you're beautiful," he utters as he breaks the kiss. "How much longer do we have to stay?"

A harsh clap on his shoulder makes him stiffen as the General's gruff voice rumbles, "Did you miss the DJ announcing it's time for the father/daughter dance?"

Roger rolls his eyes at me and sighs. "No, sir. Your turn."

Dad chuckles. "You'll get her back. Go dance with my wife, you idiot."

My mom stands close by, stifling a grin, as my husband holds his arms out to her and indignantly grumbles, "He called me an idiot."

Mom giggles. "Welcome to the family, Roger."

Epilogue

I do not deserve this woman. After observing her agony for the last fourteen hours, I'm beginning to believe no man deserves any woman. I delivered a total of two babies during my time as a firefighter, but they were crowning already and my full attention was on delivery versus labor. When there's a little head popping out of a vagina, you don't ask mom how far apart the contractions are; you deliver a kid. Until you've experienced the whole process, hour by intolerable hour, there is no way to appreciate what a woman goes through.

Seriously, how in the hell do Panda bears get off so easily? My pecker is bigger than they are at birth, thirty times over! I watched a documentary one time. The mother's bowel movements are bigger than the cubs they pop out!

Recalling Savannah telling me her grip strength had gotten a lot stronger makes my balls shrivel as she squeezes my hand in hers once more as another contraction starts. She's not a screamer, but if I thought for one moment it would loosen her grip, I'd ask her to. If I could take her pain, I would. I caused it. It was my swimmers who fought their way to the finish line, only to concede to the champion. The winner who is about the make their appearance at any moment.

Not once has Savvy blamed me, yelled at me, called me

names. No threats of castration—yet. I've heard horror stories about the L&D department, none ending in murder, but there were definite bets placed on pending divorces.

Refusing a gender reveal, my beautiful wife and I agreed the element of surprise is half the journey. Social norms be damned. Our folks never knew what they were having until we popped out. And the advice we received? Oh please.

Eat more bananas for a girl. Yeah, the fruit shaped like a dick. Made sense, not.

Sex on only odd days of the week for a boy. What the hell? We have sex every day of the week. Screw that.

Sex mid cycle for a better chance of twins. Thanks, one at a time is good.

Stand up sex—boy. Missionary sex—girl. So, doggy style gives you . . . puppies?

And the winner from Reece? Morning, noon, and night. Who the hell cares?

"Okay, Savannah," Dr. Joslin says from the end of the bed where it would seem she's speaking more to my wife's crotch, as her feet are in stirrups and she's spread eagle. "You're at ten. Next contraction, you push."

Savvy's breaths are labored and her head is sweaty, but she's never looked more beautiful. Her eyes lock on mine, pleading. I brush a few sweaty strands away from her face, and smile. "You can do this, baby. I gotcha."

The contraction hits hard and fast this time and my spitfire gives it all she's got as her back rises off the bed. She holds a death grip on my hand, and lets out a howl that is soon matched by another set of lungs that announce their arrival before Savvy drops back on the bed.

Sliding an arm under my wife's shoulders, I prop her up so she can get a better look as they lay the wrinkly little miracle on her belly.

I get lost as I stare at the perfection before me.

An exhausted Savvy grasps at my scrubs sleeve. “What did we have?”

“He’s beautiful, Savannah,” I whisper in awe of the ruddy-skinned creature.

My wife sobs and looks up at the ceiling. “You’ve got your namesake, Bro.”

As Roger and Savannah promised each other there would be no end, it feels wrong to write those words as this series comes to a close.

So instead, we all bid you farewell.

Until we meet again
Live well, laugh often, love much!

About The Author

Annie Mick

A diehard laughaholic who has learned to take everything with a grain of salt, Annie Mick loves to dish it out with a good dose of sarcasm.

If you can giggle while you wiggle, it's added exercise and spares you ten minutes on the treadmill.

It is true that if you can laugh while you cry, the tears are saltier and it makes the margaritas taste better.

If you can find your hero in one of her books, therein lies her success. If you can find a bit of yourself in one her characters, therein lies her joy.

Life is too short to not get lost in a fantasy; if only for a day, if only in a book, one page at a time.

Sweet dreams.

The Nurses of Maricopa County

Meet your caregivers and the men who love them through this series. Each with their own unique story to tell; the pain, trials, and journeys they traveled to get to where they are, which, coincidentally, happens to be the same medical center in Phoenix, Arizona.
No cliffhangers and can be read as standalones.

I Should Have Kissed Him

Lucas
It's true what they say: you never forget your first love. Liberty Collins was mine. Problem is, I not only never forgot her, I never got over her. Liberty wasn't just my first love; she was my only love, and my last.
The very memory of her and the night we parted have served well as a cruel reminder there will never be another love of my life. We made a deal that day, one I've never forgotten. One that has factored into every decision I've made since.
She's back, and I've come to collect on her 'promise of tomorrow'.
A story of young love and best friends torn apart by tragedy and tested by time. Follow the journey of Lucas and Liberty as they struggle with adult relationships, all the while searching for the one they never forgot.

But I Kissed A Cowboy

Long ago on a sunny morning in Texas, there was a boy who took a girl for a ride on his horse . . .

Reece Callahan, firefighter extraordinaire

Offering the beautiful nurse anesthetist a seat on my face probably wasn't the best approach, but it was the drugs speaking at the time – sort of. Old habits die hard. Those eyes and that kissable mouth were taking me to a place and time I'd been before. A place I wanted to revisit – something I never do. I could break those rules, at least once, maybe twice . . .

Mallory Tompkins

The rules and ethics are concise; contractual. My own are pretty clear as well. The hospital's? No patients. My own? No players.

Reece Callahan is well known as both. He's also persistent. But the day he rescues me in the hospital parking lot is the day that changes everything . . . for both of us.

He wasn't just a patient, and she wasn't just his attending anesthetist. Does history change the rules and ethics? Can they get past what was and move on to what can be?

Never Kiss A Hotshot

Other Books by this Author

The Crew series:
Amazon.com: Run To Me: A friends to lovers romance (The Crew Book 1) eBook : Mick, Annie : Kindle Store

Wicked Lemonade (The Crew Book 2) - Kindle edition by Mick, Annie. Contemporary Romance Kindle eBooks @ Amazon.com.

Amazon.com: Find Another Hero: Just Make Sure He Can Dance (The Crew): 9798685424785: Mick, Annie: Books

The Attorney Series:

Tell Me Why, Jannie: Mick, Annie: 9798595087735: Amazon.com: Books

The Fresh French Connection - Kindle edition by Mick, Annie. Literature & Fiction Kindle eBooks @ Amazon.com.

Road Trip time!

Old Farts and Pop Tarts - Kindle edition by Mick, Annie. Literature & Fiction Kindle eBooks @ Amazon.com.

Twins!

Amazon.com: Saari, Not Sorry eBook : Mick, Annie: Kindle Store

Amazon.com: The Chauffeur: Phoenix Rising eBook : Mick, Annie: Kindle Store

Navy Seals and paranormal:

Manipulation 101: Code of Ethics - Kindle edition by Mick, Annie. Paranormal Romance Kindle eBooks @ Amazon.com.

Crime and grit:

Amazon.com: Somebody's Someone eBook : Mick, Annie: Kindle Store

A touch of Christmas year round:

Amazon.com: Donner's Vixen eBook : Mick, Annie: Kindle Store

www.ingramcontent.com/pod-product-compliance
Lightning Source LLC
Chambersburg PA
CBHW060850250626
47159CB00008B/2674

* 9 7 8 1 9 6 3 5 7 2 1 8 6 *